Lola Bensky

Also by Lily Brett

LILY BRETT

COUNTERPOINT

BERKELEY

First published by HAMISH HAMILTON, Penguin Group (Australia), 2012

Design by Laura Thomas © Penguin Group (Australia)
Cover photograph © Gabrielle Revere/Getty Images
Author photograph © Bettina Strauss
Typeset in Adobe Caslon Pro 11.5/17.5pt

Library of Congress Cataloging-in-Publication Data is available
ISBN 978-1-59376-523-1

COUNTERPOINT
1919 Fifth Street
Berkeley, CA 94710
www.counterpointpress.com

Printed in the United States of America
Distributed by Publishers Group West

10 9 8 7 6 5 4 3 2 1

for David,
for decades of love,
with love

I

Lola Bensky was sitting on an uncomfortably high stool. She could feel the nylon threads of her fishnet tights digging into her thighs.

She had put a wad of tissues underneath the fishnet, on the inside of each of her thighs. The tissues, which were supposed to stop her thighs rubbing against each other and chafing her skin, had shredded, and now her flesh poked through the mesh in small, shiny, tightly packed pink squares.

She tried to move into a more comfortable position. She didn't like sitting on stools. And she didn't like heights. She noticed a sprinkling of disintegrated tissue on the floor, below her left foot. She decided to sit very still. And to go on a diet.

Jimi Hendrix, who was sitting on a slightly lower stool, looked at her. His face had a quietness about it. There was no sign of the Jimi Hendrix who, just thirty minutes earlier, had been humping the microphone stand on stage and fucking his guitar. There was no sign of the Jimi Hendrix whose guitar had whined and moaned and shuddered in a frenzied, carnal staccato with his body.

Jimi Hendrix removed the brightly-coloured patterned silk scarf that was tied around his neck. 'Are you comfortable?' he said to Lola

Bensky, in a soft, improbably polite voice. 'Oh, yes,' she said, looking at him and trying to separate her thighs.

She thought that Jimi Hendrix had probably never had to go on a diet. She thought he was probably naturally lean. She had never been lean. She had a photograph of herself in the displaced person's camp, in Germany, where she was born. She was three months old in the photograph. And she was chubby. How could a baby born in a DP camp be chubby? Lola was sure that not many of the camp's other inmates, mostly Jews who had survived Nazi death camps, were chubby.

Lola was hot. Jimi Hendrix's dressing-room, the room they were in, was small. And overheated. And Lola was overdressed. It was winter, in London. Lola wasn't used to cold winters. She'd grown up in Melbourne, Australia, where winter was barely distinguishable from spring or autumn.

She looked at the questions she had prepared. 'You're not going to ask me what my gimmick is?' Jimi Hendrix said to her.

'No,' said Lola. The question threw her a bit. She didn't know he had a gimmick. Maybe someone had suggested that playing his guitar with his teeth was a gimmick? Or flicking out his tongue? Or fondling the neck of his guitar? She didn't know.

She did know that he was born in 1942 to a mother who had just turned seventeen and a father who was away in the army. She knew that from the time he was a baby he was farmed out to various people until his father came back from the army, when Jimi was three. She knew that his parents, who were separated, got back together and had four more children, Jimi's brothers, Leon and Joseph, and his sisters, Kathy and Pamela. Joseph was born with an array of disabilities, including a clubfoot, a cleft palate and one leg shorter than the other. Kathy was premature and blind and Pamela had some minor physical problems. Soon Joseph was made a ward of the state. And so were Kathy and Pamela. By the time Jimi was nine, his parents were divorced, his mother was alcoholic and his remaining brother was in and out of foster care. Lola knew that the family was so poor that Jimi was often dressed in rags.

There was no evidence of this childhood turbulence on Jimi Hendrix's face. He had a slow gaze and a languid half-smile. His lips made lazy, playful movements when he spoke.

Lola liked accumulating information about people. She liked listing what she knew about their lives. She found it oddly soothing. She had her own lists, too. Lists of her mother and father's dead relatives. Renia Bensky, Lola's mother, had had four brothers, three sisters, a mother and father, aunts, uncles, cousins, nephews and nieces. By the end of the war, everyone Renia Bensky was related to was dead. All murdered. Lola's father's mother and father and three brothers and a sister were also all murdered. Those lists bothered Lola.

Lola preferred to list the various diets she was thinking about. She had just given up on a Mars Bar Diet she had tried for several days. All the Mars bars you could eat and nothing else. On her list of diets she had called it the Get Bored Diet. The basic principle was that the Mars bars would lose their appeal and she'd soon be eating very few of them, in fact she'd be eating very little. It hadn't worked. The Egg and Cucumber Diet was on the top of her new list of diets.

Lola didn't have time to feel sad. She was too busy being cheerful or planning her interviews or thinking about food. Decades later, Lola Bensky would not be quite as immune to the lists of the dead.

The dead would adhere themselves to her. But she didn't yet know any of this. She was nineteen.

She shifted around on her stool. Jimi Hendrix was watching her intently. The row of sequined beading around the neckline of her blue dress was starting to irritate her skin. All of her dresses had high necklines and were gathered above the bust in order to billow out and cover her hips and her thighs. One of her false eyelashes felt as though it were coming unstuck. She tried to press it back in place. It was probably because of the heat, she thought. This was a new pair of false eyelashes. Cher had borrowed the ones Lola was wearing last week. They were lined with diamantes around the rim and were Lola's favourites. Cher, in the middle of Lola's interview with her, had asked where she had bought the diamante-lined eyelashes. 'José of Melbourne, Australia,' Lola had replied. Cher had looked blank, and then asked if she could borrow them. Lola had felt as though she couldn't say no to Cher.

People sometimes said that Lola looked like Cher. Lola thought that it was their dark, heavy-lidded eyes, high cheekbones and Semitic noses. 'I'm twice her size' was Lola's standard answer to any remark about the similarity. Lola was sure that Cher didn't ever have to diet. Sonny probably didn't, either.

Lola had been in London for two months. She had already interviewed The Small Faces, The Kinks, The Hollies, Cliff Richard, Gene Pitney, Spencer Davis, Olivia Newton-John and The Bee Gees. Olivia Newton-John and The Bee Gees were easy interviews to get as she had interviewed them before for *Rock-Out*, the newspaper she worked for in Australia.

Lola's tape recorder was on her lap. She looked down to make sure it was working. Jimi Hendrix licked his lips. His mouth didn't look anything like the mobile, worryingly lascivious mouth she'd had to avert her eyes from during his performance.

'Are you religious?' Lola asked Jimi Hendrix. Lola envied people who were religious. She felt that being religious would be like being in a very large club and always having someone to talk to. Not God, just another member of the club.

Lola's mother, who had been brought up in a very religious home, wouldn't tolerate any notion of religion. When Lola now and then asked if she could go to synagogue, mostly on high holy days, Renia used to say, 'If you did see what I did see, you would not even talk about religion.'

'You only want to go to synagogue to meet boys,' Renia would add, in the tone of voice that suggested that meeting boys was akin to meeting your drug dealer or hanging out with a serial killer.

Religion was a subject that couldn't be discussed in the Bensky household. 'There is no God,' Renia Bensky would say, over and over again. 'There is no God.' She would say this in the middle of washing the dishes, or in the backyard hanging out the clothes or just sitting at the kitchen table by herself.

'Am I religious?' Jimi Hendrix said. 'I don't believe in religion. I went to church a few times when I was a kid, but I got driven out because my clothes were too poor.'

'That wasn't very charitable or pious of the church or the congregants, was it?' Lola said.

'Charitable or pious,' Jimi Hendrix said. 'They're interesting words. No, it wasn't charitable or pious. I loved listening to the choir. But I never went back.'

'What do you believe in?' said Lola.

'I don't believe in heaven or hell,' he said. 'I don't know if there is a God.'

Renia Bensky could have told him the answer to that, Lola thought.

'We all have our beliefs,' Jimi Hendrix said slowly, as though he could hear Lola's thoughts. 'I try to believe in myself. If there is a God and God made us, then believing in myself means that I believe in God.'

'I don't believe in God,' Lola said. 'I wish I did.'

'I hear you, man,' Jimi Hendrix said. Lola thought he probably did.

'Music is my religion,' Jimi Hendrix said. 'I play to go inside the soul of people.'

Lola knew what it felt like to want to go inside people's souls. She used to wish she could press herself right into people she liked so that she could be as close to them as it was possible to be. She wished she could get past the barriers of clothes and showers and clean hair and good manners.

'Are you comfortable?' Jimi Hendrix asked her, taking a packet of gum out of his pocket.

'Oh, yes, I'm very comfortable.' Lola said.

'You haven't moved at all,' he said.

She was surprised, she hadn't realised that he had been observing her that carefully. Most rock stars were so absorbed in themselves that you could have had a nervous breakdown or been dancing a jig and they wouldn't have noticed.

Lola moved her head and her shoulders in an effort to appear more mobile. She looked at the floor. She didn't think any more shredded tissue had dropped from between her thighs. 'I like sitting still,' she said.

Jimi Hendrix smiled. It was the sweetest smile. The sort of smile you'd expect to see on the face of a choirboy. The smile was so far removed from the expression on his face when he was playing to go inside the souls of people. You wouldn't think that the same face, the peaceful, almost sinless face that she was looking at now, could accommodate such diverse and possibly conflicting expressions.

Jimi Hendrix offered Lola a piece of gum. 'No thanks,' she said. She shifted slightly on the stool and tried to clamp her thighs even closer together.

'Were you a happy child?' she asked him. Lola felt that there were a lot of people who were happy children. She wasn't one of them. It made her sad to think that she mostly remembered being unhappy. There must have been happy days. She could think of happy moments. Moments when someone, particularly a man, told Renia how beautiful she was and Renia glowed from the compliment. Or moments when Renia, flushed with excitement, in a dress she'd bought at a bargain sale, looked at herself in the mirror and looked happy. Lola thought there were probably a lot of people who thought of their childhoods as happy. As a series of one happy day after another. Maybe they were taken on picnics with picnic hampers and woollen rugs to sit on. Maybe their mothers held their hands and allowed them to eat as many ice-creams as they wanted.

'I was a very shy child,' Jimi Hendrix said. Lola believed him. He still looked shy. At least here, in this dressing-room, away from the stage, he looked shy. 'My father was very strict. I didn't speak unless I was spoken to. My mother drank a lot. She didn't take care of herself. Still, she was a groovy mother.'

Lola didn't think a mother who drank and didn't take care of herself sounded at all groovy. Jimi Hendrix looked pensive. 'My mother and father used to fight a lot. Things would be quiet for a couple of months and then there'd be another fallout and I knew I'd have to be getting ready to be sent off somewhere. To my grandmother's place or to a friend of the family's place. My parents weren't around that much. They got divorced when I was nine.'

Lola felt sad. She felt sorry for Jimi Hendrix. She knew what it felt like, as a child, to feel that there was too much that was unpredictable. And too much that was incomprehensible. 'My parents didn't get divorced and never argued,' she said. 'But they weren't around. They seemed to be there. But they weren't. They were on another planet.'

Decades later, Lola would learn that she had been right. That Renia Bensky, who was in the kitchen, banging the saucepans as she lifted them out of the cupboard or grinding meat in the old, loud meat grinder, was not there. Renia Bensky was somewhere else. She was with her dead.

In the death camps, it was impossible to mourn the dead. There were no farewells, no burials, no memorials. Without the goodbyes, Renia Bensky, like many others, remained locked in a frozen dialogue with her dead. For Renia Bensky, her dead were still alive. They took up most of the space in her heart.

'Oh, man,' said Jimi Hendrix, 'having your parents around but not around, that must have been tough.'

'I don't remember it being tough,' said Lola. 'And I don't remember ever crying as a child.'

'I cried when my mother died,' Jimi Hendrix said.

An awkward silence descended on them. As though they had both been taken by surprise and were a little embarrassed at the unexpected turn the conversation had taken. Lola realised she had moved to one side when she was talking. She straightened herself up. She noticed some miniscule pieces of tissue float to the floor. Maybe Jimi Hendrix would think it was dandruff, she thought.

'Were you upset by the fighting in your house?' she said to him.

'Sure I was,' Jimi Hendrix said. 'Man, I hated it. I used to hide in a closet. Children know what's going on without being told. The fights were mostly over money. I knew and I hated it. I spent a lot of time in the closet. I slept there, too. It was my bedroom.'

Lola was impressed by the thought of having a closet as a bedroom. When Lola was small she would invent stories about her and her parents only having one blanket between them. The truth was that Lola and her parents, who lived in one room of an eight-room terrace in Australia that they shared with seven other families, had several blankets. The eight families shared one small bathroom and one small kitchen, but Renia, Edek and Lola had plenty of blankets.

People seemed spellbound when Lola described how they took turns at using the one blanket, which meant that each of them, Lola, her mother and her father, had a blanket for two-and-a-half days a week. Seriously poor kids, kids who wore no shoes and whose clothes were in tatters, would cry when Lola told that story. And Lola found that curiously satisfying.

Jimi Hendrix was right, Lola thought. Without being told, children always knew what was going on. Lola herself felt steeped in her parent's past. She'd felt this way since she was a small child. She didn't know how she knew so much.

No one ever sat down and talked to her. Renia Bensky's mouth was mostly clamped firmly shut and her head was bent over a sewing machine or a saucepan. Six nights a week Renia did piecework, sewing sleeves into dresses, for a factory in Fitzroy. Edek didn't say much when he was home. He would sit on the bed at night in a singlet, too tired to speak after his double shift at the factory.

'My parents separately survived Auschwitz, the Nazi death camp,' Lola said. 'But although they got out alive, parts of them stayed there. Parts of them got left behind.'

Jimi Hendrix nodded.

Lola thought that Jimi Hendrix would understand exactly what she was talking about. He could think of his mother as being a groovy mother, despite the fact that she drank too much and couldn't take care of herself and couldn't take care of him. He could still see the goodness in her. Jimi Hendrix wouldn't think Lola was referring to a scarf or a belt that had been left behind in Auschwitz.

'Are you Jewish?' Jimi Hendrix said.

'Very,' said Lola.

Jimi Hendrix laughed. 'My first gig was in the basement of a synagogue, the Temple De Hirsch Sinai, in Seattle. It didn't go well.'

'Why?' said Lola.

'I was fired between sets,' he said.

Lola started laughing. 'What for?' she asked.

'For showing off,' said Jimi Hendrix. 'I was trying to play from my soul and the other band members thought I was showing off.'

'Maybe the rest of the band thought that in synagogues and churches anything to do with the soul had to be very quiet,' Lola said.

For someone who made such unabashed, unequivocal, unrestricted movements with his body and his voice on stage, Jimi Hendrix's speech was surprisingly hesitant. For a man who plucked and caressed his guitar strings with such a potent urgency, Jimi Hendrix was unexpectedly measured. He spoke slowly and his voice was soft. He thought before he answered questions. He spoke haltingly, his words coming out in groups of three or four at a time.

His lips, which on stage had been disconcertingly lustful, were now carefully formulating and forming vowels and consonants. Jimi Hendrix's lips had an almost chaste purity about them now. His pelvis now looked merely functional. It no longer looked dangerous. It seemed to be just a bony frame at the base of his spine, to which his limbs were attached. A regular, everyday pelvis.

There was a lot about Jimi Hendrix that seemed regular, Lola thought. There was a sense of humility about him. His hit song 'Hey Joe' was number four in the *Melody Maker* charts in London that week. 'Purple Haze' was coming out next month. Rock stars were streaming in to his performances.

A few nights ago at the Bag O' Nails, the decidedly dank but ultra-cool basement nightclub in Soho, Lola heard Brian Jones telling everyone within earshot that Jimi Hendrix was one of the most brilliant guitarists he'd ever heard. Brian Jones had looked very excited. Brian Jones didn't seem to be an excitable person, to Lola. She had only seen him a few times, but each time he had appeared to be quite subdued. In a few months, Lola would see Brian Jones again, at the Monterey International Pop Festival in California. At Monterey he would appear even more subdued, almost comatose.

Eric Clapton, Paul McCartney, Ringo Starr, Mick Jagger and Brian Epstein, The Beatles' manager, were just a few of the other people who'd come to see Jimi at the Bag O' Nails that night. Everyone wanted to meet him. You could tell none of this from Jimi Hendrix's demeanour. He was quiet and he was thoughtful. If he inadvertently interrupted

Lola, he immediately stopped and said, 'No, please do go on.'

The large black cowboy hat adorned with brooches and badges that Jimi had been wearing on stage, was on a bench beside him. Lola looked at him. Jimi Hendrix clearly dressed with care. The sleeves of the floral-patterned satin shirt he was wearing were gathered at the shoulders and stitched into a loose cuff at the wrist. It looked as though it were made for him.

Jimi Hendrix also wore velvet trousers. Crushed velvet trousers in bright colours. No man Lola knew wore crushed velvet trousers. Crushed velvet was for girls. There was, however, nothing girlish about Jimi Hendrix.

On stage it was impossible to forget that Jimi Hendrix had a penis. He rubbed his guitar against his penis. He thrust his hips out. He made short, sharp, rhythmical movements with his crotch. His penis almost seemed to be playing the guitar. Making the music. And talking, pointedly, to the audience. Which could be a bit bothering if, like Lola Bensky, you hadn't had a lot of experience communicating with a penis.

While his penis strutted and pointed and shuddered, Jimi Hendrix was lost in his music. He had blended himself into the whining, cajoling, moaning, pleading notes. His body movements were completely intertwined and integrated with the music. It was impossible to tell what part of him was doing what to which note. Jimi had merged himself into the vibrato he was manoeuvring and controlling until each note sounded like a human voice.

Lola envied Jimi's ability to get lost like that. She couldn't. She was always on guard. Prepared. Prepared for what? A *pogrom*? A war? The Gestapo? She didn't know. Unlike other people her age, she couldn't relax and hang around the house in her pyjamas or underwear. Lola always had to be fully dressed. And ready. Ready for what? Lola had no idea.

The heat in Jimi Hendrix's dressing-room was starting to make Lola's hair frizz. She tried to straighten it by tugging on the ends.

Jimi Hendrix had been talking for about ten minutes. He was talking about the difference between playing live and being in a recording studio. Lola was trying hard to concentrate. She knew she wasn't all that interested in the technical details of his music. How he got the sounds that he did and how he had been experimenting with feedback and which notes would feed back.

Lola had asked him the question because she knew that there were readers of *Rock-Out* who would want to know. But she was having trouble focusing.

She did hear him say several times that he got bored easily and liked to move on. Both in his music, and in the other parts of his life. 'I don't like to stay in one place for too long,' he said. 'I might not be here tomorrow, so I do what I want to be doing.' Lola was startled. She didn't think when he said he might not be here tomorrow, that he was talking about leaving London. She thought he was talking about the possibility of leaving this earth.

Lola realised that she hadn't heard half of what Jimi Hendrix had been saying for the last ten minutes. She looked at her tape recorder. It was still on and recording. She had been distracted by the feedback details, her concern about her fishnet tights digging into her thighs and her rapidly frizzing hair.

Jimi Hendrix's hair was wild. His curls, which grew in great profusion, streamed and screamed in every direction. Lola loved the abandoned way his curls mingled with each other. Her own curls had been ironed flat. Tamped down. Every strand of hair had been ironed until it was ramrod straight. Flattened and battened down. Until now, when the heat and humidity in the room had started an unruly uprising. Curls were springing into action. At odd angles. And in odd places. With no co-ordination or thought about what the rest of her hair was doing. She knew she must look strange. But there was nothing she could do about it.

She decided to focus on Jimi Hendrix's hair. 'I heard that you've got a set of hair curlers,' Lola said to him. Lola had read this in an article talking about how concerned Jimi Hendrix was about his appearance.

In Australia, hair curlers were called rollers. All of the women her mother's age had hair curlers. And so did quite a few of Lola's friends. It was not unusual to visit a friend on the weekend to find the friend and/or her mother with a head full of hair curlers. Lola had never seen a man with a head full of hair curlers.

'Yes, I've got a set of hair curlers,' Jimi Hendrix said. 'I brought my hair curlers with me, from America, when I came to London. That was practically all I brought with me.'

'Really?' said Lola.

'I wear my hair in the same way I wear my scarves and rings and jackets. It's all part of who I am,' he said. He smiled, and looked at Lola. 'There's nothing weird about that,' he said.

'No,' Lola said. 'It's less weird than the fact that I iron my hair straight. I lay it out on an ironing board and iron it, with my head bent as low as I can, in order to get every curl out.'

'You do a good job,' Jimi Hendrix said. 'You got no curls left.'

'It was fine until the humidity in here started to curl it,' Lola said.

'Miss Bensky, you look mighty fine to me,' he said.

Lola was startled that Jimi Hendrix would remember her name for a start, and secondly that instead of referring to her as Lola would call her Miss Bensky. There was something strangely at odds about that with who he was, and something strangely appealing.

'I started using hair curlers because I thought it was a groovy style,' Jimi Hendrix said. 'Now everyone is running around with these curls. Most of them are perms. I've got nothing against perms. I used to get my hair straightened and they use the same solution they use for perms.'

'I know,' Lola said. 'I used to get my hair straightened, too. I hated the smell of the perm solution.'

'I didn't like it either,' Jimi Hendrix said.

Jimi Hendrix was very satisfying to talk to, Lola thought. 'Do you arrange your hair curlers in rows?' she said.

'No,' he said, 'but I know exactly where I need to put them.'

Where to put hair curlers and whether they were in rows or not was not the sort of conversation Lola had expected to have with Jimi Hendrix. Lola wasn't at all sure that this sort of stuff was exactly what her newspaper was looking for.

'You can come and see me in my hair curlers, tonight if you like,' Jimi Hendrix said. Lola had heard a lot about Jimi Hendrix's sexual appetite. She hadn't even known you could have an appetite for sex. She'd thought an appetite only referred to food. Lola had heard that Jimi often had sex with several women in one evening, sometimes with all of them present, and possibly in one bed. She'd also heard that he had sex anywhere. Everywhere. In hallways, dressing-rooms, bathrooms, and often in the presence of other people who just happened to be there at the time.

Lola didn't think a late-night visit to Jimi Hendrix would be a good idea.

'I might,' she said.

'You don't look as though you mean it,' Jimi Hendrix said, and grinned.

2

Lola stood at the front door of Mick Jagger's apartment. She took
a deep breath and tried to flatten her stomach. It didn't really work.
Holding her breath wasn't flattening her stomach. She didn't know
why she was bothering. She would have to breathe eventually. And no
other part of her was flat.

Last night she'd been to a reception for the supermodel Twiggy.
Twiggy was seventeen and one of the thinnest girls Lola had ever
seen. Twiggy's arms and legs were so thin they looked as though they
couldn't possibly have enough space for the bones, muscles, joints, ten-
dons, veins and arteries they needed to contain. Twiggy was about to
change the shape women wanted to be – a change that would last decades, and have almost every female in the developed world on a diet.

Twiggy was very pretty. Her huge blue eyes shone and her short
blond hair gleamed. Standing next to Twiggy, Lola felt as big as a
piece of furniture. A large, clunky piece of furniture. Twiggy looked
as light as a leaf. It must feel so comfortable to be that thin, Lola
thought. You must feel closer to your own heart and lungs and bones.
Lola wondered if that sort of proximity to what you were composed
of made you feel more at ease with yourself. Less worried about who

you were. The only bones that Lola could feel were the bones in her wrists and her feet.

She would have to diet for a decade to be as thin as Twiggy, she decided. Lola usually planned eight- to ten-week diets. Then she would delay the start. There was usually a goal. At the moment, she was planning to lose sixty pounds before her trip to New York and to California, to the Monterey International Pop Festival, in three months. She had already delayed the start of this diet.

It was a new diet she had devised while watching The Walker Brothers perform 'The Sun Ain't Gonna Shine Anymore'. She called it the Apple, Banana and Egg Diet. Each day she would have seven bananas, seven apples and three eggs, divided into four meals. She would have two apples, two bananas and one egg, three times a day, and one apple and one banana, once a day. It came to a total of approximately 1640 calories a day.

Lola thought that this diet sounded very promising. She would feel relatively full because of the bulk in the food and she wouldn't look odd taking an apple or a banana with her to most places. She might have to be a little more careful with the boiled egg. It wasn't easy to peel and eat a boiled egg in public with dignity, unless you were at a picnic.

Last week, just as she was about to begin the Apple, Banana and Egg Diet, the lead guitarist of The Troggs had ordered fish and chips for everyone and Lola had had to eat them. They had been in a small fish-and-chip shop somewhere in the north of England and Lola had felt too embarrassed to bring out the banana and apple and egg she had packed at the bottom of her bag. Lola had been on tour with The Troggs for six days. She had heard 'Wild Thing' and 'I Can't Control

Myself' one time too many. Lola didn't like loud music. It gave her a headache.

In her article about The Troggs, she had written about their high-voltage, explosive sound and how Reg Presley, the lead singer, lured in the audience with his sensual moves and flirtatious lyrics. She had also mentioned that despite their string of hits, The Troggs were straightforward and unpretentious. She had said nothing about her headache.

The thought of trying to be as slim as Twiggy daunted Lola. It had made her think about Caramello Bars. Caramello Bars were blocks of milk chocolate with a thick, almost runny caramel sauce at the centre of each square. Lola thought that few of the people surrounding Twiggy were thinking about Caramello Bars at that very moment.

Twiggy's blue eyes were fringed with the thickest black lashes Lola had ever seen. In the two minutes she'd had alone with Twiggy, Lola had asked her where she got her eyelashes from. 'They're just ordinary false eyelashes. I layer three pairs over my own,' Twiggy had said. Lola didn't think she would try to do that. She didn't think she was dexterous enough to glue on three layers of lashes.

'You are so pretty,' she'd said to Twiggy.

'I hate the way I look,' Twiggy said. 'I think everyone's gone stark raving mad.'

Mick Jagger opened the door. He looked more slightly built than he did on stage. Maybe all the movement he made while he was singing made him appear larger. On stage, Mick Jagger moved continuously.

He shook his head, he waved his arms. He skipped across the stage and jumped and danced. He radiated energy. The other members of The Rolling Stones looked almost static next to Mick Jagger.

'Hi,' he said. 'Come in, I'm a bit tired. I was in the recording studio till five a.m.'

Lola was thrilled that Mick Jagger was a bit tired. On stage he looked like the sort of person who never got tired.

Mick Jagger was three-and-a-quarter years older than Lola. He was twenty-three. And vilified by parents of teenagers all over the world. Lola couldn't quite understand why. Because he had sultry lips and moved his hips while singing 'Let's Spend the Night Together'? In America The Rolling Stones had had to change the lyrics to 'Let's spend some time together' when they'd performed on the Ed Sullivan television show. Lola thought that had been a stupid demand. What were the producers of *The Ed Sullivan Show* worried about? Did they think that hundreds of thousands of teenagers would rush out to spend the night with each other? Lola didn't think so. She thought it was probably Mick Jagger's hips and his defiant strutting that bothered older men. And possibly older women.

Mick Jagger wasn't skipping or strutting this morning. His movements were slow and leisurely. The apartment looked very large, to Lola. It seemed to be about half a block long. The living-room area was carpeted in a neutral sort of dark-beige tone. One wall was painted blue. Next to a long, refectory-style dining table was a huge record player with hundreds of LPs.

Mick Jagger pointed to an elongated, five-seater sofa. 'Would you like to sit there?' he said. The sofa looked very low, to Lola. She hated low armchairs and sofas. It was impossible to sit on them without your skirt or dress riding up and exposing your knees. And Lola needed to keep her knees covered. They were very chunky knees. Lola was sure they took up more space than Twiggy's hips. Lola's knees looked force-fed. As though someone had been stuffing them. Mick Jagger's sofa, which looked as though it should be on the cover of a home decor magazine, was not where Lola would have preferred to sit. The chairs at the refectory table looked much more comfortable.

'Sure,' said Lola.

She sat down, tugged at the hemline of her dress, which had already crept up to her knees, and began to arrange her equipment. She put her tape recorder on the gold-topped coffee table in front of her and arranged her pen and notebook on her lap. She wished she'd brought a larger notebook. It might have covered her knees.

Mick Jagger sat opposite her on the other side of the coffee table in a black leather armchair. He was curled up in a curiously passive position. He looked very comfortable. He didn't look like the anti-establishment destroyer of social values that he and the other Rolling Stones had been labelled.

Lola knew that Mick Jagger's father and grandfather were both teachers. His mother, a hairdresser, was also active in Conservative Party politics. At the moment, apart from his longish hair, Mick Jagger looked much more like the product of schoolteachers and members of the Conservative Party than the defiant troublemaker he was supposed to be.

'I hope you're not going to ask me what colour socks I wear,' Mick Jagger said to Lola.

'No,' said Lola, 'I'm not interested in what colour socks you are wearing. I'm not going to ask you if you know Paul McCartney, either.'

'Of course I do,' said Mick Jagger. 'He dropped into the recording studio last night and is coming around later today.' Lola wasn't
sure what to do with that piece of information. She made a note of it
in case her tape recorder hadn't caught the first couple of minutes of
their conversation.

'What do you think it is that causes the worship and hysteria
among your fans at your concerts?' she asked Mick Jagger. 'Is it love?'

Lola wasn't sure she knew a lot about either worship or love. Mick
Jagger looked perplexed. He brushed his hair away from his face and
put his foot on the coffee table as he pondered the question. Lola felt
that Mick Jagger wasn't about to toss off a blithe answer. He looked as
though he cared about what he was quoted as saying, and he treated
interviews as seriously as he treated his performances. Even interviews
with an Australian rock newspaper.

'I'm sure it must be a highly sexual thing, sexual and violent,' he
said. 'You asked if it was love. I don't think it's love. I believe that there
is affection. The audience have bought tickets because they want to
see us; we are there because we like doing concerts, we like audiences.
There is a rapport, a tremendous basic affection.'

Lola looked at him. He was linking basic affection with violence
and hysteria. It seemed like a very odd coupling to Lola. 'But on top of
that affection is violence,' Mick Jagger said. 'And on top of the violence
is sex. It is a strange escalation of emotion.'

Lola decided not to argue with him. She felt he must know a lot
more about sex and violence than she did. Mick Jagger was looking at
her intently. As though he wasn't sure if she had understood what he
was saying.

He was strangely attractive, Lola thought. He certainly didn't have the regular, symmetrical features that were usually associated with being considered handsome. He did have beautiful eyes. They were a hazel, a brown that easily changed shades. And he had a very pleasing puffiness under his eyes, as though his eyes had their own pillows. His large lips were perfectly delineated. They had a natural pout even when he was saying something serious.

He didn't dress with the flamboyance of some rock stars. He wasn't wearing striped satin trousers and strange hats like his fellow Rolling Stone Brian Jones. In fact he was dressed more like the London School of Economics accounting and business student he once was. He was wearing a thin navy woollen sweater with the sleeves rolled up to his elbows and grey cotton trousers.

'It's a strange thing,' Mick Jagger said. 'You feel a tremendous energy directed at you from the audience. You feel as if they are try- ing to say something to you. They need something but they're not sure what it is.'

Lola knew that feeling of needing something. And not knowing what it was. It often made her feel scared. Or lonely.

'Do you ever feel scared or lonely on stage?' she said to Mick Jagger.

'No,' he said, looking perplexed. 'I'm not alone on stage. I'm one-fifth of The Rolling Stones. We always have fun on stage, always have a laugh.' He paused. 'I was a bit scared recently,' he said. 'We were play-ing a huge stadium in Zurich, and we were on a platform thirty or forty feet above the crowd. As we walked on stage somebody jumped on my back. There were ten guys pushing and pulling me, they nearly had me over the edge. I looked down and I was frightened.'

'Ten guys?' Lola said,

'Yes,' Mick Jagger said. 'It was frightening.'

'I thought your audiences were mainly girls,' Lola said.

'No,' he said. 'In Britain, maybe, but not in other countries. In France, it's predominantly boys who come to the concerts. In Berlin we just had a concert with twenty-thousand people. As far as we could see, they were all boys. Not a girl anywhere. Maybe it's some sort of nineteenth-century leftover, you know, a young lady must not appear at the theatre unless correctly chaperoned. Or maybe it's simply that the girls do not have the money that boys earn. They just don't earn as much. It shouldn't be that way, but it is.'

Lola found that interesting. Few people, especially men, were thinking about the disparity in income between men and women. 'Do you think men and women should have equal pay for equal work?' Lola said.

'Of course they should,' he said. 'Otherwise they'll never get anywhere. You know guys are going to get somewhere, but most women aren't. If it sounds like I'm making an anti-feminist statement, I'm sorry, but I'm just speaking from practical experience.'

Mick Jagger was right, Lola thought. This was not a woman's world. It was a man's world. Lola was one of the few females working in the rock world. The performers were mostly men, the journalists were men, the managers were men, the stagehands were men, the road crews were men. Where were the women? Some of them were go-go girls, animated decoration in nightclubs or on television. And the others were screaming in the audience or scrambling to get into the beds of one of the rock stars or their entourages.

Linda Eastman, the talented photographer who later became Mrs Paul McCartney, was one of the few women working in the rock world. Lola had met Linda a few times. They had a mutual friend, the New York-based, Australian journalist Lillian Roxon. Linda was American and very confident. She had lots of blond hair and a wide stride. She wore reasonably short skirts. Often when she leaned back to take group photographs, whatever underwear she was wearing was completely exposed. Lola thought that Linda must have fabulous balance to be able to lean back like that.

One day, Lola was waiting to interview Dave Dee, Dozy, Beaky, Mick and Tich. The group had had several hit records, including 'Save Me' and 'Touch Me, Touch Me'. Lola loved the song titles, if not the songs themselves. She was sitting in the waiting area of the group's management company offices, when the door to one of the rooms flew open. Linda Eastman came out. Lola could see Dave Dee, Dozy, Beaky, Mick and Tich in the background. 'Oh, it's you,' Linda said. 'They said there was a fat Australian journalist waiting and I thought it was Lillian.'

The door to the room Linda had come from was still open. Lola knew that everyone in there had heard. 'Wrong fat Australian journalist,' Lola had said to Linda, in what she had hoped was a nonchalant tone. She felt humiliated and flat. And very fat. Not even her new purple false eyelashes could distract her from the fact of her fat.

Lola could hardly remember anything about the interview with Dave Dee, Dozy, Beaky, Mick and Tich. She remembered that they had all been polite, not the sorts to describe someone as a fat Australian journalist, especially Dave Dee, a former policeman, who had been very polite. Lola didn't know if it was Dave Dee who had described her. Maybe being a former policeman had made him feel obliged to be more factual in his descriptions.

'I don't think you're being anti-feminist or sexist,' Lola said to

Mick Jagger. 'I think you're right. It's a boy's world. The rock world is full of boys. Boys in bands in love with themselves and in love with being who they are.'

Mick Jagger laughed. 'And you're not in love with any of them,' he said.

'No,' she said.

She was particularly not in love with Pete Townshend of The Who. She'd had to interview The Who in their dressing-room after one of their performances. Lola was sitting on a chair adjusting her tape recorder when Keith Moon, The Who's drummer, walked in, stood beside Lola and removed his trousers. Keith Moon's crotch was exactly at Lola's eye level, and uncomfortably close to her face. She concentrated on her tape recorder and pretended not to notice his hairy legs and peculiarly coloured, tight underpants.

The Who were known as the group that hated each other. They were also known for ending their shows with a spectacular display of destruction. They smashed guitars and drumsticks and amplifiers until the stage was littered with the very expensive debris of broken musical instruments.

'Are you getting along better with each other?' Lola asked John Entwistle, the bass guitarist. She'd asked him the question because it meant she could turn away from Keith Moon and his tight underpants. 'We get along much better now,' said John Entwistle. 'Sometimes we still get into a fight, but usually as a group and not against each other individually.'

Lola was trying to come to terms with the notion of fighting as a group – did he mean that they punched each other or other people? Keith Moon and Pete Townshend did seem to have explosive tempers.

Pete Townshend moved his chair closer to her and said, 'The Who aren't getting on any better. We're just pretending to get on better. It's easy to pretend. Everyone pretends. You pretend to get on with your parents, you pretend you're happy at home because it suits you to keep living there.'

Lola wished she hadn't asked the question. There was something about his derisive, indifferent tone that bothered her. 'The working atmosphere in any group is probably similar to ours,' Pete Townshend said. 'There's got to be friction there. What about The Kinks? They've got two brothers in the group. There's always friction between brothers of any kind. The Walker Brothers. There must be friction there.'

He'd said the name with a particularly dismissive sneer. Lola wondered what he had against The Walker Brothers. She didn't have to ask. 'The Walker Brothers come on stage looking fabulous and fantastic and within weeks they're on top of the charts,' he said. 'Our group is really not glamorous at all. It's one of our big problems, there's no glamour.' Lola thought Pete Townshend might have problems more complex than a lack of glamour. His churlish and unpleasant demeanour, for a start.

Pete Townshend started talking about how he began smashing up his guitar on stage. Twenty minutes later he was still talking about it. Lola wanted to turn to one of the other members of The Who, but they were both sitting next to Keith Moon, who by now had also removed his shirt.

Pete Townshend was talking about the sound he achieved by crashing his guitar into the amplifiers when he suddenly stopped talking, looked at Lola, and said, 'The best sound you can get is Awaah.' Or maybe he'd said 'Uwuuh'. Lola had no idea what Awaah or Uwuuh meant. She wasn't sure he was speaking English. It could have been Urdu.

'Awaah, Awaah. You should know, because you're Australian,' he shouted. Lola didn't think this was the moment to mention that maybe she wasn't all that Australian. Maybe being born in a DP camp in Germany meant she had missed out on something basic about being Australian.

Awaah or Uwuuh, he kept repeating. Lola didn't have a clue about what he was trying to say. Pete Townshend was becoming more and more agitated. He got up and paced around her. 'Awaah,' he shouted, 'Awaah.'

Lola racked her brains. She'd never heard of 'Awaah'. He said it made a good sound. That eliminated most food or drink or plants. Maybe it was an animal. Australia did have a lot of peculiarly named animals.

About twenty minutes later, Pete Townshend had calmed down and was in the middle of a monologue on British music, British fashion and British identity, when Lola suddenly got it. She looked at him. 'Do you mean AWA?' She said, enunciating each letter with care. 'AWA. Amalgamated *Wireless* Australasia?'

Lola's parents had bought a beautiful AWA radio in 1952. Lola had loved the look of it, with its curved lines and dials. On Saturday nights from the time she was eight or nine she would sit, glued to that AWA radio, listening to the latest murder-mystery thriller. Then she would be too scared to go to sleep.

'Awaah, yes, awaah,' Pete Townshend had said, and sneered. Lola didn't think that sort of imagined pronunciation transgression warranted a sneer.

'AWA,' she repeated.

'Awaah,' he shouted, 'that's right. Awaah.' He looked at her with disdain. 'You should have known that,' he said. Pete Townshend whined a lot and seemed to have that sneer semi-permanently smeared on his face.

He whined about the quality of pop music. 'There's no quality in pop music. I was listening to a stereo recording of The Beatles in which the vocals come out of one side and the backing track comes out of the other. When you hear the backing track without the vocals, it's lousy.'

Lola looked at him. His features seemed to feel the pull of his personality. His nose hung low, his eyes drooped at the outer edges, his mouth curled down. Even his earlobes frowned and looked down. 'Are you looking at my nose?' Pete Townshend said.

'No,' said Lola. She had read that Pete Townshend had been taunted about his nose from the time he was a child.

'My nose has bothered me my whole fucking life,' he said. 'I played the guitar to take attention away from my nose. I'm not bothered by my nose any more. In fact, I hardly think about it.'

He didn't sound as though he was no longer bothered about his nose, Lola thought.

'His bad moods show more than most people's,' John Entwistle, the bass player, said to Lola. Lola thought that he had probably been trying to make her feel better.

'I heard a journalist saying the other day that your sexually charged gyrations are the secret to your success,' Lola said to Mick Jagger.

'That's utter crap,' he said. 'There's no secret to anyone's success. It's not about a secret. It's about doing the best you can, putting everything into it and hoping people will like it. People have to know about what you are doing, but once they know you exist and they can listen to what you've got to offer, they either like you or they don't. It's got nothing to do with having a secret.'

'Do you think you're a great singer?' Lola said. Lola couldn't, on the whole, tell who sang well and who didn't. She couldn't tell if a singer was in tune or was hitting the right notes. Despite years of forced piano lessons, she wasn't at all musical. When she reviewed records, it was generally the lyrics or the personality of the singer she responded to more than the music.

'Am I a great singer?' Mick Jagger said. 'No. I can hardly sing. I'm not Tom Jones or Scott Walker and I couldn't give a fuck.' A lot of people had it in for Scott Walker, Lola thought. Pete Townshend fumed about The Walker Brothers. And Mick Jagger wasn't exactly sounding enamoured of them.

'I've got nothing against Scott Walker,' Mick Jagger said. 'He's a good singer. I'm not, but I like to sing. I've always liked to sing. I was always singing when I was a child. I used to sing around the house. I used to sing in the church choir. I loved singing.'

Everyone went to a church or to a synagogue, even Mick Jagger, Lola thought. That thought made her feel quite deprived. There seemed to be something so cosy about belonging to a group. It was a sense of belonging, Lola thought. Lola never really felt as though she belonged. As a family, Renia, Edek and Lola seemed too decimated to be called a group. When you were part of a formal group, you were officially declared a member. Unlike families, in which your membership seemed to be more a matter of random or haphazard occurrence. Your role in a church group, or Boy Scout's group or knitting group was clear. It all seemed straightforward, you went to meetings, people were friendly. There was order and structure and what seemed to be cohesion. There were rituals and rules and, often, food. Lola's next-door neighbour when she was a child, Mrs Dent, was always baking apple pies or jam tarts for the church picnic, or other church functions. She was a devout Methodist. Lola often wished she could go to church with Mrs Dent and have a piece of apple pie or a jam tart.

Lola knew being in a group wasn't as clear-cut as it seemed. When she was twelve, she had persuaded Edek to join a school friend's father in a game of tennis one Saturday afternoon. Edek had resisted her pleas for months. 'Are you crazy?' he had said. But eventually, he had relented. Lola had been elated. She had planned a tennis club. A series of tennis afternoons with her school friend Suzy and Suzy's father Bill. 'Bill' was an Anglicised version of something Hungarian.

Bill Gantner was a dark, moustached, handsome man. He was wearing white shorts, a white shirt and white tennis shoes. Edek arrived in his grey weekend trousers and a plastic parka. The match did not get off to a good start. Bill Gantner had to show Edek, who was a more than reasonable table-tennis player, how to hold the racket. Edek swung the racket violently at every ball. He ran all over the court. He sweated profusely and cursed in Yiddish.

Apart from a series of grunts, all that could be heard from Edek's side of the court was '*Oy, cholera*', which could be literally translated as 'Oh, cholera', but really meant 'Oh, fuck'. Edek didn't manage to hit one ball. Play had to be suspended when Edek tripped, ripped his trousers and grazed his knee. Edek had been in a terrible mood in the car on the way home.

'I am finished with such games,' Edek had said to Lola.

'Mr Bensky needs to practise,' Lola's friend Suzy reported her father had said. The tennis team disbanded before it had even had a chance to bond.

'I also loved listening to singers on the radio or watching them on television,' Mick Jagger said. Listening to singers on the radio or on television didn't seem like the activities of someone who would grow up to be called a scruffy, rebellious, lawless, licentious bad boy.

Nothing about Mick Jagger or his apartment was remotely scruffy. His apartment, which Lola heard he'd decorated himself, was orderly and spotless. A grey square box with lights that flickered on and off was artfully placed slightly to the left of the middle of a wooden mantelpiece. Mick Jagger saw her looking at the flickering lights.

'You can't switch them off,' he said. 'It's a nothing box. I like to sit and look at it.' Lola had no idea what a nothing box was, but sitting and looking at it seemed harmless enough.

'This has got nothing to do with a nothing box, but you have been accused of being depraved,' Lola said. 'Are you depraved?' Mick Jagger thought for a minute.

'What constitutes depraved behaviour?' he said. Lola was startled. She hadn't thought about what constituted depraved behaviour in a rock star. Maybe the journalist who had called Mick Jagger depraved was envisioning a sexual orgy of some sort.

Lola knew that the snippets that slipped out of her mother about the Gestapo forcing women to go down on their hands and knees and be raped and violated by large, well-trained SS dogs contained depraved behaviour. And the slivers of sentences about doctors

infecting hundreds of men, women and children with typhus, cholera, bubonic plague or leprosy and subjecting them to whimsical,
nonsensical medical experiments were also about depraved behaviour.

Renia and Edek had a group of eight friends. They called them-
selves The Company. The Company went to the movies together on
Saturday nights and on Sunday nights they played cards. Mostly at the
Bensky's house, as Renia, who didn't like to play cards, usually volun-
teered to make supper. One Sunday night, Mrs Feldman asked Mrs
Lipschitz why she looked so tired.

'Don't ask,' Mrs Lipschitz said. 'I couldn't sleep last night.'

'She was thinking all night about Willhaus,' Mr Lipschitz said.
'Obersturmführer Willhaus was the commandant of the Janovska
Camp, Lvov. He did live there with his wife and daughter.'

'I did hear about him,' Edek said. 'He did like to stand on his balcony with his wife and his daughter and shoot at the prisoners. It was
a bit of fun for them.' The Company went very quiet. 'Lvov is maybe
three-hundred-fifty miles from Lodz,' Edek said to Lola, who had
been watching Edek play. Lola wasn't sure why Edek thought she
needed the exact geographical location of the shootings.

'Sometimes Willhaus would order someone to throw three- and
four-year-old children in the air while he did shoot at them,' Mr
Lipschitz said. 'When he did shoot a child, Willhaus's daughter, who
was nine years old, would clap her hands and cry out, "Do it again,
Papa."' Mrs Lipschitz started to cry.

'Have a chocolate,' Edek said to her. 'The ones with a prune in the
middle are very good.'

'In 1943, on Hitler's birthday, Obersturmführer Willhaus did
count off fifty-four prisoners and did shoot them himself,' Mrs

Lipschitz said. 'Hitler was fifty-four that day.'

Lola was sure that Willhaus was depraved.

'I think the journalist accusing me meant *decadent*,' Mick Jagger said. 'I may be decadent, but I'm not depraved. I try to look after myself. I don't eat much meat. I prefer fish. I don't drink milk or eat a lot of starchy foods.'

Lola was going to ask him why he didn't drink milk, but she decided against it.

'I believe in that adage, you are what you eat,' Mick Jagger said. 'If you eat an enormous amount of potatoes, you end up looking like a potato.'

'I don't eat a lot of potatoes,' Lola said.

'I wasn't talking about you,' Mick Jagger said, looking surprised.

'I eat a lot of chocolate,' Lola said. 'I should look flat and rectangular. But I do look more like a potato.'

'No you don't,' he said.

'I am fat,' said Lola.

'You're very pretty,' Mick Jagger said.

'Thank you,' said Lola.

That was nice of him, Lola thought. He probably wasn't even decadent, let alone depraved.

Lola wanted to move the conversation well away from food or body size or shape.

'What made you leave the London School of Economics?' she said.

Mick Jagger's tutor at the London School of Economics had described him as 'A highly promising, intelligent pupil'. Mick Jagger shrugged his shoulders.

'I suppose I was just drawn into being an entertainer,' he said.

Lola thought 'entertainer' was an odd word for him to use to describe himself. Rock star, musician, singer would have been more appropriate words to use.

'I like entertaining,' he said. 'It helps me, as a person, to get rid of my ego.'

How could he or anyone else separate themselves from their ego, Lola wondered. Unlike toes or knees, egos were not easy to locate.

'If I get rid of the ego on stage, then the problem ceases to exist when I leave the stage. I no longer have the need to prove myself.'

Mick Jagger's tutor had said that he was welcome to return to the London School of Economics at any time. Lola didn't think Mick Jagger would be taking up his offer. 'He would certainly have graduated if he had stayed,' the tutor had added.

Lola had not graduated from her high school, a high school for gifted children. She had failed the final year. Well, she hadn't actually failed, failed – she hadn't sat for two of the compulsory exams. She had gone to see the Alfred Hitchcock movie *Psycho* instead. And then been shocked to see her exam number missing from the published list of graduating students.

Edek didn't say much about Lola failing to finish high school, except for mentioning, again, that she would have been a better lawyer than Perry Mason. Renia had said nothing at all. All year Renia's sole focus had been on the fact that Lola was twenty pounds heavier than Renia thought she should be. At the beginning of the year, Renia had enrolled Lola in a slimming program where a thick vibrating rubber belt was strapped around her hips while an electric current jiggled the fat around. After eight weeks, the vibrating rubber belt had failed to remove even half a pound from Lola's hips. Halfway through that final year of high school, Renia had announced, as she packed

Lola's pyjamas and a dressing-gown, that she was putting her in hospital for a week. Lola spent a week in the Royal Melbourne Hospital on a 500-calorie-a-day diet. At every meal, the menu would have no butter, no oil, no cheese, no toast, no jam, no sauce neatly handwritten across the top. Lola was also allowed no visitors.

Lola couldn't remember how she got through those seven days. She had no memory of eating anything, no memory of reading or talking on the phone. She had no memory of showering or brushing her teeth or walking or talking to anyone. She had no visitors. She couldn't remember either Edek or Renia visiting her.

What she could remember was the humiliation she felt when she went back to school. Apparently the school had been told that Lola had been in hospital, but no one knew why. Lola whispered to anyone who asked her what had happened that she had had a throat operation and couldn't speak. At home, even though it was unnecessary, Lola kept up the charade. She hardly spoke. Renia didn't notice – they weren't a family who chatted much, anyway.

Lola could also remember eating two family-size blocks of Cadbury's chocolate the day after she got out of hospital. She had lost seven pounds in the week she'd been in hospital. Those seven pounds didn't remain lost for long. They found their way back to Lola's hips and thighs as though they'd never been away.

A recurring nightmare of having to go back to high school and pass those exams would haunt Lola for years. She would have decades of dreams in which she was back at school and in a big mess. But she didn't yet know this. She didn't yet know she would spend years and years in analysis trying to figure out, among other things, why she went to see *Psycho* instead of sitting for her exam. She was sixty-two when she woke up one morning and realised she was too old to go back to high school.

The phone rang in Mick Jagger's apartment. 'Can you excuse me for a moment?' he said, and got up and walked to the phone. He had a very ordinary brisk walk. There was no evidence of sexually charged gyrations in his pelvic area. He didn't half-skip, as he sometimes did on stage. He just walked. He answered the phone. 'I'm okay,' he said. 'Not great. I didn't get much sleep last night. The session didn't finish till early this morning. It didn't go well.'

Lola knew that Mick Jagger had been brought up a Catholic, but he sounded so Jewish. That list of what was wrong was very Jewish. Asking any Jew how they were inevitably resulted in a series of grievances. Yiddish phrasebooks never included 'I'm excellent' or 'I'm very good' as an answer to the question, 'How are you?'

In most Jews, merely being asked that question provoked both an anxiety and an opportunity to complain. '*Nish-koshe*', 'not too bad', and '*a-zoy*', 'so-so', as well as '*s'ken alemol zayn erger*', 'it could always be worse' or '*s'ken alemol zayn beser*', 'it could always be better' were considered positive replies. The responses were always accompanied by a pained facial expression, a weary shrug or the wringing of hands.

Lola used to love the list of complaints that came out when any of her parents' friends were asked how they were. 'My children are giving me a heartache.' 'I have a pain in my head.' 'My Harry is killing me. He won't study.' 'My husband works too hard. My own feet are swollen.' 'How should I feel?' These were not atypical answers.

When Lola's school friends' parents in Australia were asked how they were, they would inevitably reply, 'Very well, thank you.' What did that tell you, Lola thought? Nothing. You had no idea whether they were very well, or on the verge of death. If you said how are you to a Jew, you usually learned something about them. Renia's friend Mrs Littman, when asked how she was, mostly had the same reply. 'What Yitzhak wants from me every night, dear God, don't ask.'

Nobody ever asked.

Lola liked Mrs Littman. She was blond and busty and wore tight tops and even tighter skirts. On card nights, Mrs Littman always passed Lola a slice of cake, or a chocolate wafer, when Renia wasn't looking. For years, every time Lola saw Mrs Littman, she wondered whether Yitzhak was still wanting whatever it was he wanted every night.

'No, it was really bad, man,' Mick Jagger was saying on the phone. 'The session was a mess.' He looked very bothered. Lola was drawn to people who were bothered, people who talked about what was wrong. People who were worried. She thought that being cheerful, too much of the time, was unnatural.

She was also drawn to anguish. She could detect anguish at a distance. From the other end of the house, from the other side of the street, possibly even from a block or two away. She could spot anguish even if it came in the disguise of a smile or was hidden behind a grin.

A few days ago, she had been walking in Carnaby Street with Cat Stevens. They were on their way to Cat Stevens' manager's office. There was, Lola felt, a small hint of anguish waiting to emerge in Cat Stevens.

Cat Stevens already had two smash hits with 'I Love My Dog' and 'Matthew and Son', and was about to have a third hit with 'I'm Gonna Get Me a Gun'. He was eighteen, almost two years younger than Lola.

Carnaby Street was awash with bright colours and mini miniskirts. Lola had told the readers of *Rock-Out* that young women and girls were wearing fluorescent pink, yellow and green mini-dresses with matching shoes. They also wore silver, gold and bronze eye make-up and had earrings and brooches made out of old belt buckles, table-tennis balls, old necklaces and even plaited shoelaces. Some of the skirts and dresses were so short they barely reached the wearer's thighs. Lola saw several young women with bloomers that matched their dresses. Now that the weather was warmer, girls were also decorating their bare knees with glued-on pieces of jewellery or artificial flowers.

This was definitely not the year to have fat knees, Lola thought. She had been contemplating seeing a Harley Street specialist who guaranteed a minimum weight loss of four pounds a week. His weight-loss program consisted of daily hormone injections and a diet of five hundred calories a day. Lola wasn't sure she could afford to have herself injected and starved. It was bound to be expensive.

Cat Stevens knew these streets well. He'd grown up in the area. He lived above the Moulin Rouge, the restaurant his Greek father and Swedish mother owned. He seemed much older than his years. He had a thoughtfulness and an introspection you didn't usually see in eighteen-year-olds. It wasn't quite anguish, but it looked as though it could maybe head in that direction later.

Lola liked Cat Stevens. He had a straightforward, yet quirky seriousness about him.

Lola asked him if he got on well with his mother. She didn't know why she asked him that question. She wasn't sure if she knew how to tell whether she was getting on well with her mother or not. How could you tell? She had left home when she was eighteen, but she used to speak to her mother three or four times a week and visit her at least once or twice a week. Was that getting on well? She and Renia didn't argue. Maybe that was getting on well.

Renia had cried for over a week after Lola had moved out, Edek had told her. Lola had felt bothered. But she didn't think that Renia was crying because Renia was missing her. She thought Renia's crying had more to do with no longer having Lola there. Lola knew that there was a distinction between these two things, she just found it hard to pinpoint exactly what that distinction was.

'Do I get on well with my mother?' Cat Stevens said. 'I like both my parents very much. I get on well with them, but I haven't always. If you get on well with them in the beginning, maybe you won't get on so well with them later on.' Lola thought that was probably a shaky principle to operate on. She thought getting on well in the beginning sounded more promising, as it could possibly give you a backlog of goodwill when things started to go wrong.

She wasn't sure when things started to go wrong between her and Renia and Edek. She wasn't even sure if things were wrong. When Edek spoke about her as a baby, he always said what a beautiful baby she was. But as Lola got older, there didn't seem to be a lot of praise or admiration coming from either of them.

They were horrified when at fifteen she decided she was beatnik. She dyed her hair black and found the palest, whitest face make-up she could. Already looking ghostly, she practised and perfected a suitably sombre expression for a serious beatnik.

'My parents got divorced when I was eight,' Cat Stevens said.

'Really?' said Lola. She didn't know many people whose parents were divorced. Maybe divorce was less common in Australia. It was certainly less common among Jews. Maybe there was already too much loss in Jewish genes to be able to willingly part with another person.

'I sometimes wish my parents would get divorced,' Lola said to Cat Stevens. 'They never disagree about anything. They never argue or contradict each other. Well, my father never contradicts my mother. I might be able to get a second opinion about something, anything at all, if they were divorced.'

'A second opinion about what?' said Cat Stevens.

'I don't know,' Lola said. 'It would be good, occasionally, just to get another view. About anything. About me being fat.'

'You're okay,' Cat Stevens said. 'It's probably your thyroid.' How did Cat Stevens know about thyroid glands, Lola wondered.

'My mother had my thyroid tested when I was twelve,' Lola said. 'It was fine.'

There was a loneliness about Cat Stevens, despite his jaunty black hat and round, wire-rimmed, dark glasses. In less than a year's time, he would be hospitalised for months with tuberculosis. That hospitalisation and the yearlong convalescence would change his life. He would become vegetarian, take up meditation, write very introspective songs, read about different religions and question every aspect of his life.

'Do you have a lot of friends?' Lola said to him.

'I don't have any really close friends,' he said. 'There are people I meet and talk to. But close friends, no, I don't have any.'

Lola wondered if Cat Stevens was lonely. She herself didn't feel lonely. She wouldn't feel her loneliness for years. She would wait until she was living with a man who told her he loved her every morning and every night and, often, at several other times during the day, before she could feel her loneliness. Once she felt that loneliness, it would feel limitless, immense and immeasurable.

'I don't go to clubs,' Cat Stevens said. 'I don't like them much, really. I like home life, anyway. I'm a funny sort of person. Even as a little kid I could never mix with people. I was different from the other kids.'

'How has fame affected you then?' Lola asked.

'I don't really notice it,' he said. 'As I said, I was a queer kid and people pointed and stared and laughed anyway. The other day I suddenly thought, Gee how many people know my name? It was a gas thought.'

Lola couldn't understand what could have been so queer about Cat Stevens and why people would have pointed and stared and laughed. He was often described as being nervous. Maybe that's what they were pointing at. Journalists had written descriptions of him tapping his knees or hugging cushions or shredding napkins. Lola didn't think any of that was weird.

Lola mentioned the knee-tapping she'd read about and asked Cat Stevens if he was a nervous person. 'People keep telling me I've got nerves,' he said. 'I did tap my knees all the time and twitch a bit, but I've lost that habit. I don't think I'm nervous.'

She asked him why he changed his name. She knew he hadn't been born Cat Stevens. 'Can you imagine people asking for a record by Steven Demetre Georgiou?' he said.

'Probably not,' Lola said. 'Do you like Cat Stevens?'

'I'm getting to know him more and more every day,' he said. 'I'm looking forward to growing old. There's so much you don't understand when you're young. Getting older brings wisdom, and wisdom is a beautiful thing.'

Lola had never thought about acquiring wisdom or getting old. It never occurred to her to think about the future. The future seemed nebulous. How did you know you were going to have one, anyway? 'Do you think about the future a lot?' she said to Cat Stevens.

'I do,' he said. 'I want to build a house in Greece one day.' Lola thought that not many eighteen-year-olds would be thinking about building a house.

'Being half-Swedish and half-Greek and living in England, you sort of get to wondering where your home is,' he said. 'I went to Greece two years ago, and I've been dreaming about going back ever since. It's a great land. I'm going to build a house there one day made of stone. I like the idea of stone. I don't know why. I'll have a melon vine, a stream, a tape recorder, a piano, a guitar and a flute, and live there forever with my woman.'

Lola thought this seemed to be a much better ambition than her own plans to lose weight. She wondered if Cat Stevens was referring to a particular woman he planned to live with in Greece.

'Are you thinking about getting married soon?' Lola said.

'I never think about marriage. Yet I want to love someone desperately,' he said.

For a long time after she had left him, Lola thought about Cat Stevens' need to love someone desperately. She had never thought about loving someone desperately. There was an intensity to the word 'desperately' that Lola had never coupled with love.

Lola walked along Carnaby Street. She knew every store in the street. Carnaby Street was in the Soho area, where many managers, publicists and song publishers had their offices.

It was also the epicentre of the teenage-fashion industry. Lola didn't even try to shop for clothes there. She knew that nothing would fit her.

Lola had been shopping in Carnaby Street with Barry Gibb, the eldest of The Bee Gees brothers. Barry was exactly Lola's age. Technically, he was four days older than her. They knew each other from Australia, where the Gibb family had migrated when Barry was twelve.

Barry Gibb had found a cream-coloured suit he liked. He had tried it on and asked Lola what she thought. She thought he looked smashing in it. 'Smashing' was her new word. Everyone in London seemed to be using it. Lola had been trying to eliminate it from her vocabulary. It had an inbuilt violence that bothered her. Still, Barry Gibb did look smashing in that suit.

'You look fabulous,' she'd said to him.

'What colours does this suit come in?' Barry asked the salesgirl. She showed him the suit in three more colours, a pale blue, a pale pink and a bright white. 'I'll take them all,' he said. Lola had been thrilled. She'd never seen anyone buy clothes in bulk. Lola liked Barry Gibb. He was calm and kind and easy to be with. He had a solidity about him. Not a physical solidity. A psychic solidity, as though he'd never do anything too stupid or too crazy.

Lola knew that Barry Gibb hadn't had an easy childhood. When he was two and a half he spilt a hot cup of tea over himself and spent more than two months in hospital with serious burns. When he came home he was very quiet, cried a lot and wouldn't talk. He was three when the twins Robin and Maurice, the other two Bee Gees, were born. The family was very poor. A neighbour described the three boys as skinny and always hungry.

Lola was glad that Barry Gibb could now afford to buy four suits at a time. She thought that he could probably buy four thousand suits at a time. Lola had asked Barry Gibb if he thought she should ask Cher if she could have her diamante-lined false eyelashes back.

'I don't see why not,' Barry had said. 'Why wouldn't you ask for them back?'

'I think I'd feel too embarrassed,' Lola had said.

Lola didn't think she would ask Mick Jagger if she should ask Cher to return her diamante-lined false eyelashes. Mick Jagger had finished his phone call and was back in his black leather armchair. 'You are so admired by so many young people, do you feel a responsibility to set an example for them?' Lola asked him.

'A responsibility to set an example for them?' Mick Jagger said. He looked irritated. 'No,' he said. 'I don't. I don't think people in the public eye have as much influence as people think they do. I believe that individuals really do make their own minds up much more than they're given credit for. They don't just follow blindly, like sheep, what some pop singer says or does. I don't like it when pop stars preach about drugs, politics or religion. I don't do it because I don't consider myself knowledgeable enough or responsible enough to lead other people or make public statements. I'm not a bishop or a minister of religion, someone who is setting themselves up as an example to the community. I'm not a great philosopher or a headmaster. I'm a pop star.' He paused for a moment. He still looked irritated. 'My responsibilities are only to myself. My responsibility to the public is to do my work, my records, as well as I can. My knowledge isn't enough for me to start lecturing or pontificating on some of the subjects some pop stars try to get into. I don't propagate religious views, such as some pop stars do. I don't propagate drug use as some pop stars do.'

'Propagate? Do you mean promote?' Lola said. 'I thought propagate was to do with plants, like germinating a plant from a seedling. Not that I know much about plants or seedlings,' she added.

'It can also be used to mean to widely promote knowledge or an idea,' Mick Jagger said.

Lola felt embarrassed. 'English wasn't my first language,' she said, and then felt awkward because she had learned English by the time she was four or five.

'You speak it extremely well,' Mick Jagger said.

Mick Jagger and her parents were in accord about that, Lola thought.

'What was your first language?' Mick Jagger asked.

'German,' she said. 'I was born in Germany to two Polish Jews who had separately survived Auschwitz.'

'That must have been terrible,' Mick Jagger said. '*Terrible* isn't a strong enough word for what your parents must have experienced.'

Lola was surprised that Mick Jagger knew what Auschwitz was. So many people didn't.

'In some countries, like America, a lot of children grow up with no real understanding of World War II,' he said. 'I'm not saying that people in America didn't have terrible experiences then. They had rations and shortages and they had people killed but, unlike people in Europe and Russia, they didn't have the experience of the block opposite you being destroyed when you woke up in the morning. All of his irritation at her question about his responsibility as a public figure had vanished. He looked pensive and moved.

Lola hadn't really thought about what people in America were doing when her mother and father's families were being murdered. In general, she had understood that not many people anywhere in the world had seemed to care.

'You've been called rebellious,' Lola said. 'Do you think you are rebellious?' It was a ridiculous question to ask someone who was sitting in an armchair looking sensitive and concerned. Mick Jagger laughed. 'Do I look rebellious to you?' he said.

'I'm not sure what rebellious looks like,' Lola said, feeling a little stupid.

'Look, I question things about society,' Mick Jagger said. 'But my generation isn't the first generation that's questioned the values of the previous generation. That doesn't mean I am a rebel. My generation is one of the first generations that hasn't had to worry about material things like food and shelter. We're questioning things, like fighting wars, in a way that other generations couldn't. They couldn't question the morals of their society, because you don't have enough time to worry about morals if your stomach is empty and you're hungry.'

Lola knew you could be very hungry and be concerned about morality. 'My mother weighed seventy pounds when she was liberated from Stutthof, the death camp she was sent to after Auschwitz,' Lola said. 'She had severe malnutrition, typhus and all her teeth were loose. She had been hungry for six years. But she said over and over again, "It wasn't enough to survive, you had to survive as a human being." When I was small, I didn't know what she meant. I used to wonder if human beings could suddenly turn into elephants or rats, and I thought if they could it would be important to try and avoid that. When I was older, I understood that she was talking about not turning into an animal, in quite a different sense. She tortured herself and still does, wondering if she did anything at all at anyone else's expense in order to survive. She was always talking to herself about that in Yiddish.'

'Do you know much about what your parents experienced?' Mick Jagger said.

Lola knew that she didn't know much. She knew miniscule, barely visible molecular scraps of a crushing calamity. A calamity neither of her parents seemed to want to talk about, and neither of them seemed able to avoid talking about.

'When the Germans did first come into Lodz, it wasn't too bad,' Edek had said. He came from a very wealthy family that owned apartment blocks, knitting mills and a timber yard. 'We was used to *pogroms*. My mother did say, "This will pass." The Germans did come and take our jewellery and fur coats, but my mother said, "Let them take what they want, we don't need it." Me and my two brothers were seized for forced labour. We did have to clean toilets with our hands and we did have to scratch the dirt off with our nails. They did make the women take off their underwear and wash the floor with it.'

Lola used to hate that detail. Even when she was eight or nine, she understood that that was just to impose extra humiliation. 'We was allowed to go home at night,' Edek said. 'Things did still seem a little bit normal.' A few months later, they were forced to leave their homes and their possessions and were imprisoned in the Lodz Ghetto.

Nothing was going to be normal for Renia and Edek for a long time. Nothing was going to be normal, and nothing was going to be ordinary.

'Nobody did have a cat in the ghetto,' Edek had said to her out of the blue one day. Lola hadn't asked for a cat. She didn't want a cat. She didn't think she'd even talked about cats to Edek. 'The only people what was allowed to have a cat was the people what did run the food-distribution centres,' Edek said. 'The cats did have to work for their rations like the prisoners did. But for their work, which was to catch mice, they did get one kilogram of fresh meat a week. I did work in the food-distribution centre for a few months, and me and the other workers were so jealous of the cats. We didn't get any meat. We did get turnips and radishes and a terrible, thin soup. I did decide, one day, to steal the meat from the cat. And you wouldn't believe that that was the week the meat for the cats did run out. Not even the poor cats did get meat.' Edek had laughed and laughed at the end of this story. Lola hadn't thought it was funny.

'I know weird things about my parents' past,' Lola said to Mick Jagger. 'I know that at one stage, the ghetto got a huge shipment of cabbage. Vegetables were scarce and prohibitively expensive. But suddenly the ghetto was flooded with white cabbage. About two hundred kilos of it. The price of cabbage dropped. The prisoners, who had to work for six months to buy one loaf of bread on the black market, were suddenly having cabbage three times a day. My father said the whole ghetto smelled of cabbage and everyone was walking around with their stomachs distended. Then, everyone started feeling nauseous. The nausea was soon followed by widespread diarrhoea.'

'That's sad,' said Mick Jagger.

'That's not one of the sad stories,' Lola said. Mick Jagger looked disturbed.

'What were some of the other stories?' he said.

'They weren't stories,' Lola said. 'I shouldn't have called them stories. They were just things my parents said.'

She hesitated. She had come to interview Mick Jagger, not to talk about the Lodz Ghetto or Auschwitz. She started to feel uncomfortable. She was sure Mick Jagger didn't want to hear more about distended stomachs or death camps.

'What sort of things did your parents say?' he said.

'Odd things,' she said. 'My mother used to talk, almost to herself, about the fact that in Auschwitz, they used human meat, rather than animal meat, as a medium to grow culture in. She didn't explain much about it to me, except to say that it was done in the Hygiene Institute in Block 10 and that a culture medium was material that you could grow bacteria or other microbes in. A bit like a flowerbed in which you grow flowers.'

Why was she talking about flowers and flowerbeds? She'd already mentioned plants and seedlings. Mick Jagger would start thinking she was a keen gardener. She knew nothing about gardening. She knew that if you wanted to grow bacteria, you needed to supply it with nutrients and a good environment to keep it alive. Scientists usually used a nutrient broth, made out of meat extract, Lola had heard Renia say. In Auschwitz, human flesh was more expendable than animal meat. Renia said members of the SS inevitably stole the animal meat that was put aside for so-called scientific use. Lola knew all of this from hearing snippets of Renia's conversation with herself.

'My mother talked about four women from her barracks being shot and half an hour later seeing their discarded bodies with large, very deep pieces of flesh cut out of them. One of them was a girl she'd gone to high school with,' Lola said.

Mick Jagger looked disconcerted. Lola thought she should change the subject.

'Is this something a lot of people know about?' he asked.

'I don't know,' Lola said. 'My mother said that some of the prisoners who worked in the laboratory talked about the slabs of meat that had no hair or fur that was being used. My mother was interested in medicine. She wanted to be a paediatrician. She was about to start medical school when she was imprisoned.'

'Did she get to be a paediatrician?' Mick Jagger said.

'No. She ended up working in a garment factory,' Lola said.

'What were they growing in the culture medium?' Mick Jagger said.

'They were growing pneumonia, typhus, cholera and other diseases to inject into prisoners for various experiments,' Lola said. 'They experimented with abandon in Block 10. Experiments were going on everywhere. Organs and limbs were being removed. People were injected with poisons. People were frozen and then reheated.'

'They did do it for fun,' Renia used to say. 'Like children who throw their food on the floor, because it is fun and the floor is there.' Lola felt awkward. Her family's past was so messy. It was all one big mess. She wished she came from a family who had library shelves full of books, a piano and spent their holidays by the seaside.

She had no idea that this was exactly what she had come from. She had no idea that her father's family had had hundreds and hundreds of books in Polish, Russian and Yiddish, or that they had vacationed by the sea, or that the piano had been an ornate Bösendorfer baby grand.

Lola looked down at her questions. She had reams and reams of questions. She had talked about bodies with flesh gorged out of them and Nazis stealing meat intended for experiments. But she hadn't

asked Mick Jagger about his relationship with Brian Jones or Keith
Richards. What was she doing? She hardly ever talked about this sort
of stuff. She didn't talk about it at home. She never mentioned it to her
colleagues at *Rock-Out*. At the highly acclaimed high school she went
to in Melbourne, no one suggested that Lola and several others in the
classrooms had a direct link to a very recent piece of history. It was a
subject that wasn't talked about by anyone, other than the few solitary
survivors talking to themselves. Now here she was chatting to Mick
Jagger about cabbage in the Lodz Ghetto.

'I've never met anyone whose parents survived Auschwitz,' Mick
Jagger said.

'I guess there aren't a lot of us,' Lola said. 'Most of the Jews in death
camps were murdered.'

'Did your parents have siblings?' Mick Jagger asked.

'Yes, they both did,' she said. 'My mother had three sisters and
four brothers.'

'What happened to them?' he said.

'They were all murdered,' she said.

She felt bad. That was such a bleak answer. Maybe she should have
made up a story and said that Aunty Bluma and Aunty Malka and
Aunty Hinda were all doing well. And that Uncles Abramek, Felek,
Jacob and Shimek lived in Melbourne, Australia, and that they all
often went on outings together.

'It must have been hard to grow up in a family like that,' Mick
Jagger said.

'Oh no, it wasn't too bad,' Lola said. 'I thought everyone's mother
woke up at night screaming in Yiddish for their mother.' She wished
she hadn't added that. She wished she could have mentioned something

that she and Renia did together. Like cook together. But cooking the Jewish dishes of Renia's childhood was not something Renia could share with Lola. Renia cooked her latkes and chicken livers and chicken soup in an impenetrable cocoon of saucepans and frying pans and ladles and wooden spoons. She really must ask Mick Jagger about his relationship with Keith Richards and Brian Jones.

'Would you like a cup of tea?' Mick Jagger said.

'I'd love one,' she said. She followed him to the kitchen. Mick Jagger had obviously thought a lot about the decor of his apartment. The kitchen was the swishest kitchen Lola had ever seen. Not that she'd seen that many kitchens. Mick Jagger's kitchen had a series of bright-red enamel cast-iron pots hanging from one wall, and the biggest fridge Lola had ever seen. She thought you could probably fit three grown men in that fridge.

'You wouldn't ever run out of food with that fridge, would you?' Lola said.

Mick Jagger laughed, and said, 'You would run out, eventually.'

Lola thought that it would take Mick Jagger a long time to run out of food. He didn't look as though he was a very big eater.

The kitchen stove and oven had more clocks and knobs and handles than any stove Lola had ever seen. It looked fabulous. More like an interplanetary laboratory than a cooking appliance, to Lola.

Mick Jagger poured the tea and carried the cups back to the sofa. Lola hoped that she hadn't exhausted him. Other people's misfortune or misery or tragedy could be exhausting. Mick Jagger didn't even look tired.

He didn't seem to want to talk about Brian Jones or Keith Richards, although he did say that he and Keith had gone to school together. 'We became friends at Wentworth Primary School in Dartford, Kent, when I was about seven or eight,' he said. 'But I've known him almost all my life. We lived one street away from each other and my mother knew his mother.'

'So you were close friends,' Lola said

'We weren't close friends, but we were close,' Mick Jagger said.

That was a subtle differentiation, Lola thought.

'Were your parents pleased by your choice of career?' Lola said.

'No, they weren't. My father was furious with me. He couldn't have been angrier if I'd said I was going to join the army. And I don't blame him. Who knows how long this will last.'

'You're very successful,' Lola said. 'Are they still not pleased?'

'I don't know,' he said.

'But you are very successful,' she said.

'Success means different things to different people,' Mick Jagger said. 'I don't know what success means to my parents. To a lot of people, success means marriage and the monotony of suburban life and planning for your old age. I've always had the feeling that I won't live to an old age.'

'Why?' said Lola. 'You're not eating potatoes and not drinking milk.'

'I am trying to take care of myself,' he said. 'But I wouldn't want to be old anyway. There are not many old people who are happy.'

Lola didn't know if he was right or not about old people being happy. She didn't know anyone older than her parents.

She was bothered by the fact that Mick Jagger's parents might still not be pleased. 'Your parents must be pleased,' she said. 'You've got this beautiful apartment, you're world famous.'

'I don't know,' he said. 'I don't want to please my parents. Why would I want to please my parents?'

'It's possibly a natural response,' Lola said. She didn't know why she was so concerned about what his parents thought.

Mick Jagger laughed. 'I don't want to please them,' he said. 'I also don't want to displease them. Do you want to please your parents?' he asked her.

'I think I do,' she said. 'Although, maybe I don't. If I really wanted to please my mother, I'd lose weight. I do plan new diets all the time.'

'Your mother gets strung-out by your being heavy, does she?' Mick Jagger said.

'*Strung-out* would be a good way to describe how she feels about it,' Lola said. 'If you had any fat on you at all, in the ghetto or in the death camp, it meant you were doing something untoward to get food. The *kapos* and the Jewish police were always well fed, as were the *Sonderkommando* who pulled the bodies out of the gas chamber and loaded them onto the trolleys that went into the ovens.'

'Shit,' said Mick Jagger. '*Untoward* might not be exactly the right word.'

Lola switched off the tape recorder. She thought she'd asked Mick Jagger everything she wanted to ask. 'Thank you very much for the interview,' she said. Mick Jagger walked her through the wood-panelled hallway to the front door. He opened the door and looked at Lola. 'Would you like to meet Paul McCartney?' he said. 'He'll be here at four o'clock.'

Lola was surprised. She hesitated. She was torn. She would really like to meet Paul McCartney. She hadn't managed to get an interview with any of The Beatles, not that meeting Paul McCartney would mean that she would be able to arrange an interview with him. But she had an interview with Manfred Mann at four o'clock. It had taken her about twenty phone calls to arrange the interview. Manfred Mann's 'Semi-Detached, Suburban Mr James' was still selling well, and 'Ha Ha Said the Clown' was already at number four.

'I can't,' said Lola. 'I've got an interview with Manfred Mann at four o'clock.'

'That's a pity,' Mick Jagger said.

She knew he was referring to the fact that she could not meet Paul McCartney and not the fact that she had to interview Manfred Mann.

'Thank you, again,' she said.

Lola's tape recorder jammed three-quarters of the way through her interview with Manfred Mann. One of the band's road managers was trying to fix it. Lola wasn't too bothered. She'd got most of what she wanted from the group. She wasn't too worried about the tape recorder, either. She had a spare one in the apartment she was sharing with an Australian rock group, The Browns. Lola didn't know why they were called The Browns. Not one of the six Browns was named Brown, or even had brown hair, which was, statistically, against the odds.

She had a headache. The room she and Manfred Mann were in was small and felt a bit airless. There was too much cigarette smoke and too many men in too small a space, Lola thought.

She seemed to have been surrounded by males ever since she'd arrived in London. For a start, she was sharing an apartment with six of them. And then there were the groups she was interviewing. They were all men. In the last three weeks, she had interviewed The Kinks, The Hollies, The Small Faces and The Spencer Davis Group. There was not a female member among the lot.

It had been a relief for Lola to see Cher. She had interviewed Cher again, briefly, at her hotel. It was for a silly new column she had to write called 'Say Your Piece'. Pop stars made two- or three-sentence statements on half-a-dozen subjects that needed novella-length answers. Subjects like love and happiness.

She hadn't asked Cher about her eyelashes. And Cher hadn't brought them up. She had complimented Lola on the green false eyelashes Lola was wearing, but didn't ask to borrow them. Lola thought it was probably hard to ask anyone to return false eyelashes they had borrowed. But it seemed even harder to ask someone who had a wardrobe of clothes that filled an entire hotel room.

Lola noticed that Sonny hovered around Cher as though he were her father. And Cher seemed to check with him before she answered questions. Sonny and Cher were leaving London soon. They had been on the road for a while. 'When you finally settle down, what part of the world do you think you will live in?' Lola had asked Cher.

'We're already settled to a degree,' Sonny said. 'We have our own home in California. We don't have a family yet, but when we've got through some of the work that is waiting for us, we'll have a family.' Lola felt a bit stupid. Of course they were already settled. They weren't sharing an apartment with six members of The Browns. Lola hoped that maybe she would be able to pluck up the courage to ask Cher to return her false eyelashes when she saw her in Los Angeles.

The rest of Manfred Mann had packed up and left Mike d'Abo, the relatively new lead singer, to comment on some Australian records

Lola had brought with her. Mike d'Abo seemed nice enough. Lola had already interviewed Paul Jones, the lead singer Mike d'Abo had replaced.

Paul Jones was considered a bad boy. Lola couldn't see what was so bad about him. Maybe leaving Manfred Mann to go solo was considered bad, or the fact that he was very direct. He didn't seem to modify his thoughts to make them more palatable for public consumption. And he had plenty of thoughts.

They had touched on the subject of education. 'When people talk about children, they start with premises like the super-imposition of discipline from outside is necessary and good,' Paul Jones had said. 'And they say things like discipline has been going on for thousands of years.' Ten minutes later he sighed and said, 'If you want to say something, you need a whole day for a subject like education or else you end up talking in slogans.'

Lola had said that she didn't think *Rock-Out* was looking for discussions that took a whole day, although she hoped they were looking for more than slogans. She'd asked Paul Jones if when in 1962 Brian Jones had asked him to join a band that he was forming, he'd said no because he wanted to complete his Oxford degree.

'No,' he'd said. 'I'd just auditioned to be a singer in a dance band in Slough.' That had been the question that had led to the education discussion. It should have led to the matter of whether he regretted the decision to not join Brian Jones, as that group had gone on to become The Rolling Stones.

'People say I'm conceited, and maybe I am,' Paul Jones had volunteered. 'I'm confident, and that can get you a reputation for being conceited. When I'm asked how the show, the concert, the film, the record is going, I answer truthfully as I don't believe in false modesty.

I say, 'The show is going great for me.' Then they rush off and say, 'My God, he should have said he was humbly grateful.' Show me the guy who says he's humbly grateful and I know he is a hypocrite and a liar. Mind you, he's very show business.'

Paul Jones had just co-starred with England's top model, Jean Shrimpton, in a movie called *Privilege*. Lola had asked him if he enjoyed working with Jean Shrimpton.

'She's a very warm and wonderful person with whom it was a pleasure to film,' he said. 'We hope to make a follow-up with Twiggy called *Underprivileged*.'

It had taken Lola a moment to see what was funny about that and then she'd laughed. It had been strangely uplifting to be laughing about someone who was too thin.

Lola knew that Mike D'Abo was the son of a London stockbroker, although she didn't know what a stockbroker did. She knew they were mostly rich. She had had several letters from readers of *Rock-Out* asking if she could ask an English artist to comment on some Australian records. She'd brought five records with her for Mike D'Abo to comment on.

An hour later, she thought she may well not be able to use any of them. It had started off on a promising note with The Bee Gees' 'Spicks and Specks'. 'Absolutely first class. A beautiful song,' Mike D'Abo had said. Things had gone rapidly downhill from there. 'The limitation, of course, of the song,' he said, 'is that it is only about eight bars long, and then it goes on over and over again.'

His comments on the next four songs ranged from 'I was incredibly bored by that record', or 'His singing is diabolical', or 'He's got an incredible voice, unfortunately it gets a bit boring and it's not a very good song' to 'I don't like this song at all. I loathe hearing elevator, whiskey, waiter, decorator and commentator. I think it's a filthy idea. The whole song is so ugly.'

Lola thanked Mike D'Abo. He looked quite cheerful as though listening to what he thought were terrible records had somehow buoyed him. She briefly contemplated asking him a few more questions about himself but decided against it. She was tired. She started packing up her things, when an older woman came into the room and told Lola that there was a phone call for her in the front office.

Lola wondered who it could be. She knew very few people in London. She couldn't think of anyone who knew exactly where she was. She knew it couldn't be Renia or Edek. They barely had any idea of what it was that she was doing, let alone where she was on a daily basis. Maybe it was the Australian photographer she worked with. She had given him all the contact details for the interview she was doing.

She picked up the phone. 'Hello,' she said. 'This is Lola Bensky.' Every time she said that, Lola thought of herself scrambling as a three-year-old to get up on the stool that was kept near the phone on the wall in their house in North Carlton. 'This is little Lola,' she would say. She couldn't say that now. She tugged at her dress, which had ridden up a bit.

'Hello,' she said again.

'Hi, this is Mick,' a voice said.

'Mick?' she said.

'Mick Jagger,' the voice said.

'Oh,' said Lola. 'Hello.'

'Paul is still here, and he'll be here for another couple of hours,' Mick Jagger said. 'A few other people are coming over. Would you like to come over?' Lola didn't know what to say. She was not expecting this.

'How many people are coming?' she said.

'Three others,' he said. It's just for an hour or two. I have to be back at the studio at eight o'clock.'

Lola didn't really want to go. She was tired. It had been a long day. In between interviewing Mick Jagger and Manfred Mann, she had had to find out which bank her salary had been sent to. It seemed to arrive at a different bank every month. No one at *Rock-Out* seemed to know why, or how to trace it.

She thought about Mick Jagger's invitation. She really should go. How many people got calls from Mick Jagger asking if they'd like to come over and meet Paul McCartney?

'Oh, okay,' she said to Mick Jagger, and realised that she had sounded a little half-hearted.

'So, you are going to join us?' Mick Jagger said.

'Yes,' she said, and then added, 'thank you,' in an effort to sound more enthusiastic.

'I'll send a car around to pick you up,' Mick Jagger said. 'It should be there in fifteen minutes. Does that suit you?'

'That would be great,' Lola said.

She hoped that it wasn't a Rolls-Royce. She had been picked up in a Rolls-Royce by one of The Shadows, Cliff Richard's backing group. He had told her that one of his children had had the top of one of their fingers cut off by the electric windows. Lola had never seen an electric window in a car and had made a mental note to avoid Rolls-Royces. She had wondered at the time if the top of the finger being cut off had been some sort of punishment for driving a car that cost more than most people's houses. She had had to remind herself that there was no God and, therefore, not only was it impossible for God to help people, he also couldn't dole out punishments.

She looked at her watch. There was definitely not enough time to diet before meeting Paul McCartney. She wondered if Mick Jagger had asked the receptionist if he could speak to the fat Australian journalist. That thought made her cringe.

3

One of the first things Lola noticed about New York was that there were no miniskirts and no Rolls-Royces. 'If you sometimes think that we in Australia are behind the times, one trip to New York will put that notion in perspective,' Lola had written in a letter to the readers of *Rock-Out*. 'You can walk around all day and not see one miniskirt,' she wrote. 'All the fashions are years behind. Stiletto heels are still in. The scene really is square.'

Two days later, she'd seen the shallowness of her statement. New York wasn't behind. It was different. Unlike London, it was hard to detect who was very wealthy and who was relatively poor. There was a uniformity to the clothing. And to the cars. Huge wealth wasn't on display. Certainly not below Thirty-first Street, where Lola was staying at the Horwood Hotel.

The Horwood Hotel was seedy. Friends of friends of Renia and Edek knew the owner. Lola met the owner, Abe, a fat, sweaty man with what looked like a mustard stain down the front of his shirt. He bought Lola an orange juice and gave her a five-per-cent discount on the room.

Everything in the sparsely furnished room looked dirty. The corpses of half-a-dozen cockroaches were scattered across the once beige carpet, which now had a greasy sheen so thick it looked slippery. Everything in the room looked dead.

Lola wondered if being in a room so stripped of all human comforts made you closer to God. Why was she thinking about God? She didn't believe in God. Anyway, if a prerequisite for closeness to God was a lack of amenities, her parents, as death-camp inmates, would have qualified as God's best friends. The other inhabitants of the Horwood Hotel, a ragtag group of moth-eaten men, didn't look particularly close to God. Lola decided to get God out of her head and spend as little time as she could in her hotel room.

Lola was walking down MacDougal Street when she realised she was beginning to feel more in tune with New York. She could feel the intellectual heft in the city. The conversation in cafes and clubs was about politics and art. No one was talking about the latest fashions.

New York was a heated city. Heated by passion and purpose. Nothing much was prettied up or hidden. The yellow cabs that had traversed the streets had often seen better days. The spring seemed to have gone out of the upholstery in most of the passenger seats, and the cars' suspension systems, more often than not, were shot.

New Yorkers were not afraid of a few rough edges and were certainly not afraid to express an opinion or ask a question. 'Why are you fat?' a woman on Fifth Avenue had said to Lola yesterday. Lola had stopped in shock. She had only been in New York for five days. She tried to think of an answer that had a degree of complexity. Before she could come up with anything, the woman said, 'You eat too much.'

'I think you're right,' Lola said, and hurriedly walked on.

'You've got a very pretty face,' the woman called out after her.

Lola tried to take her mind off the fact that a perfect stranger had felt compelled to tell her that she was eating too much. She should have suggested that the woman speak to Renia. They could have had a very long and satisfying conversation.

Lola had to buy some tapes for her tape recorder. She was hoping to interview Jim Morrison of The Doors. The Doors were not yet internationally well known, but the talk in the rock world was that they soon would be.

Lola did have an interview arranged with The Young Rascals, whose hit record, 'How Can I Be Sure', she had reviewed for *Rock-Out*. She was very taken with the indecision in the title and had given the record a rave review.

She had also organised to interview The Lovin' Spoonful, whose hit, 'Did You Ever Have to Make Up Your Mind', Lola had also reviewed well. At the moment, The Lovin' Spoonful's 'Summer in the City' seemed to be on the airwaves all the time. The song's lyrics about summer making your neck dirty and gritty made even more sense now that Lola was in New York.

It was hot. And humid. And crowded. The heat and the humidity and the density of the population gave downtown New York a thin coating of something less than wholesome. Uptown, everything looked swanky and polished, but downtown things looked a bit tarnished and burnished. Lola liked this semi-rundown, demi-matte world, with its whiff of crime and other times.

It reminded her in a strange way of the world of the vaudeville shows she used to go to with Edek. Edek used to take Lola out on Saturday afternoons, when she was younger, to give Renia a break. Edek sometimes took Lola to the Melbourne Zoo. He would buy her a long ribbon of tickets for rides on the elephant. Edek would sit in the rotunda and read his detective-fiction books, while Lola, who always sat as close to the elephant's head as she could, rode round and round on the elephant. Up high, with the elephant's ears flapping close to her arms, Lola used to feel on top of the world. At that height, everything looked so promising. Every now and then when the rides were over, Lola used to find Edek, who was working double shifts in the factory, fast asleep in the rotunda.

Sometimes they would do boring things like drop off piecework to half-a-dozen women, mostly in the outer suburbs, who sat at home and hemmed hemlines, sewed in sleeves and added pockets to various garments that the factory Edek also worked for produced. But once a month, from the time Lola was eleven or twelve, they would go to the two p.m. matinee at the Tivoli Theatre in Bourke Street, Melbourne.

The program was always a mix of singers, jugglers, magicians, dancers, hypnotists, comedians and strippers. And Lola and Edek always sat in the second or third row from the front. Just the scent of the theatre was exhilarating to Lola. She wanted to submerge herself in that heavy perfume of pancake make-up and high heels.

If a hypnotist or magician needed a volunteer from the audience, Edek was the first to jump to his feet. He laughed so hard at the comedians that they always played to him. And he clapped louder than anyone else at the dancers.

The dancers didn't do that much dancing. They were weighted down with feather-and-glitter headdresses, but at least once during every show they did the cancan or another choreographed number. Edek would clap so hard that Lola thought his hands must hurt.

Apart from the feathers and glitter, the dancers wore a legless, flesh-coloured mesh leotard with a built-in sequined bikini bottom and small sequined caps to cover their nipples.

There were also showgirls, who were distinguishable from the dancers by two things. Their nipples were uncovered. And they didn't move. The nude showgirls stood very still. It was illegal, in Melbourne, to move on stage if you were nude.

Lola used to wish she could be one of the dancers or showgirls and be part of it all. But she knew that she would have to slim down quite a bit and possibly would never be able to balance all those feathers and glitter on her head.

The singers who appeared at the Tivoli never looked or sounded as though they had just flown in from La Scala or some other world-famous opera house. They were mostly breathy women. One of the most successful was Sabrina. She whispered her way through the songs. She didn't need to do much more. Sabrina had a forty-two-and-a-half-inch bust, most of which was exposed, an eighteen-inch waist and thirty-six-inch hips.

Lola had never seen a bust that size. The size of Sabrina's breasts was amplified by the size of her waist. It was tiny.

'She is very talented,' Edek had said to Lola when Sabrina finished her act.

'She's got very big breasts,' Lola said.

'That is true too,' Edek had replied.

Sabrina's talents had possibly not really been put to the test, Lola thought. Lola had seen Sabrina in the movie *Blue Murder at St Trinian's*. Sabrina, who appeared in posters for the movie, had a non-speaking part. She sat in a bed, in a nightie, reading a book. No one had nominated her for an Academy Award for that role.

At interval at the Tivoli, Edek would buy two ice-creams, a chocolate one for him and a vanilla ice-cream for Lola, and a packet of Fantales, chocolate-coated hard caramels with a biography of a movie star on each wrapper.

All the way home in the car, Edek and Lola would talk about the show and finish the last of the Fantales. Edek would park the car outside the house. That was the demarcation line. After the car was properly parked, all conversation about the jugglers and magicians ceased. They would arrive home with no hint of where they had been. There were no stray feathers or remnants of perfume. Renia never asked where they had been or what they had been doing. Lola sometimes wished that Renia would, just once, come out with her and Edek. Maybe not to the Tivoli, but somewhere else. Anywhere else. But Renia never did. The three of them never went out together unless it was to a bar mitzvah, or a wedding or birthday.

Lola loved going to the Tivoli. There was an underwater stripper who mesmerised Lola. Lola and Edek had seen the underwater stripper's act three times. The underwater stripper had long blond hair that floated slowly as she swam, languorously disrobing, in a giant glass pool on the stage. She swam with her eyes wide open and a smile on her face. Every now and then she would press her face against the glass and blow kisses to the audience. A small trail of bubbles would float up after each kiss.

The underwater stripper also danced as she stripped. She pointed her toes, elongated her arms and did horizontal pirouettes as she removed one item of clothing after another.

She wore shorts, socks, a blouse, a camisole and several layers of undergarments. It can't have been easy to remove wet socks, Lola thought.

The underwater stripper stripped and danced to the sound of Bobby Darin singing 'Beyond the Sea'. She never once came up for air. Listening to 'Beyond the Sea' often made Lola feel a bit sad. She had a feeling that beyond the sea was where she wanted to be. Somewhere. A vast somewhere with endless possibilities. Not here in North Carlton or St Kilda, to where she and Renia and Edek were about to move.

Lola spent ages trying to work out how the underwater stripper could breathe, let alone take off her clothes, underwater. She persuaded Edek to let her go backstage one day. 'I want to know how she can breathe underwater,' Lola had said to Edek.

'It is a big mystery to me too,' Edek said. 'I did watch her very carefully each time and I did not see how she was breathing.'

At the stage door, a man with long black hair told Lola that the underwater stripper had gone home.

'How did she have time to get dry and put her clothes on?' Lola said.

'She's very quick,' the man said.

'Are you sure she's gone?' Lola said. She felt quite devastated.

'I saw her leave,' he said. 'I said goodbye to her.'

'Do you know how she breathes underwater?' Lola said.

'I don't know how she breathes out of water,' the man said.

'What do you mean?' said Lola.

'Breathing is a complicated business,' he said.

'Do you have the underwater stripper's phone number?' Lola said.

'No,' he said. 'How old are you?'

'I'm thirteen,' she said. 'I've seen the show three times and I can't figure out how she can breathe underwater.'

'Maybe you don't need to know,' he said. 'Do you spend a lot of time underwater?'

'No,' said Lola.

'Who did you see the show with?' the man at the door asked her.

'My father,' she said. 'He's getting the car at the moment.'

'If you've got a minute, do you want to meet my wife, Margot?' he said. 'She's the other stripper, the above-water stripper.'

'Yes please,' said Lola.

'My name is Jackie,' he said. 'Jackie Clancy.'

Backstage, the Tivoli was organised chaos. The chaos of people, costumes, shoes, props, magic tricks and a performing dog. The hypnotist was removing his moustache in the hallway. Lola was agog at how unremarkable and un-hypnotic the hypnotist looked without his moustache.

'Are you Jewish?' Jackie Clancy said as they walked to his wife Margot's dressing-room.

'Yes,' she said. 'How can you tell?'

'You look Jewish,' he said.

'I didn't meet the underwater stripper,' Lola said to Edek when she got into the car. 'But I met the other stripper.'

'She is very talented too,' Edek said.

'She is very nice,' Lola said.

Lola started meeting Jackie Clancy for coffee after school on Wednesdays. Jackie would buy Lola a hot chocolate with melted nougat at Hoagey's on Collins Street, while they waited for Margot to join them when her Wednesday matinee performance was over.

Jackie, a comedian who was formerly a boxer, sometimes looked depressed, almost on the verge of tears. Other times he would be so hilarious that Lola would kill herself laughing. They made a strange trio, the stripper in her street clothes, the schoolgirl in her University

High School uniform and the former-boxer-turned-comedian, with his unkempt and often greasy black hair.

Jackie and Margot Clancy were both English. They'd migrated to Australia in 1956. Lola felt at home with the two of them. Margot and Jackie listened to each other. And to Lola. And they laughed together.

Lola started leaving school early on Wednesdays so she could spend more time with Jackie while they waited for Margot. A short, stout man, he was very unpredictable. He would argue with anyone, call out to strangers, mimic people and animals and ruminate on the end of the world, and the possibility of nuclear radiation or the invasion of the Chinese. 'You better plant a rice paddy in your backyard,' he said to Lola. 'You'll want to befriend the enemy.' Lola adored him.

Jackie Clancy seemed part of a larger universe to Lola. He wasn't nervous. He wasn't afraid to be provocative. He didn't care about what anyone thought of him. All of the adults Lola knew were, even when they were out dancing or at the movies, clustered in small claustrophobic huddles. Jackie Clancy was out in the world, taking people on, taking a stand. He had big dreams and big ideas.

By then Jackie Clancy was appearing regularly on radio and television in Melbourne. He was also regularly being fired from radio and television shows in Melbourne. Among other things, he would be fired for not watching his language and arousing the ire of the Australian broadcasting censors.

When Lola had told Jackie that she'd gone to see *Psycho* instead of sitting for her final-year high-school exams, she thought he would find it amusing. He didn't. 'That's really going to upset your parents,' he said.

Lola hadn't seen Jackie Clancy or Margot since she left high school. She would think about Jackie Clancy for years and years. He was the only adult who had ever suggested to Lola that her parents' history was catastrophic. For her, as well as for them. Years later, she would pay more than one analyst a fortune to point out the same thing. And years after that, she would hear that Jackie Clancy had helped to smuggle Jews out of Germany.

Lola had been walking across Fourteenth Street. It wasn't easy to work out which stores might even stock recording tapes. Fourteenth Street had a particularly rundown quality about it. A shabbiness that seemed both at odds with and an integral part of the intellectual core of New York City. There were dilapidated doorways and stores and foyers that looked worn down. She passed a dimly lit luncheonette with a sign painted above the front window that said 'Furs Sold Upstairs'. An arrow pointed to a hallway at the side of the luncheonette. Lola looked inside the hallway. It didn't look as though those stairs could lead to a fur salon. But New York was full of surprises. Shabby exteriors were not a good indicator of the interiors they contained.

Lola really liked this part of New York. She liked the fact that you could have a twelve-storey building right next to a three-storey building and a vacant lot. And that cheap luncheonettes seemed to have very good food, and there seemed to be a Jewish deli on almost every block. You could buy a chopped liver sandwich or *matzoh* balls and chicken soup at any time of the day or night. Lola had never seen either of these items anywhere other than in a private house in Melbourne. It was a strange feeling to think that a lot of people here knew what chopped liver was.

One of the storekeepers on Fourteenth Street suggested that Lola try Canal Street. She began walking in that direction. The short sleeves of her dress were digging into her upper arms. Lola thought the sleeves felt tighter than they were the last time she had worn this dress. Maybe it was just the humidity.

She tried to stretch the sleeves with her hand. The air was so humid she had been sure the fabric would stretch. But the rickrack edging on the end of the sleeves wouldn't budge. Her efforts to dislodge her flesh from the tight vise of the sleeves had left red circles around the tops of her arms.

She must have put on weight, she thought. She never weighed herself. The only way she could tell whether she was putting on weight was when various parts of her clothes got a little snug or more than a little snug.

Lola never looked at her body. Other girls would notice a bruise on their leg or a mark on their knee. Lola noticed nothing. She made every effort not to look at herself below the neck. It wasn't that hard. She just had to avoid most mirrors, look up when she was in the shower and look away when she was in the bath.

Lola concentrated on her hair and her face. Especially her false eyelashes. She felt they decorated her and covered some of her discomfort. Decades later, Lola would read that children of survivors were beset by fears of bodily damage and illness. She would also read that children of extermination-camp survivors, who were typically more traumatised than other survivors, tended to be more tormented by the traumas of their parents' past than children of other survivors.

When Lola finally noticed her body, everything about it terrified her. A twinge in an arm signified a stroke or heart attack. A mouth ulcer looked like oral cancer, a callus on her foot metamorphosed into a tumour. Any ache or pain made her heart pound. She felt nauseated as soon as she made a doctor's appointment, aged ten years over every medical test and planned her funeral over and over again. Life had been much easier when her body didn't seem to be attached to the rest of her.

Lola found recording tapes in a store that sold bulbs, screwdrivers, tape measures, saucepans and strainers. She bought a box of twenty tapes. She looked at her watch. She would have just enough time to get to midtown, where she had to meet Lillian Roxon. The other fat Australian journalist, as Linda Eastman had so bluntly put it.

Lillian had asked Lola to help her choose some new summer clothes at a large department store. Lillian was almost fifteen years older than Lola and quite beautiful. She had dark-blond hair and large green eyes with pale purple shadows under them. This dark area under her eyes added a mysteriousness to her already exotic looks. It suggested late nights and intriguing encounters. She also had flawless porcelain skin and a smile that uplifted and embraced friends and perfect strangers.

Lillian was quite short and fluctuated between being plump and just plain fat. At the moment, she'd been on a strict diet for about four weeks, she'd told Lola. 'I've got a new very young boyfriend,' Lillian had said to her on the phone last night. 'I lied to him and said I've always been skinny but have just let myself go a bit in the last year.' She shrieked with mirth and said, 'I've never been skinny in my life, not even for a day. But I can't bear to say to him that this, for me, is thin.'

'How old is he?' Lola said.

'He's nineteen, your age,' said Lillian.

'I'm twenty now,' Lola said.

'Oh, no, he's even younger than you.' Lillian said.

Lillian was Australia's first female foreign correspondent. She was the New York correspondent for the *Sydney Morning Herald*. She covered arts, entertainment and women's issues, areas she would stick to for the rest of her life.

In her first week on the job, Lillian was interviewing Elvis Presley's manager, Colonel Tom Parker, and Rock Hudson. Soon she would be interviewing Elizabeth Taylor and Richard Burton, scouting out talent in the newly exploding rock world, writing a weekly column, 'Top of the Pops', for the *New York Sunday News* and dispensing psychological theories and views about sex in the monthly column 'Intelligent Woman's Guide to Sex', for *Mademoiselle* magazine.

Lillian was the first Australian journalist to establish a high profile in America. Lola liked her enormously. She was warm and generous. And she could be so bitchy. Lola admired well-executed bitchiness. She admired it in her mother. Renia would say anything. And so would Lillian.

Lillian had called Lola on her first night in New York, when Lola was trying to accustom herself to the company of cockroaches and the sounds coming from the public toilet in the shared bathroom located right next door to her room.

'Hi,' Lillian had said. 'Do you want to come over? I've got a cake of soap stuck in my vagina.'

'Oh, how awful,' Lola said. She couldn't bring herself to ask why Lillian would have even tried to insert a cake of soap in her vagina. 'You could try sitting in some water. That could dislodge it,' Lola said.

'I'm in the bath,' Lillian said. 'And it's not moving. It's stuck.'

'Maybe you should get someone to take you to the hospital,' Lola said.

'There are quite a few people here,' Lillian said. 'I'm having a small party.'

Lola didn't feel there was much she could do for Lillian. Frankly, she was puzzled and bothered by how you could end up in the bath, in the middle of a small party, with a cake of soap stuck up your vagina.

'I'm really tired,' Lola said. 'I think I'll go to bed.'

'You can't be tired. You're only nineteen,' Lillian said.

'I'm twenty now, remember,' Lola said. 'And twenty-year-olds seem to need more sleep.'

'Okay, okay. I better keep working on the soap,' Lillian said. 'I'll see you tomorrow. Don't forget, we're going shopping. Don, come and help me,' Lola heard Lillian call out as she hung up the phone. Who was Don? There was an Australian disc jockey, Don Dunlap, in town. Maybe it was Don Dunlap.

Lillian was waiting outside the department store when Lola arrived. Lillian looked fresh and animated. She showed no sign of having had a bar of soap stuck in her vagina. She took Lola to the section of the store where she liked to shop. It was called the Chubby Teens department. 'You get the best deal in the Chubby Teens department,' Lillian said.

Yes, but did you get the best clothes, or even acceptable clothes, Lola wondered. She had never seen a Chubby Teens department. She didn't think there was one in Melbourne. Or possibly anywhere else in the world. She bet chubby teenagers hated the Chubby Teens department.

All Lola could see in the girls' section of the Chubby Teens department were flounces and frills. She didn't think that chubbiness needed to be amplified with trails of frills and mountains of flounces. All the merchandise was brightly coloured and vividly patterned. The cacophony of clashing colours and geometric and floral prints was enough to give the most detached Buddhist a headache.

'I think you're too tall for the Chubby Teens department,' Lillian Roxon said. 'I love this place.' Lola was surprised at Lillian's enthusiasm. She didn't want to say anything that might dampen it.

'I think I'm definitely too tall,' she said. Her height had finally saved her, she thought. Renia was always telling her that she was too tall. Lola was five-foot-nine and that did seem tall for a girl. But whether it constituted too tall, unlike whether too fat was too fat, was something Lola was unsure about.

Once, when Renia was looking at Lola, she had sighed and said, 'You are too tall.'

Lola had tried to answer her. 'I thought you like tall,' Lola said. 'You're always saying you weren't short like the other Jewish girls.'

'I'm not short,' Renia said. 'But you are too tall. It is because you ate so many sweets.'

Even at twelve Lola knew there was no correlation between a person's height and how many sweets they ate. If there were a correlation, all of the kids at her primary school would have been giants. Australia had a candy culture. There were stores on almost every block that sold dozens of varieties of candies for just a few pennies per bag. Lola hadn't really minded the height conversation. It had been a relief to get away from the subject of being fat.

Lillian bought herself a short-sleeved cotton blue-and-white gingham dress. It was one of the most subdued dresses in the Chubby Teens department. 'It really suits you,' Lola said. And it did. The dress looked cool and youthful and few people would ever guess it came from the Chubby Teens department of a department store. Lola noticed that there were no other 35-year-old women trying on clothes in the Chubby Teens department. She thought it was so smart of Lillian to shop there.

'Why don't you get it in the green-and-white gingham too,' Lola said. 'It really, really suits you.'

'That's a good idea,' Lillian said. 'They're very cheap.'

'Well, get the brown one too,' Lola said.

Lillian and Lola left the Chubby Teens department with Lillian carrying three short-sleeved cotton gingham dresses and looking very pleased with herself.

'I learnt that from Barry Gibb,' Lola said.

'Learnt what?' said Lillian. 'I don't think Barry Gibb goes shopping in Chubby Teens' departments.'

'I learned about buying in bulk from him,' Lola said. 'He bought four suits in Carnaby Street. They were the same style, but in different colours.'

'He's a very good-looking guy,' Lillian said.

'He is,' said Lola. 'And he's a really nice person.'

'Lola, you sound positively middle-aged,' Lillian said. 'You're not supposed to be thinking about what a really nice person a handsome rock star like Barry Gibb is.'

'What am I supposed to be thinking about?' Lola said.

'How much you'd like to fuck Barry Gibb,' said Lillian.

Lola nearly fell over a tall stack of very large men's overalls. They were now walking through the Tall and Big Men department. She was shocked, firstly, that Lillian could talk like that in the Tall and

Big Men section of a very sedate department store, and secondly that Lillian thought that Lola should have been thinking about how much Lola would like to fuck Barry Gibb, instead of being reassured by what a nice human being he was.

'There must be something wrong with me,' she said to Lillian.

'It's possibly the same thing that's wrong with many women,' Lillian said. 'They're just too passive. You've got to be aggressive. Aggressive socially, aggressive in the workplace and you've got to be sexually aggressive, like a man.'

Lola felt a bit light-headed. They had just passed through the perfume department. The thick odour of too many scents combined with the notion of being sexually aggressive was making her feel queasy, and a bit dizzy.

'Are you okay?' Lillian said. 'You look a bit pale.'

'Yes,' said Lola. 'I'm okay. It's just the perfume.'

Lola wasn't sure what being sexually aggressive involved. Did it mean you said mean things, or punched the guy? Or did it mean you chased him and had sex wherever and whenever you or the guy wanted to? What if you didn't want to have sex all that much? Sex was not on Lola's mind, a lot of the time. Interviews were on her mind. Her diets were on her mind. Her mother and father were on her mind. This made for an already over-crowded mind.

'Let's have something to eat,' Lillian said. They stopped at a cafe on Thirty-Sixth Street. 'They have fabulous non-fat, soft-serve ice-cream here,' said Lillian.

Lola had never had non-fat ice-cream. It sounded promising, if not utterly thrilling.

The cafe had rows of red booths. Lillian chose a booth at the back.

Lola thought the booths were a brilliant idea. She assumed that they were designed to give fat people privacy and peace while they ate their non-fat ice-creams. She didn't realise that half the diners in New York had booths like this and that they were not designed with fat people in mind. They were designed mostly for comfort and economy of seating. 'You can have non-fat thickshakes here, too,' Lillian said. Lola ordered a non-fat chocolate thickshake and a tomato and lettuce salad. Lillian ordered the same.

'Are you going back to Australia when you're finished working in the US?' Lillian asked her.

'I have to go back to London first and then I'll go back to Australia,' she said.

'Why are you going back to Australia?' Lillian said.

'Because that's where I live,' said Lola.

'You don't just live where you've been placed,' said Lillian. 'You're not an immovable object.'

'It's my home,' said Lola.

'Lvov was supposed to be my home,' said Lillian. 'I'm sure glad I don't live there.'

'Your parents came from Lvov?' said Lola.

'Yes,' said Lillian.

'My parents came from Lodz, which is three-hundred-and fifty miles from Lvov,' Lola said. Lola knew this because Edek had three aunts who lived in Lvov. He used to talk about Cha Cha Hannah and Cha Cha Taube and Cha Cha Ruchel. Lola loved the sound of all the *cha chas* and the sound of the words Lvov and Lodz. Several times she had wondered whether she could slip Lvov and Lodz into one of her articles. She knew that one of The Lovin' Spoonful, Zal Yanovsky, was

Jewish. Maybe she could ask him where his family was from and slip Lvov and Lodz into the sentence.

'Not many people I know have heard of Lvov,' Lillian said. 'I certainly didn't expect to meet someone who knew exactly how many miles from Lodz Lvov was. Or is,' she corrected herself.

'My dad had three aunts who lived in Lvov,' Lola said.

'Maybe we're related?' Lillian said. 'We used to be the Ropschitzes. My parents were Doctor and Mrs Ropschitz. When I was eight, my parents wanted to change their name in order to become more Australian. I was looking at some rocks and suggested Roxon.'

'You were a smart kid,' Lola said. 'We used to be the Berkelmanns. I wanted to change to Beer because all Australians, it seemed to me even then, drank a lot of beer. But my parents said no and we became the Benskys. Renia, Edek and Lola Bensky. We didn't exactly sound like a gathering of Episcopalians.'

'No, you still sounded like recently arrived Jews,' Lillian said.

'Not to my parents,' Lola said. 'They were convinced they'd Anglicised us.'

'When I get home, I'll ask my father if the Berkelmanns were related to any Ropschitzes,' Lola said.

'Why do you have to go back to Australia?' Lillian said. 'Why don't you move to New York? Try it for a year. You are very talented. You shouldn't be going back to Australia.' Lola was surprised and bewildered. No one had ever suggested that she was talented. What did Lillian mean, she thought. She knew she couldn't sing or dance or play the piano or the violin.

'I've got a boyfriend in Australia,' Lola said.

'That's no reason to go back,' said Lillian.

'He's probably already going out with someone else,' Lola said. She thought that her boyfriend, who played in a popular band, probably was going out with someone else.

'Going out?' Lillian said. 'What do you mean going out? Do you mean he's probably fucking someone else?'

'I think so,' said Lola.

'He's an arsehole,' Lillian said. 'Why would you want to go back to a boyfriend who's fucking someone else?'

'I don't know,' said Lola.

She hadn't missed him. She hadn't missed talking to him. She wasn't sure if they did talk much. She tried to list his good qualities and realised she'd never thought about what they might be. She did like him. Or maybe she just liked having a boyfriend. Having a boyfriend did make her feel settled. And normal. He was just part of how things were. He was her boyfriend, and in about six months when she finished her work in America, she was going back to Australia to be with him.

People had told her that they had seen him with a very quiet, mousy sort of girl. But Lola had somehow filed that information in a part of her brain she had no access to. She seemed to have an unnerving ability to overlook the obvious. When she was sixteen she had gone out with Philip Hughes, an engineering student, for two years. After a year, she had begun to feel that there was something she didn't know about him. Something she didn't trust.

Renia and Edek had been hoping for an engagement announcement. They liked Philip Hughes. Well, they liked the fact that he was male and taking Lola out. Renia and Edek thought that his parents, Iris and Fred Hughes, were Jewish. They thought they were English Jews, which explained their lack of Yiddish and their bewilderment about Jews not celebrating Christmas. Iris and Fred Hughes had gone along with the deception as they lived with Philip and his sister in a two-bedroom apartment, and Renia and Edek by now had moved into a three-bedroom house. Iris and Fred saw Lola as proof that their son Philip was moving up in the world.

At a party in a house by the seaside, when Lola was seventeen, someone had told her that Philip Hughes was kissing a boy behind the fridge.

'There's no room behind the fridge,' Lola, who was standing in the garden, had replied.

She had had to wait until a year later, when she came home one day to the apartment she shared with a *Rock-Out* colleague, to find Philip Hughes in her bed with an older man. Lola hadn't been sure whether it was the man's age or gender that had shocked her most. She did know that it was all over between her and Philip Hughes.

'Don't get married young,' Lillian Roxon said to her. 'It's a big mistake. Live your life and then get married.' Lola thought that getting married was living your life. 'You can come to New York and live with me,' Lillian said. 'Think about it.' Lola did think about it. It seemed like an invitation to become a Martian or turn into a pumpkin. She'd never thought of living anywhere other than Melbourne.

Lillian's apartment on East Twenty-First Street was across the road from the Thirteenth Precinct police headquarters, which, Lillian had pointed out, made it a very good location. Despite the location, Lola noticed that Lillian had three locks on the door of her third-floor walk-up apartment. Lola was sure that no one in Melbourne had three locks on their front door.

'I think I'll have an ice-cream,' Lola said to Lillian.

'Why not?' said Lillian. 'They're non-fat.'

'It doesn't say on the menu how many calories they have,' Lola said.

'How many calories can non-fat ice-cream have?' Lillian said.

'I don't know,' said Lola. 'I've never had non-fat ice-cream before.'

'Do you count the calories of everything you eat?' Lillian said.

'Only when I'm on a diet,' said Lola.

'I told you I'm on a diet at the moment,' Lillian said.

'I've been on a diet half my life,' said Lola. 'My mother used to serve me meals that always came in under two hundred calories,' Lola said. 'She used to give me grilled something and a salad. Grilled chicken and a salad, grilled fish and a salad, grilled liver and a salad, grilled anything and a salad. I had to keep a constant supply of chocolate in my bedroom cupboard so I wouldn't starve.'

'My father hated me being chubby,' Lillian said. 'And I was chubby then, not fat. I was getting ready to go out on my first date, when I was sixteen, when he came into my room and said, "If you could see yourself from behind, you wouldn't leave the house."' When we ate out, he'd say to the waiter, "No potatoes for my fat daughter."'

'Your father and my mother would have got on very well,' Lola said. 'My mother believes in slimness above all else. She doesn't believe in God, so she doesn't value godliness. Nothing beats being slim.'

'It's crazy, and sad,' said Lillian.

'What went wrong?' Lola said. 'I thought we Jews were supposed to be constantly overfeeding our children, our guests and our relatives, if we had any.'

'I think I'll have an ice-cream too,' Lillian said.

'It was very good,' said Lola.

'Next week, I want to take you to see a new group, The Doors,'

Lillian said. 'They're going to be huge. Particularly their lead singer, Jim Morrison.'

'I've heard of them,' Lola said.

'Linda is coming too,' Lillian said. Lola almost mentioned that she'd bumped into Linda while Linda had been photographing Dave Dee, Dozy, Beaky, Mick and Tich, in London. But she decided against it.

Lola had been walking all day. It was another hot day. She had decided that she really liked New York. The city absorbed you. Took you into itself like a sponge or a piece of blotting paper. New York made you feel less aware of being on your own, less aware of being a foreigner, less aware that you weren't at home. No one asked you why you were in New York. People from everywhere were there. You were just one of them.

Lola found it easier to arrange interviews here. In London she had to do a lot of talking to persuade people that interviews that would come out in *Rock-Out*, in Australia, were worth doing. On the whole, the English were suspicious of Australians and looked down on them.

In New York, no one questioned the value of an interview with an oddly named Australian newspaper. Lola felt unexpectedly at home in this semi-rundown, not quite spick-and-span city. She wasn't frightened of New York. She wasn't frightened by the talk of how dangerous the city was. She wasn't frightened by the police who all carried easily seen guns. She wasn't frightened of anything. She didn't yet know that within a decade, she would be frightened of everything. That she would experience panic attacks that would leave her gasping for breath.

Lola had begun to feel more accommodating towards the cockroaches in her room at the Horwood Hotel. She used to sit and watch them scurrying across the floor. Unlike ants, cockroaches seemed to frequently pause. Lola wondered what they were doing during their pauses. They just seemed to stand very still and then, suddenly, move on again. Maybe they were eating, but their movements were too delicate and refined for Lola to detect any activity.

Lola had also worked out that if she got up early in the morning, she could usually be guaranteed an empty bathroom that was still clean. She was becoming fond of the Horwood. She and Lillian and Linda Eastman were going to see The Doors at The Scene, a downtown club, that night. They would be a trio of Ls.

She was meeting Lillian and Linda in an hour. She put on her purple false eyelashes. When she finished positioning and gluing them and painting thick black eyeliner above and below the lashes, she remembered that neither Lillian nor Linda wore make-up. Lola briefly contemplated scrubbing her face, but it had been a long time since she'd gone out anywhere without her pancake make-up, her eyeliner and her lashes.

The Scene was in the basement of a building on the corner of Forty-Sixth Street and Eighth Avenue. The area was called Hell's Kitchen and wasn't the most salubrious part of town. You emerged from The Scene, late at night, to a parade of prostitutes in hot pants on Eighth Avenue. Lola had never seen a prostitute close up before. They looked like ordinary girls only more made-up, more worn out and less clothed.

The Scene was one of the in places to go. The best bands played there. The 23-year-old owner, Steve Paul, seemed to be able to spot stars well before they were stars. Fleetwood Mac, Traffic, The Lovin' Spoonful, The Young Rascals and Jimi Hendrix had all played there. Tiny Tim, a ukulele player with a very high falsetto-vibrato voice who sang vintage popular songs, was the warm-up act for all the performers.

A lot of the regulars who frequented The Scene were serious hippies. There was always a clutch of celebrities – Liza Minnelli, Andy Warhol, Sammy Davis Jr, Mick Jagger. And there was also a smattering of uptown people slumming it for the night.

Linda Eastman didn't look at all embarrassed to see Lola. She gave her a hug and a kiss. 'Did you like London?' she said.

'I did like London,' Lola said.

'I could easily see myself living there,' Linda said. Linda really looked like the well-bred, upper-class girl from Scarsdale, New York, that she was. Everything about her was well put together, but unfussy. She clearly didn't feel the need to embellish herself with jewellery or the latest hairstyle.

Her shoulder-length thick blond hair was sensibly cut, and her clothes were well made, subdued and practical. She carried herself with an innate confidence. She spoke with an aristocratic Scarsdale accent and an air of authority. There was a sense of affluence about her and the entitlement that affluence can bring. She stood out from the other *habitués* of The Scene, most of whom were in kaftans and far from perfectly groomed.

Linda looked just like the receptionist for the upper-crust *Town and Country* magazine that she had been. Except for three things. First, the two Nikon cameras that were always hanging around her neck. And second, her determination. She had a determination that was evident in every syllable and consonant that came out of her mouth. And then there was her sexuality. Her sexuality, which was not displayed in low-cut necklines or see-through tops, was clearly visible in the way she looked at certain pop stars. Her gaze was very direct and purposeful.

Lola knew that Linda's mother had died in a plane crash five years ago, when Linda was twenty. Linda had become pregnant in the month after her mother died. She had got married three months after her mother died and given birth to her daughter, Heather, six months after that. Lola thought it was hard not to look at those events and to think they were not, to a degree, a consequence of Mrs Eastman dying. Linda divorced Heather's father when Heather was two and a half.

'Could you really see yourself living in London?' Lola said to Linda.

'Yes,' said Linda. 'I loved London. I really like English people.'

'You should visit Australia,' Lola said. 'It's full of English people.'

'So London must have felt like home to you,' Linda said.

'Not really,' said Lola. 'The English don't really like Australians. I think they see us as their uncouth relatives.'

'Well, we're not their relatives,' Lillian said. 'Lola's relatives didn't come from London and neither did mine. They came from Lvov and Lodz. Lvov and Lodz were in Poland, three-hundred-and-fifty miles from each other. Lvov is now part of Ukrainia.'

'So did your relatives know each other?' Linda said.

'I don't know,' said Lola.

'You should ask them,' Linda said.

'I haven't got any relatives apart from my parents to ask,' Lola said.

'Well, ask your parents,' said Linda.

'She's going to,' said Lillian.

'My father's family came from Russia,' Linda said.

'I thought your father was born in America,' Lillian said.

'He was. Just,' said Linda. 'My grandparents, Louis and Stella, met at Ellis Island while their documents for entry into the United States were being processed. My father was born the following year.'

'That's why he seems so American,' Lillian said. 'He doesn't act very Jewish. And neither do you. You love to ride horses, and you love the countryside. You're not afraid of snakes and spiders and you're a nature lover. That's not very Jewish at all.'

'We were Jewish but we didn't make a big deal out of it,' Linda said. 'I don't think about being Jewish much, if at all.'

'She barely knows what Passover is,' Lillian said.

'That's true,' said Linda. 'My father didn't feel very Jewish. Or maybe he didn't want to feel Jewish. I remember when we bought a beach house in East Hampton, he didn't want too many Jews to buy houses there. He thought it would provoke anti-Semitism.'

'You mean more anti-Semitism,' said Lillian. 'East Hampton is about one hundred miles from New York,' Lillian said to Lola. 'It has huge, secluded estates of old blue-blood families. It's where they go to get away from New York. And part of getting away from New York means getting away from Jews.'

'You don't need Jews to have anti-Semitism,' Lola said. 'You just need anti-Semites. That's one of my father's favourite sayings. It sounds even better, in Yiddish.'

'You can speak Yiddish?' Lillian said.

'Yes,' said Lola.

'Linda probably doesn't even know what Yiddish is,' Lillian said.

'I do,' said Linda. 'I just can't understand any of it. I think my father really wanted nothing to do with his Jewishness.'

Even if they had wanted to, Renia and Edek would not have been able to discard their Jewishness, Lola thought. Their anguish, their sadness, their wariness was as clear as if it had been printed on them and illuminated and enlarged. And their lack of language sealed the deal.

Lola would later learn that a lot of people wanted nothing to do with Jewishness. It wasn't just Linda's father, Mr Leopold Epstein, who became Mr Lee Eastman, who wanted to ditch all Jewishness.

Some of America was also eager to have nothing to do with Jewishness. Breckinridge Long, the assistant secretary in charge of the visa division of the US Department of State, wrote in a memo in June 1940 to his colleagues, 'We can delay and effectively stop for a temporary period of indefinite length the number of immigrants into the United States. We could do this by simply advising our consuls to put every obstacle in the way and to require additional evidence and to resort to various administrative devices which would postpone and postpone and postpone the granting of visas.'

'A temporary period of indefinite length' was a clever phrase, Lola thought, when she read Breckinridge Long's words. Breckinridge Long, a wealthy man and a personal friend of president Franklin Delano Roosevelt, was a smart man.

He was a good liar, too. In order to crush a proposed government resolution to establish a secret agency to rescue Jewish refugees, he gave false testimony to the House Foreign Affairs Committee saying that everything was being done to save Jewish refugees. Ninety per cent of the quota places for Jews and immigrants from Fascist regimes were left unfilled.

The nightclub was filling up. Lillian had told Lola that The Scene, along with Max's Kansas City, was the place to be seen and to see everyone you wanted to see. Linda was talking about her horses. Lola wondered if anyone else at the club that night was talking about their horses. Thinking or talking about horses was for the idle rich, Lola decided. Neither Renia nor Edek would ever be rich. And they couldn't afford to be idle. Being idle made it easier for errant, aberrant and abhorrent thoughts to seep in. Once they got in, they made themselves at home and seemed impossible to evict.

The only time horses were mentioned in the Bensky house was when Renia talked about her very pious father giving her a piece of horse meat, in the ghetto. The eating of horsemeat was prohibited under Orthodox Jewish dietary laws. 'He said to me,' Renia said, "I can't eat this meat, but you must eat it. It is more important to live than to be kosher."' Renia usually cried after telling this story.

Lola couldn't understand Linda's love of horses. She couldn't really understand people's attachment to any sort of pet, although she wasn't sure that horses fell into the category of pets. They seemed too big to be pets. Surely, pets had to be small enough to be able to be picked up and petted. Or maybe petting something had nothing to do with being able to pick up the animal.

Lola wasn't interested in horses. She didn't even like dogs or cats. Edek had brought home a dog from the dog pound when Lola was about ten. A black dog with a mean demeanour. Because the dog was black Edek named it what he'd heard was a popular name for black dogs in Australia – Nigger.

Nigger barked a lot. And liked to bite people. Every now and then Nigger escaped and Edek would go running after him, down Nicholson Street, North Carlton, shouting, 'Nigger, Nigger, come back.' Edek had no idea what the word *nigger* meant. Neither did Renia, or Lola. When Lola found out, several years later, that *nigger* was a derogatory, racist term, she was mortified. Luckily by then Nigger had bitten the postman, the milkman, the doctor and several passers-by and had to be returned to the pound.

'Did you two know each other in Australia?' Linda said.

'Lola would have been in kindergarten when I left Australia to live in New York,' Lillian said.

Lola laughed. She knew Lillian had been living in New York for about six years. 'I think I was just about to start high school,' Lola said.

'Yes, while I was interviewing Rock Hudson you were a good little schoolgirl,' Lillian said.

'I don't think I could have been all that good,' Lola said. 'I was always being kicked out of class. Mainly French and German class.'

'You were kicked out of class?' said Lillian. 'So was I. I was kicked out of French and maths, and I was constantly kicked out of Latin class. I asked too many questions, and girls weren't supposed to do that. The Latin teacher would kick me out before the class even began. I'd go outside and sit on the verandah.'

'I used to crawl along the brick wall below the panes of glass that made up the upper half of the classroom wall to get to the boys' classrooms, which were at the other end of the hallway. There was always some boy who'd been kicked out I could talk to.'

'Why were you kicked out?' Linda said.

'For talking too much, I think,' Lola said. 'I wasn't doing anything terrible. Most of the time, I was planning what to have for lunch.'

'Hey, the two of you were destined to meet,' Linda said. 'You're both Australian, both journalists, both fat and both got kicked out of class.'

Lola wanted to kick Linda. What she had said, even if it were all true, was just plain mean. She didn't think Linda was a mean person. She was just a bit blunt. More truthful than she needed to be.

'You forgot that we're both Polish Jews,' Lillian said.

Linda was about to reply when she spotted Jim Morrison just near the stage. She ran over to him. Something was clearly going on between them. Linda was gesturing and reddening. And Jim Morrison had his back to her half the time. Linda looked as though she was pleading with Jim Morrison, although she didn't seem to Lola like the type to plead. Jim Morrison was looking into the distance. He didn't look like the type to be moved by pleas of any sort.

'They have a thing going,' Lillian said.

'It looks as though whatever thing they had going has gone,' said Lola.

Lillian laughed. 'I think you're right,' she said. 'Linda won't take this lying down, although I'd guess it's all about lying down.'

'Looks to me like the lying down is over,' Lola said.

By now, Jim Morrison was shaking his head. And Linda was looking a bit tearful. Lola felt sorry for Linda. She looked defeated. But Lola knew Linda well enough to know that the defeat wouldn't last long.

'Are you going to come back to New York after you've been to Los Angeles?' Lillian asked Lola.

'By the time I leave Los Angeles, I'll have been away from home for over a year,' Lola said.

'Melbourne is too small to be your permanent home,' Lillian said. 'You can visit Melbourne from time to time, but don't stay there. Think about it. I'm being very serious.'

Melbourne didn't seem that small to Lola. It did seem far away, though. Far away from everything. She tried to change the subject. 'Do you know who's playing at Monterey?' she said to Lillian. 'They've got an incredible line-up. The Mamas and the Papas, The Who, Simon and Garfunkel, Jefferson Airplane, Jimi Hendrix, Otis Redding, Ravi Shankar and a lot of others.'

'I know,' said Lillian. 'There's a band called Big Brother and the Holding Company playing. Their singer Janis Joplin is sensational. Call me after Monterey and we can talk about your plans.'

'After Monterey, I'm going to Los Angeles,' Lola said. 'I'm interviewing Sonny and Cher in their house.' Lola hesitated for a moment. 'In London, Cher borrowed my false eyelashes,' she said. 'They were my best pair, diamante-lined. I couldn't get them back from her in London. Do you think I should ask Cher to give them back to me when I see her in LA?'

'Why wouldn't you?' said Lillian.

'Because I feel silly,' said Lola.

'Just ask her,' Lillian said. 'She's supposed to be very nice. I've heard she depends on Sonny for everything. Poor thing.'

It was hard for Lola to think of anyone who had a body as sleek as Cher's and a mane of thick straight black hair and wardrobes full of glamorous clothes as 'a poor thing.' Maybe Cher was a poor thing. Lola had been bothered by the way Sonny hovered and answered too many of the questions Lola had asked Cher. Maybe she should just let Cher keep the diamante-lined false eyelashes.

Lola saw Linda sitting on the floor at the side of the stage. The Doors were setting up. Linda was already photographing them. Everyone at the tables quietened down. The Doors started playing. After half an hour of The Doors, Lola had a headache. It wasn't just the volume of the music or the theatre of what seemed like a well-rehearsed provocative piece of carelessness and abandon. It was Jim Morrison himself who disturbed her.

He was long and lean and swayed sideways like a snake when he sang. He had the sultry good looks of a movie star. His mouth seemed to be part of a permanent pout. His blue-grey eyes appeared to be unattached to a heart or a soul. There was something dead at his core, Lola thought. Jim Morrison was wearing low-slung, black leather pants that were so tight they could have been painted on to him. Lola would read later that he had his trousers especially made to emphasise the crotch. Jim Morrison licked his lips with a reptilian slitheriness while he sang. He looked poised and poisonous. And disconnected from everything around him.

Lola was surprised at her reaction to him. She hadn't expected it. But inaccessible people bothered her and Jim Morrison appeared to be completely inaccessible. The Doors finally finished their set. 'That was unendurable pleasure,' Lillian said to Lola.

'Unendurable pleasure?' Lola said. 'What was pleasurable about it?' she said.

'The music,' said Lillian.

'There's something about Jim Morrison that really freaks me out,' Lola said.

'Do you think it's because he appears hypnotised or in a trance?' Lillian said.

'I don't know,' she said. No one else in the audience appeared to be freaked out by Jim Morrison. Most people looked high from the performance.

Lola could see why Jim Morrison was compelling. His movements on stage were suggestive, aggressive and unleashed. There was an intensity and an arrogance to him. He was surly, sullen and sexy. He screamed and caressed or throttled the microphone. He was wild and dangerous. Every now and then, he lurched and staggered blindly around the stage as though he could fall at any second. As though he were more than a little out of control.

'Come over with me. I'll introduce you to him,' Lillian said. Lola had been to Max's Kansas City with Lillian a few times. Each time Lillian, who appeared to know everyone there, had introduced Lola as Australia's best journalist. Lola would follow that introduction with an embarrassed insistence that she was far from Australia's best or top journalist. Until one night when Andy Warhol stared at her with his stark, white face and said, 'Don't be so humble, you're not that great.' Lola would later hear that quote attributed to Golda Meir, but even if it was not an original Andy Warhol, it did the job. Lola kept quiet and let Lillian pronounce her greatness.

Andy Warhol was one of the weirder-looking people in Max's Kansas City's raucous crowd of exhibitionists. The bar was where Lillian held court every night when she wasn't at The Scene. Max's Kansas City was frequented by painters, sculptors, filmmakers, musicians, writers, poets, actors, fashion designers, models and the occasional socialite or member of the Kennedy family. The very elegantly dressed Duke and Duchess of Windsor were there the night Andy Warhol addressed Lola's lack of greatness.

'I don't want to be introduced to Jim Morrison,' Lola said.

'You have to meet him,' Lillian said, 'He's going to be huge. Make arrangements to interview him. He does his own publicity, so do the interview now, if he agrees.'

'Now?' said Lola.

'Yes, now,' Lillian said.

'Jim,' Lillian said, 'I want you to meet Lola Bensky. Lola is one of Australia's top journalists. Her stories are read from one side of the country to the other and she's a fabulous writer. She's interviewed, among many other people, Mick Jagger and Paul McCartney.'

'I haven't interviewed Paul McCartney,' Lola said to Lillian. Lillian elbowed her in the side. 'I had a cup of tea with him,' Lola said. 'He told me his mother died when he was fourteen. I said my mother lost her parents at seventeen and her brothers and sisters three or four years after that. He said *loss* was a pretty stupid word to use. I said I couldn't agree more. You can lose socks and umbrellas and even underpants, but you can't lose your mother or your father.' Jim Morrison barely looked at Lola. Up close, his face had a chubbiness that could have looked innocent on someone else, but on him looked malevolent.

Lillian spotted Paul Newman and went over to talk to him. Lola was left standing next to Jim Morrison not sure what to do or say. She would have infinitely preferred to be talking to Paul Newman.

'Could I arrange to do an interview with you?' Lola said to Jim Morrison.

'Why do you want to do that?' Jim Morrison said.

'Because I think you're going to be very, very famous and that's what I do – I write about famous rock stars,' Lola said.

She thought it was a lame answer and was trying to think of a better one when Jim Morrison said, 'These days in the United States you have to be a politician or an assassin to be a superstar.' He spoke very slowly, as though each word was weighted with a meaning that needed to be digested. 'Sit down,' he said to Lola.

'Here?' she said.

'Yes,' he said.

'Now?' she said.

'Yes, now,' he said.

Lola grabbed her chair and got out her notebook. *Has a sullen demeanour and a brutal ruthlessness about him*, she'd written in her notebook while she'd been watching him perform. She quickly turned the page, although she thought he would probably be quite pleased by that description.

Lola knew that Jim Morrison was born in Melbourne, Florida. She hadn't known there was a Melbourne in Florida. She'd thought that she lived in the only Melbourne there was. She didn't think she'd mention the Melbourne connection. It didn't seem like the sort of bond that would move Jim Morrison.

There was a carefully applied carelessness about Jim Morrison, Lola thought. Jim Morrison, despite his world-weary gestures and postures, was only three years older than Lola. She knew that Jim Morrison didn't get on well with his parents. Jim's father was a highly decorated naval officer. On the official biographical information about Jim Morrison, he had listed his parents as dead. Lola knew that they weren't dead.

'You look as though a lot of things bother you,' Lola said to Jim Morrison. Oh God, she thought to herself, she hadn't meant to say that. She didn't have a list of questions prepared.

'A lot of things do bother me,' he said. He spoke very slowly, as though the words and the spaces between them were freighted with other interpretations. 'A lot of things do bother me.' That was a pretty clear sentence. Lola thought there was a limit to the number of ways it could be interpreted.

'What sort of things?' Lola said.

'I hate the sound of heavy breathing,' he said. 'Especially when I'm trying to sleep.'

That sounded reasonable. Lola was a very light sleeper herself and was woken up by the slightest sound. She thought it probably had something to do with the fact that Renia used to regularly wake up screaming in her sleep and Lola and Edek would have to reassure Renia that it was a dream, before they could all go back to sleep again.

'My brother had chronic tonsillitis,' Jim Morrison said. 'His breathing was very noisy. A couple of times I taped his mouth shut while he slept. He used to wake up gasping for breath.' Jim Morrison started to laugh at the memory. It was clearly a memory that amused him. Lola watched him laughing. Even his laugh had a cruel, almost feral component.

'I used to throw rocks at him, too,' Jim Morrison said.

'Why?' said Lola.

'For the fun of it,' said Jim Morrison. 'I rubbed dog shit on his face once. Nice fresh dog shit.'

'Was that funny too?' said Lola.

'Of course,' Jim Morrison said. 'Don't you think it's funny?'

'Not at all,' said Lola. She felt disconcerted and uncomfortable. She thought Jim Morrison was enjoying her discomfort.

'Why are you so angry?' she said to Jim Morrison.

'I'm not angry,' he said. 'I just hate some people.'

'Who do you hate?' she asked him.

'My mother,' he said. 'My brother.'

He looked at Lola for a few seconds. 'You probably love your parents,' he said with a smirk lurking behind his grin.

'I think I do,' she said. 'Do you love anybody?' she asked him.

'No, not even myself,' Jim Morrison said. 'I love poetry. And Satan.'

Lola looked at him. How could he love Satan? Satan was a concept of evil, of darkness and destruction. Maybe he saw himself as the physical embodiment of Satan? An adversary. Someone who was against everyone.

'My father was the captain of one of the biggest naval carriers in the world,' Jim Morrison said. 'My father commanded three thousand men but in our house my mother was in command. She hollered at him. She told him to take the garbage out. And he did it. He took the garbage out.'

'He's very moody,' Linda Eastman had said to Lola about Jim Morrison. Moody? Moody would have been fine. Lola understood moodiness. This wasn't moody. Jim Morrison started irritatedly unbuttoning his shirt. He looked as though he not only wanted to shed his clothes, but would have liked to remove his skin. He was scratching at the shirt. As though he wanted to get through to something he had no access to.

Lola could see Lillian on the other side of the club. She was still talking to Paul Newman. They looked as though they were best friends. She wished she could join them.

'You don't like me, do you?' Jim Morrison said to Lola.

'Not really,' she said, surprising herself. 'But I think you're going to be very successful.'

She felt a little bad. Maybe she should have just said, 'Of course I like you.' She thought Lillian was right. Jim Morrison was going to be huge.

Two months later, 'Light My Fire' would hit number one in the charts and sell more than one million copies. Jim Morrison's mother would track him down in New York. She would speak to him on the phone and ask him to come home for Thanksgiving. 'I'll be pretty busy,' he would say. He also said he might see her when he performed in Washington, where his parents now lived. 'Could you do your mother a big favour and get a haircut?' she had said.

'I don't want to talk to her ever again,' other people in the room heard him say when he hung up.

Jim Morrison's mother and brother came to his concert in Washington. He avoided seeing either of them. From the stage he screamed, 'Mother, I want to fuck you,' and looked at his mother with a vacant stare. Lola thought that Jim Morrison would not be a good candidate for her 'Say Your Piece' column.

It was getting hot at The Scene. The club was still crowded. Jim Morrison gestured to the waiter closest to him. The waiter seemed to know what he wanted and brought him two drinks. Lola knew that Jim Morrison drank a lot and that he dropped acid. Lola wasn't sure why it was called dropping acid instead of taking acid. LSD was a pill like any other pill. You didn't drop an aspirin or an antibiotic.

Jim Morrison's speech was slowing down even more. It was hard not to look impatient or prompt him when the silences between his words felt interminable. The only advantage of this snail's-pace speech was that she had no trouble taking notes.

'Music and poetry are things everyone can take part in,' he was saying. 'They're natural things like child's play. It's a good way to move through life. If there were more people playing, things would be a lot smoother.'

If there were fewer people throwing rocks, things might be smoother still, Lola thought.

Lola didn't know much about either music or poetry. They had very little music and no books of poetry in the house when she was growing up. They had no books at all.

Edek borrowed his detective-fiction books from a library in the city. Lola thought he had learnt most of his English from the detective-fiction books. Edek knew the terminology used in post-mortem laboratories and police stations all over the English-speaking world. Edek could talk about thoracic aortas and windpipes and sternums and how to detect the difference between a suicidal hanging and a homicidal hanging.

Linda Eastman had come over and was standing behind Lola. She was taking photographs of Jim Morrison. He took no notice of her.

'Have you read *The Doors of Perception* by Aldous Huxley?' Jim Morrison said to Lola.

'No,' said Lola.

'That's too bad,' Jim Morrison said.

Lola knew that The Doors were named after a line by William Blake, 'If the doors of perception were cleansed everything would appear as it is: infinite.'

'He eats acid pills like they were peanuts,' Linda muttered to Lola.

'And he smokes bags of grass.' Lola knew that Linda didn't mean lawn cuttings. Everyone was talking about marijuana, grass. Grass, which currently seemed to be coming from Mexico.

'What is important to you, apart from music and poetry?' Lola said to Jim Morrison.

'Art, literature, philosophy,' Jim Morrison said. 'The thing that really changed my life happened when I was very young. I saw a family of American Indians scattered all over the highway, bleeding to death. There was blood everywhere. Blood all over the highway. Blood, blood, blood.' The word blood was a very graphic word, Lola thought. Jim Morrison repeated the word a few more times.

Blood was one of the things Renia talked about. 'They took so much blood,' she used to say to herself. 'So much blood. They didn't take it from a vein in a prisoner's arm, they cut straight into the carotid artery,' she would say, pointing to her neck. 'They took as much as they wanted and would leave the person to die. The blood went to the German army,' she would sometimes add.

Lola wished she could talk to Renia about normal things. If the conversation had to be about blood, then maybe they could have talked about menstruation. When Lola was eleven and came home with blood on her underpants, all Renia had said was, 'That is your period.' Lola had thought that this 'period' was something that was only going to happen once. She got a terrible shock when it happened again, a month later.

'As one of the American Indians was dying,' Jim Morrison said, 'his soul passed into my body.'

'How old were you?' Lola said.

'About five,' said Jim Morrison. Lola didn't know why she'd asked

Jim Morrison that question. She thought that it was because she didn't know what else to say.

Lola didn't really think that souls could travel. She certainly didn't think they would make dumb travel decisions, like landing in Jim Morrison's body. She wondered if souls really could inhabit other people. Was she carrying other people's souls? The souls of her mother's dead relatives? Or her father's dead relatives? She didn't think so. Decades later, she wouldn't be so certain.

'Do you get on well with the other members of the band?' she said to Jim Morrison. She knew it wasn't exactly a smooth transition from the story of the American Indian whose soul had passed into his body.

'Do I get on well with them?' Jim Morrison said. 'They can't think, they can't fight, they can't fuck. They're okay.'

Lola didn't think *Rock-Out* would publish that quote. They couldn't print the word *fuck*. The sentence lost its punch without that.

She decided she had enough material. And she had had enough of Jim Morrison. She turned around to Linda, who was still taking photographs. 'I'm finishing,' she said. 'Can we have a cup of coffee?' She felt a strong need to talk to someone who was easier to understand and more friendly than Jim Morrison.

'Sure,' said Linda.

'Thank you very much for the interview,' Lola said to Jim Morrison. Jim Morrison looked a little bewildered. As though he was just getting into the flow of things.

'He's not stupid,' Linda said to Lola as they looked for a table. 'He's just mixed up.' Lillian, who had just finished talking to Steve Paul, the owner of The Scene, joined them.

'Shall we have a drink before we go home?' Linda said. 'Soda, seltzer or coffee all around,' she said, and laughed. 'You two are probably the only two people in here who don't drink alcohol or do drugs.'

'I don't like being out of control,' Lola said.

'If you don't let things get out of control, you miss out on some of life's adventures,' Linda said.

Lola was tired. There was something about Jim Morrison that had depleted her. Or possibly more than one thing. He had seemed untouchable. And out of control.

'I think maybe I'm not looking for adventure,' Lola said to Linda.

'Adventure isn't a bad thing,' said Linda.

Less than two years later, Lillian would call Lola and say, 'Linda says she's going to marry Paul McCartney.'

'Do you believe her?' Lola said.

'I think I do,' said Lillian. 'She's never lied to me.'

Anyone who could spread her legs that wide could probably get anyone they wanted, Lola thought. And then felt ashamed of herself for that thought. She thought that it was more likely to be Linda's certainty, her fearlessness and her direct, no-holds-barred attitude that attracted Paul McCartney. 'I believe her,' Lillian said.

'I think I do, too,' said Lola.

4

Lola Bensky woke up on her thirtieth birthday to the shocking reali-
sation that she had turned thirty and both her mother and her father
were still alive. Lola had been living with the prospect of Renia and
Edek's imminent demise for most of her life. For years she had jumped
at every late-night phone call. For years her heart had started racing if
they were not home when she expected them to be.

The thought that her parents wouldn't be alive for very long had
come from her parents themselves. 'Daddy and me won't live for very
long, not after what we went through,' Renia Bensky had said regularly since Lola was a small child. Each time she said it, Edek would
nod his head in agreement. Lola occasionally wondered if her parents
had some sort of pact about not living long. She didn't really think
they did. Edek just agreed with everything Renia said. He never con-
tradicted her. He never offered another point of view. He didn't even
roll his eyes.

'You are killing me,' was another one of Renia's periodic statements to Lola. It was often followed by, 'You will cry on my grave but
it will be too late.' Lola had a sinking feeling, even when she was seven
or eight, that Renia was right about this.

Once, when Renia and Edek had been in a car accident, they had called Lola from the hospital. From the moment Lola had answered the phone she had been almost unable to breathe, even though her mother had said that they were both only bruised. Lola had been sure that this was finally the moment Renia had been talking about when, any second, Renia and Edek would both be dead.

Yet here she was, thirty years old and both of her parents were still alive. She decided to relax. Her mother and father were both probably going to be around for quite a while. She thought that there was still enough time to fix things up. She wasn't sure what it was she wanted to fix up. If she'd known that she had less than a decade left with Renia Bensky, she would not have relaxed.

Lola got out of bed. Her husband was still asleep. She was married and had two children. She thought she was probably happy. Sometimes, in the middle of the night, she had to get out of bed and sit on the floor at the end of the hallway of the old, Edwardian-style house she lived in, in Melbourne. She would sit on the floor and try to calm herself down. She would have woken up with her heart pounding. The pounding was so forceful that it felt as though her heart might burst through her chest. This mostly happened after she had eaten too much. Sometimes, her husband stirred slightly when she came back to bed, but he never asked what she had been doing. Lola felt that she was lucky to have her husband.

From the time Lola was ten and taller than her mother, Renia had fed Lola a daily barrage of advice and admonitions. They all amounted to the same thing. In Renia's words, 'No boy wants to marry a fat girl.' They had started as 'No boy wants to have a fat girlfriend' and moved on to 'No boy will be serious about a fat girl.'

Lola's husband was a tall, blond, former rock star. Well, a former rock star in most parts of Australia. He had made it clear that he would prefer someone slimmer. She wasn't at all clear about why he had married her.

Lola wasn't at her heaviest at the moment. In fact, she was lighter than she had been for years. She felt so light, she feared she might vanish. Her ankles, which, even now, were thicker than your average ankles, felt too weak to carry her. Lola, who was five-foot-nine, felt so insubstantial. The scales said she was still thirty pounds heavier, or five inches shorter, than she should be. But she felt slight.

She had been dieting for ten weeks. Every morning she made herself a huge salad for the day. She mixed two cans of tuna with one large shredded cabbage, two large shredded carrots, five shredded zucchinis and twelve chopped radishes. Lola chopped the radishes, as shredded radishes, she found, became too watery. She dressed the salad with salt and pepper and half a cup of lemon juice. It wasn't fabulous, but it did involve a lot of chewing and contained a lot of fibre.

In the kitchen, Lola prepared breakfast for her children. She loved her children. They were beautiful children. Worth being married to someone you felt too fat for. Lola didn't think her husband was a bad husband. She thought whatever unhappiness she felt had more to do with herself than him.

Lola and Mr Former Rock Star had been married for nine years. Their wedding had been a complete fiasco. On the morning of her wedding, Lola had had to do the four-hour live television show she did every Saturday morning. Every Saturday morning, Lola sat behind a desk in the studios of Channel 0, in Nunawading, Melbourne, and interviewed rock stars and reviewed records. The other three women on the show mimed and danced to whatever music was at the top of the charts that week. Lola stayed seated behind her desk.

Lola drove home from the studio on her wedding day to find that the hairdresser who was supposed to do her hair had had a meltdown over her boyfriend, and wasn't there. Lola put some talcum powder through her hair to mop up the oiliness of the cream she had used to wash off her television make-up. The talcum powder only made her hair look worse.

Renia Bensky had started crying when she had seen Lola's floor-length, maroon velvet wedding dress. 'You've seen it before,' Lola said to her mother.

'It didn't look so bad,' Renia said, sniffling.

At the reception, the guests clung to their own groups. The groom's family and family friends, the Church of England Brigade, as Lola thought of them, were stiff with each other, but they were almost frozen in the presence of the Jews.

The Jews were too loud. Too emotional. And too obsequious to the Church of England crowd. There was also a lot of kissing from the Jews. And too much kissing for the non-Jews.

Several Jews offered their condolences to Renia and Edek in sympathy for the fact that their daughter was marrying out. Renia and Edek brushed off the condolences. Neither of them looked as though they really cared. Renia shook her head when anyone mentioned it. She seemed much more concerned with the thought that Lola's wedding dress already looked a little tight.

'Did you put on more weight?' Renia had said to Lola as they walked into the reception hall.

'I don't know,' Lola had answered. She had almost said, 'Since when?' But she'd known her mother would have known exactly how long it had been since Lola had had the dress made.

Everyone at the wedding, Jews and non-Jews, told Lola how beautiful her mother looked. Renia was wearing a sleeveless, cream, embroidered shot-silk gown. The back of the dress had a large circle scooped out, which exposed most of Renia's back. Lola thought that her mother must be wearing one of her many strapless or backless bras. Lola's maroon velvet wedding dress covered Lola from her neck to her ankles.

With her large eyes, high cheekbones, bouffant hair and shiny, sun-tanned skin, Renia sparkled. She looked like a combination of Sophia Loren and Gina Lollobrigida, the two women in the world she most wanted to look like.

Edek was trying to make sure that the guests mingled. It was a futile mission. Later, Lola saw Edek consoling himself with a choco-late-coated wafer he must have brought from home. He finished the chocolate-coated wafer just before he began his speech.

The Church of England contingent didn't understand a word that Edek said. He had tried to be very formal and in the process had lost some of his already shaky English.

Lola thought that her new father-in-law's speech would never end. So did most of the guests, particularly the Jews. They wore anxious expressions of intense concentration on their faces, as Jack Weldon Worthington Sr spoke and pontificated and quoted.

Lola started thinking about her hair. She shouldn't have put talcum powder in her hair. It was a really stupid thing to do, to put talcum pow-der in your hair on your wedding day. By the time Lola came out of her talcum powder reverie, Jack Weldon Worthington Sr was in full swing.

'Marriage is an evil that most men welcome,' he was saying. 'And, as the old expression goes, keep your eyes wide open before marriage and half shut afterwards.' He cleared his throat. 'Well, our son certainly had an ace up his sleeve,' he said. There was a puzzled rustle among the Jews. Even Lola, whose English had been praised by her parents and their friends since she was a small child, didn't know what ace Jack Weldon Worthington Sr was referring to. Edek, a keen card player, nodded and said, 'Yes, it is always good to have such an ace.' He leaned over to Renia and added, in a whisper, 'But maybe not in your sleeves.'

'We are not able to make head or tail of it,' Jack Weldon Worthington Sr said, smiling. 'But then again, there is no hard and fast rule.'

'*Er ret far fayer un far vaser,*' Lola heard Mr Dunov say to Mr Pincus. Loosely translated, this meant 'He is a motor mouth'.

'If they had to put his brain in a chicken, it would run straight to the butcher,' Mr Pincus replied. The saying had even more flourish in Yiddish. Lola tried not to laugh.

Jack Weldon Worthington Sr sat down. There was silence. Edek started clapping and the rest of the guests joined in. Edek led Lola and Mr Former Rock Star into the centre of the room. All five members of the Chaim Rappaport Big Band launched into a song called '*Chosen Kale Mazel Tov*'. The lyrics '*chosen, kale mazel tov*', 'groom, bride, congratulations', were repeated and repeated.

Lola had heard '*Chosen Kale Mazel Tov*' at so many Jewish weddings. It often made her want to cry. Probably because of the high hopes embodied in most marriages. And the plaintive tones of the flute that carried the melody. A melody that felt linked to another world.

All the Jews knew what to do. They formed two circles, one for the men and one for the women. Holding hands, they started dancing in large circles around the bride and the groom. The guests took turns at stepping into the centre of the circle to dance with either the bride or the groom.

The Jews beckoned to the non-Jews to join in. Some of them did. The groom's parents sat with stiff smiles at the bridal party's table. 'It is a Jewish dance,' Edek shouted as he passed Lola's new mother- and father-in-law.

The dance lasted a long time. Or so it seemed to Lola. She had never been good at this dance. Even though you could get away with only the ability to move sideways. She looked at her father. He knew all the correct steps. Even though he was a little tubby or, as Renia put it, 'a fatty', Edek was very light on his feet. He was flying around the circle.

Luba Lipschitz and Martin Schenkel and Fay Feldman sat at their table, dumpy, slumped and silent. Their parents, who were on the dance floor, were all survivors of death camps. Some of the other guests were survivors of labour camps or had been in hiding during the war. Australia had the highest percentage of Holocaust survivors per capita outside Israel. Their children were the survivors of their parents. Quite a few of them were the product of an overly vigilant neglect. They had parents who noticed every pound they gained or when they wore their hair the wrong way, but they didn't notice any sadness, any bewilderment, any loneliness or anxiety in their children. They didn't notice absences at school or money stolen or most other symptoms of a child in trouble.

The space that most parents had available for their children's current lives was taken up by the past. Lola could see it in her mother. Her mother couldn't hear her. On the whole, Lola had to say things three or four times, and even then it was hard to get a response. Whenever Lola was around, her mother would busy herself doing other things. Hanging out the laundry. Putting away the dishes. If Lola asked Renia a question, Renia would immediately seem to have something urgent or unnecessarily complicated to do. For example, Renia would sometimes balance one kitchen chair on top of the other and climb up, using the kitchen bench as leverage, in order to get something out of a very tall kitchen cupboard. It was such a precarious balancing exercise that Lola inevitably forgot whatever question it was that she wanted to ask. When Lola was a teenager she would demonstrate this balancing act of Renia's to some of her school friends. All she had to do was ask Renia a question, any question, and the two chairs would be dragged out. It would take Lola many years to understand that Renia couldn't answer questions. That Renia was terrified of questions. And terrified of the answers.

Edek had trouble hearing Lola, too. He would come home after work, eat and settle into an armchair and bury himself in one of his detective-fiction books. He seemed to hear nothing that Lola said unless she said it in a very loud voice, and then he would look startled.

Lola found that having parents who were unable to live in the present made living in your own present much more complicated. Lola did get the attention of both of her parents once. She was arrested for shoplifting when she was ten. Renia and Edek did not react well. Renia was hysterical and kept asking Lola how she could do that to them. And Edek was furious. Renia slammed doors and banged pots in the kitchen with even greater force than usual. And Edek stopped speaking to Lola other than to let her know, periodically, that she was lucky not to have been put in jail. It took months for things to go back to normal.

Lola married Mr Former Rock Star because he had asked her to marry him. She also thought that she loved him. For Lola, the clincher that came with the marriage proposal was the fact that her husband-to-be said he'd never wanted to get married, as he was frightened that the person he married would leave him. Lola promised that she would always love him and never leave him. She didn't know that she would break that promise.

At the wedding, Lola looked at her new husband. He was all blond hair and flushed skin. She felt proud to be marrying him. They were getting married despite a few hiccups in the relationship. Lola didn't know why she called these incidents hiccups. The incidents should have been harder to tolerate than the hiccups. But for Lola, they weren't.

The incidents or hiccups involved other girls. In his bed. Once, just minutes after she had left that very bed. She had returned unexpectedly just twenty minutes after she had left for the newspaper office where she worked, to find him in the middle of his final heaves and grunts. Very firmly she had asked the girl, a blonde with straight hair and very narrow hips, to leave. And with great disdain, she had asked Mr Former Rock Star to put fresh sheets on the bed.

She had been rattled, but not as rattled as she should have been. Mr Former Rock Star had come around to her office later that day, looking both sheepish and apologetic. And a little distraught. Lola couldn't tell what aspect of the incident was causing his distress. He promised that it would never happen again. Lola wasn't sure that it would never happen again. But for some reason, apart from wondering how he could have gone from heaving and grunting inside her to pumping away at Miss Slim Hips in twenty minutes, it was not a subject she dwelt on.

Lola wasn't going to think about that, now, on her wedding day. It was late in the evening and she was dancing with her parents' friend Herschel Ryza, to the music of the Chaim Rappaport Big Band, whose music was now more subdued. Herschel Ryza was a sweet, short man. He and his wife Topcha were childless. On weekends, Topcha baked small, horseshoe-shaped almond cookies and honey cakes. She always kept some for Lola.

Next to Lola, Mr Grynbaum was dancing with Mrs Mendel. Mrs Slotkowski was dancing with Mr Mendel and Mrs Grynbaum was dancing with Edek. She could see Renia at the far side of the dance floor, moving gracefully in unison with Mr Slotkowski. Lola suspected that her mother was having an affair with Mr Slotkowski. She'd found them in the house one afternoon, years ago, looking blotched and dishevelled, when she'd come home from school early. Her mother had said that Mr Slotkowski was helping her with a surprise birthday present for her father, so Lola mustn't mention his visit. Edek's birthday had come and gone with no surprises that Lola could see. Still, she kept quiet about Mr Slotkowski's visits and the number of phone calls he seemed to make to Renia.

Lola knew that Mr Grynbaum was having an affair with Mrs Zucker. Mrs Zucker was wearing a pearl-encrusted, aqua silk, one-shouldered dress and a smouldering expression. Lola could see her leaning over and saying something in Mr Grynbaum's ear. Renia had told her about the affair. 'Regina Zucker thinks that Josef Grynbaum loves her,' Renia had said. 'But Josef Grynbaum has already had a big affair with Mrs Slotkowski's sister.' Lola wondered what constituted a big affair as opposed to a little affair. Was it the length of time, the frequency or heat of the sex? She had no idea. She didn't think she would ask Renia. Judging from what Lola had seen of Renia's blotched skin and the way Renia would dart out of the room, holding the telephone, each time Mr Slotkowski called, Lola thought that their affair probably fell into the big affair category.

Lola looked at Mr and Mrs Former Rock Star Sr. They were talking to their friends Annabelle and Alistair Pilkington and the Honourable Judge Wilkinson-Powell. Lola wondered if the Church of England guests also had affairs with their friends' spouses. They all looked a bit too uncomfortable to have affairs. They looked uncomfortable standing up chatting to their close friends. Lola couldn't imagine them crushing their clothes as they grappled with each other, or how they would deal with the aftermath of that grapple. The mess that had to be wiped up and washed away. Or the unplanned and unpredictable nature of the noises and sounds that might accompany a less than orchestrated encounter. Maybe they just had more polite, controlled, well-mannered affairs. Happy together, in their shared discomfort.

Lola's parents, who were now dancing together, had decided to skip the part of the wedding where the bride and the groom are each lifted up in the air, on a chair, and carried around the room, often to another chorus of '*Chosen Kale Mazel Tov*'.

Lola had heard Edek and Renia discussing the subject. 'She is too fat for anyone to lift her up on a chair,' Renia Bensky had said.

'It is not one person who does lift the chair, it is four people who do lift the chair,' Edek had replied.

'She is too fat for four people,' Renia had said.

After a couple of minutes, Lola had heard Edek say, 'Mr Kirschbaum's son was very fat and they did lift him up in a chair.'

'She is too fat,' Renia had replied, and left the room. Lola didn't mind. She didn't like heights. Heights made her feel nauseated.

Lola finished making her tuna salad. The house was quiet. Not even her one-year-old was awake yet. Lola didn't feel thirty. But then how did she know what thirty felt like? She did know that she still had two parents. And that thought was strangely uplifting.

She had a small portion of the salad. It really wasn't a great break-fast dish. But it certainly was fibrous. She went into the bathroom and sat on the toilet. Lola loved sitting on the toilet in peace. She thought that she had inherited this from Edek, who always checked before he used the toilet that no one else wanted to use it. 'I do like to sit there in peace,' he would always say. Edek would also sometimes add, 'Even the Queen of England does have peace on the toilet.' It was the only refer-ence to the Queen of England that he ever made. Lola had no idea that either of her parents were aware of the Queen of England's existence, let alone know about the peace that she felt when she went to the toilet.

It was not easy to get peace on the toilet when you had children, Lola had discovered. Her six-year-old liked to keep her company when she went to the toilet. He would use the time to ask her endless questions, like where did the tampons she inserted go when she had a period? It was hard to sit and concentrate when a six-year-old was asking you to show him where the tampons went.

Lola, like Edek and possibly the Queen of England, loved sit-ting on the toilet in peace. The peace enabled things to work like they should work. She imagined her sphincter muscles giving her anal canal instructions to relax and open her anus. She thought about the muscles of the colon contracting and relaxing while they rolled the food that had been eaten, in Lola's case a lot of cabbage, carrots, radishes and zucchinis, around and around, like clothes in a washing machine, all the time breaking the food down and extracting the water. She knew that several times a day, mostly after meals, the colon made large, muscular contractions that dumped the newly made faeces into the rectum. When the faeces arrived in the rectum, it sent a message to the nerve centres in the spinal chord and they sent a message to the sphincter muscles of the anal canal telling them to relax and open the anus. If it wasn't a convenient time to have your anus open, the brain delivered a message to the spinal chord to prevent the 'open anus' message being sent.

Lola was staggered at this system of communication. All the parts of the body spoke the same language. Unlike her own family. Renia, Edek and Lola had never spoken the same language. Renia and Edek spoke Polish and Yiddish. Their German was also quite good. Their English was, for years, non-existent, and even after that it was fractured and broken and battered.

When they lived in Germany, where Lola was born, they all spoke German. But once they got to Australia, Renia and Edek insisted that Lola speak only English. And they would only speak English to Lola. This meant that Renia and Edek didn't understand three-quarters of what Lola said. And Lola had no idea of most of what Edek and Renia were trying to say.

Edek and Renia spoke to each other in Polish and Yiddish. Luckily, Lola understood Yiddish, but she could never join in. As soon as Lola uttered one Yiddish word, Renia would snap, 'English, please.'

Renia and Edek's English was full of patched-together and completely made-up words. Edek called faeces 'bikpeeses'. Lola had thought that 'bikpeeses' must have been Polish for faeces until she was about twenty and realised that what Edek was saying was 'big pieces'. Lola felt sad. If only the three of them could have spoken the same language, there would have been less room for confusion, distraction, dismay and uncertainty.

Renia and Edek had never really stood a chance of learning English. Three days after they arrived in Australia, they were both working in factories. The only person who spoke English in those factories was the owner, who never spoke to workers like Renia and Edek. In the factories, Renia and Edek had learnt smatterings of Italian, Greek, Maltese and Chinese.

It was seven a.m. Lola knew that her son, who was about to turn seven, would soon get out of bed. He never slept in. He was a bit like her. Always alert. Lola could hear her one-year-old babbling in her cot. She went into her daughter's bedroom. A small girl with a mass of strawberry-blond curls beamed up at her. 'Good morning, Mrs Gorgeous,' Lola said to her daughter.

Mrs Gorgeous really was very gorgeous. She had very fair skin and large, cornflower-blue eyes. Lola loved the colour of Mrs Gorgeous's eyes. The blue held a hint of the sea and the sky. Hints that suggested happiness. It wasn't just Lola who loved the colour of Mrs Gorgeous's eyes. All Jews seemed to be crazy about blue eyes. 'Look what blue eyes she has,' passers-by would say when Lola had Mrs Gorgeous in a stroller in Acland Street, St Kilda.

When Renia had first seen Mrs Gorgeous in the hospital, hours after Lola had given birth to her, she suddenly paled. All the colour drained from her face. 'She looks just like Hanka,' Renia had said, before rushing out of the room. Hanka was the daughter of Bluma, Renia's favourite sister. When Renia and Edek no longer had work papers in the ghetto and were in hiding, nine-year-old Hanka, who was still working, brought them her soup every day.

Hanka and Bluma were on the last transport out of the Lodz Ghetto to Auschwitz with Renia and Edek. Renia, who on the arrival platform in Auschwitz had been pushed into the line for life, tried to grab Hanka. But Bluma, who was headed to the gas chambers, although she didn't know it, clutched Hanka tightly.

Mrs Gorgeous was a cheerful child. She smiled easily. Lola hoped that Mrs Gorgeous would retain that cheerfulness. Lola knew that cheerfulness could easily get lost. The few people who'd known Lola in the DP camp and when she first came to Australia, when she was three, were always telling her what a lovable, agreeable, cheerful child she was.

Lola didn't think that anyone who knew her now would rush to describe her as cheerful. How had she lost her cheerfulness, Lola wondered. Where did it go? Was there a finite amount of cheerfulness in the world? Maybe unless you kept a close eye on your cheerfulness it could disappear, in a flash.

It wasn't that Lola was dour. She wasn't. She laughed a lot and thought many things were very funny. It was just that she had a sadness about her. A sadness that was hard to shake off. Even with Mrs Gorgeous beaming at her.

After breakfast Lola drove her son to school, despite his protestations that he had done enough school, was bored and didn't want to go any more. Then she dropped Mrs Gorgeous off at the day-care centre and drove to her office. Lola often daydreamed while she was driving.

Car accidents were what she was daydreaming about. She would picture a scene, just after a terrible collision. She never envisaged the collision itself. Her daydreams started half a minute after the collision with a scene of chaos. Blood, shattered windscreens, mangled car doors and bonnets, crushed roofs and glass everywhere.

Inevitably, the injured person was someone Lola knew. In these fantasies, Lola would pull up at the side of the road, grab the first-aid kit she kept in the glove box, and rush over to help. She would clear away glass, stem bleeding, bandage wounds, gingerly lift the victim out of the wreckage and reassure them that everything was going to be all right.

Afterwards, the victim's close relatives would be overwhelmed with gratitude to Lola. They would cry, and say, 'Thank God that Lola was there.' Wealthy people often offered Lola money to show their gratitude. Even though Lola could have done with the money – Mr Former Rock Star was now a public servant, working for the government as an accountant – she always said no.

Many years later, Lola would read a book about children of survivors of death camps not feeling entitled to live their own lives until the child went back to the psychotic, chaotic world of the concentration camp, and rescued her parents. Lola had immediately linked this to her car-accident rescue fantasies. Fantasies that took up thousands of hours of her life.

In the book, *No Voice Is Ever Wholly Lost* by the psychoanalyst Louise J. Kaplan, Lola learned that a major issue for children of death-camp survivors was the need to re-enact or live in their parents' past. By doing that, they were turning their parents' humiliation, disgrace and guilt into a victory over their oppressors. Lola was astonished when she read that. It fitted her car-crash daydreams perfectly.

Lola entered her car-crash daydreams and fantasies with the same sense of anticipation and excitement that other people experienced when they went to the movies. Movies bored Lola. She'd sat through endless Ingmar Bergman melodramas wondering when the movie was going to end. She was bored by *Jules et Jim* and was almost in a coma by the end of *Mary Poppins*. But Lola emerged from her car-crash daydreams invigorated, satisfied and victorious. Not once in any of her tragic fantasies was she unable to triumph.

Lola had also recognised the feeling of not feeling entitled to live her own life. She often felt that she was an imposter. Someone pretending to be a real member of the Bensky family. The real members were of course the dead and those who had suffered with the dead. Even when she and Renia and Edek lived in one room, Lola felt like a spoiled little rich girl. Renia and Edek regularly told her how lucky she was. 'You are so lucky to have parents,' Renia would say. 'You live in a free country. You have it so easy,' Edek would add. Her life was so easy, she felt. She would spend a lot of her life trying to rectify that. She would make sure that her life wasn't easy. If only she'd known that was what she was doing.

Lola didn't know that she was double-stitched to the dead. Tied to them with an invisible thread. And beginning to feel their weight.

She didn't know she would soon begin to have panic attacks. The panic attacks started, out of the blue, on a sunny day, when she was driving her son and his friend home from school. She was turning into Toorak Road, one of the wide, shop-lined streets that ran through several of Melbourne's wealthier suburbs. Mothers were out shopping with their children, people were walking their dogs, sidewalk cafes were full of Melburnians talking and enjoying the spring weather, when Lola's head started spinning and she broke out into a sweat. She gripped the steering wheel. She felt dizzy and as though she were going to faint.

Her son, who was eight, and his school friend were in the back seat. Mrs Gorgeous, who was two, was at home with the babysitter. Lola wound down the window and tried to take deep breaths. She had no idea what was happening to her. She did know that whatever it was, was not good. The after-school traffic was heavy. Lola drove with her head half-hanging out of the car window and her heart pounding. She dropped her son's school friend off and managed to drive home.

She saw three neurologists and had her head measured, prodded and X-rayed. There was talk of tumours and seizures and infectious diseases, but no evidence of any of these. She went back to her analyst, Dr Silver, whom she would later refer to as her first analyst. 'Panic attacks,' he said. 'A sudden and overwhelming feeling of acute and disabling anxiety.'

Lola had first seen Dr Silver when she was twenty-five. She had thought she was going to a weight-loss doctor. She lay on Dr Silver's couch, twice a week, for four years. She put on twenty pounds in her first year with him.

Lola's second analyst would suggest, when Lola was in her late thirties, that the panic attacks could have been triggered by her need to punish herself for getting what she had wanted. When Lola was pregnant with Mrs Gorgeous, she had really wanted a girl. After her birth, a C-section under general anaesthetic, Lola's obstetrician told Lola that she had kept saying, 'Somebody very lucky had a girl,' and that no matter how many times he or the nurses told her that it was she herself who had had the girl, Lola had kept repeating, 'Somebody very lucky had a girl.' By the time Lola saw her third analyst, she knew that feeling of being lucky was not that easy to live with.

The panic attacks always took Lola by surprise. They could happen in the supermarket, in the street, in the car. She tried to drive as little as possible, which, in a city like Melbourne, was not easy. She hired a part-time assistant so she wouldn't be in the office on her own. And she took half of a five-milligram Valium tablet when she had to do interviews.

She had spent years doing things on her own. Working late in the office, navigating airports, driving long distances. Now, she wanted someone with her all the time.

Lola knew nobody who had had a panic attack. She'd never even heard of panic attacks.

There were so many things Lola didn't know about. She really knew very little about being Jewish. She didn't know what most of the Jewish holidays meant. She didn't know anything about the religion. She couldn't understand a word of Hebrew. Although she was Jewish, Lola was not allowed to join either of the two Jewish youth organisations that most Jewish teenagers in Melbourne belonged to. She was also not allowed to go to synagogue. On Yom Kippur, the Day of Atonement, the holiest day of the Jewish calendar, when Jews were supposed to fast and not drive or do any work, Edek would drive past the synagogue waving a ham sandwich. 'Hypocrites,' he would say loudly to himself. 'Who are you praying to?'

Renia and Edek were angry with God. They weren't really angry with the Germans. They were upset about the number of Poles who seemed to be more than happy to get rid of their Jews, but they were very angry with God. They were both adamant that there was no God. And they were both furious with him. For the rest of her life Lola would feel disloyal whenever she entered a synagogue. In synagogues, she would also feel like an intruder, an outsider, a stranger. She would feel she wasn't a real Jew.

Over and over again, Lola was told how important it was to marry a Jewish boy. Where she was supposed to meet one was never discussed. Was she supposed to nab Harry Mendel, the son of Renia and Edek's friends Mr and Mrs Mendel? Harry had said to Lola when she was about thirteen that he would consider going out with her if she lost weight. Lola had stared at Harry Mendel for a long time after he'd said that. Then she'd reached over and taken a large slice of Mrs Mendel's freshly baked cheesecake.

Lola parked her car outside the small cottage in Carlton that she rented as her office. The cottage was very small. Two rooms and a kitchen. It reminded Lola of the cottage in North Carlton that she and Renia and Edek moved into when they moved out of their single room in Brunswick. The North Carlton cottage was a few minutes' walk from Lola's office.

Lola was working for a glossy monthly magazine. The magazine was considered to be both hip and high IQ. Lola wrote profiles of people. Substantial profiles of three- to five-thousand words. This month she was doing a profile of a Melbourne psychiatrist who was using meditation in an attempt to cure or arrest the growth of cancerous tumours in patients. Lola had had to sit in on several meditation sessions. Lola wasn't the meditation type. She'd found it hard to sit in silence, for an hour, in a room full of people she didn't know. It had

made her anxious. She had decided that if she had to do the meditation again, she would take a Valium.

Lola wasn't good at anything that required her to be inert.
Meditation, massage, facials, facemasks, mud baths. They all made her
very anxious. Lola didn't think she would have to attend another of the
meditation sessions. She thought she probably had all the material she
needed to write the article.

She liked writing profiles. Putting pieces of people's lives
together. Most people had parts and components that fitted together.
The snippets and scraps were connected. There weren't large gaping
holes or disturbing absences. With most people, Lola found that if
she asked enough questions, she could get enough information to
form a whole picture. She also liked observing the people she interviewed. Watching their gestures, listening to the tone in their voice,
looking at their demeanour, noting their responses. Seeing how their
habits and their histories came together to make them who they
were.

She thought that her own history was on display, although she
took great care to disguise it with a calm voice and slow, thoughtful
movements. But all you had to do was look more closely, look past the
measured smile, and you could almost see Nazis goose-stepping like a
well-rehearsed chorus line.

To Lola, some people seemed to come from a patch of blue sky and
perpetual sunshine. She envied them. Although she was slightly suspicious of people who seemed overly optimistic or overly cheerful. Lola
was drawn to the more morose type. To people who had doubts. To
people who had struggled. To people who had suffered. She thought
that part of why she probably loved Mr Former Rock Star was that

his parents were so cold. So detached. Mr Former Rock Star was their youngest child and she thought that it must have been very difficult for him growing up with his very wealthy, very disconnected parents.

His parents had an indifference to their children that Lola found frightening. Mrs Former Rock Star Sr used to say, 'Hello, darling,' to her son, and proffer up her lips for a quick peck on his cheek. But there was nothing behind that peck. It was an empty peck.

Mrs Former Rock Star Sr also played a lot of golf. She didn't work. And she didn't cook, which was just as well, Lola thought, as on the few occasions that Mrs Former Rock Star Sr did cook, the food was always the same. And always terrible. Tomatoes sliced in half with a raw onion ring on top of each half was the appetiser she almost always served. What sort of appetiser was that? Lola was used to Renia Bensky cooking for hours and preparing enough food for triple the number of people they had coming. For an appetiser she would often make a series of dishes to go with the dense black bread she would buy in Acland Street. She would make a chicken-liver pâté, a cream-cheese spread with chopped radishes and scallions and some thinly sliced, freshly boiled tongue with black peppercorns.

Mr Former Rock Star loved Renia's food. And they ate at Lola's parents' place at least once a week. Mr Former Rock Star couldn't cook, but he liked to bake. He particularly liked to bake shortbread cookies. He zealously practised making the perfect shortbread. Whenever Lola worked late, she would come home to racks and racks of hot shortbread coming out of the oven. Apparently the secret to perfect shortbread was the quality of the butter. It was necessary to use very, very good butter. Lola's fridge seemed to be constantly full of local and imported butters. Shortbread contained one cup of butter for every half a cup of sugar and two cups of flour. It was not good for Lola's diet. It was a catastrophe.

When Lola decided to leave Mr Former Rock Star, she told Renia and Edek not long after she had told Mr Former Rock Star. Lola hadn't expected Renia and Edek to take the news well. She had dreaded telling them. But the hysteria that had ensued after she had told them was far worse than she had expected. It had been worse than telling Mr Former Rock Star himself.

Mr Former Rock Star, after he'd got over the initial shock of someone else falling in love with Lola, or maybe it was the shock of Lola falling in love with someone else, had seemed almost pleased. After not eating for a week and losing twelve pounds, Mr Former Rock Star asked Lola if they could always remain good friends. 'Of course,' Lola had said. She felt she loved Mr Former Rock Star, in a sisterly sort of way.

'You were always a bit too intense for me,' Mr Former Rock Star had said.

'Really?' said Lola. Her guilt at leaving started to evaporate. A cheerfulness that she hadn't seen in years appeared on Mr Former Rock Star's face. She could tell that he was wondering whether, although he was now an accountant, he could resume his former rock-star ways.

Edek had not taken the news as calmly. '*Oy, Gott*,' he had said, several times. He seemed stunned.

Renia cut straight to the chase. 'Hitler didn't kill me,' she shouted, 'so you want to finish me off.' Before Lola had had time to say anything, if she had thought of anything to say after being partnered with Hitler, Renia wailed, 'I should have died in Auschwitz rather than live to hear this news.'

'Liebala, Liebala,' Edek said, using her pet name, 'do not do this to us.'

'I'm not doing it to you,' Lola said. 'I'm doing it to myself. I'm the one who is leaving my marriage.'

'She wants to kill us,' Renia said.

'I don't want to kill you,' said Lola.

'I should have died in Auschwitz,' Renia said, again, sobbing.

Lola was alarmed. She had only ever seen Renia crying quietly. Crying quietly for her dead. For her father or her mother or one of her brothers or sisters. Once, when Lola was about five or six, she had watched Renia crying silently. Renia's body had been heaving with sobs, yet not making a sound. Lola had put her arms around her mother, but Renia hadn't appeared to notice.

Edek had come home and seen the two of them, sitting side by side, in silence. Edek said something to Renia in Polish. 'Your mother is crying about a small baby boy who did die in the ghetto,' Edek had turned and said to Lola. Lola had known that her mother was crying about something very sad. What it would take her years to know was that the small baby boy was her brother. Renia and Edek's baby boy.

Lola wished she had waited a while before she told Edek and Renia about the fact that she was leaving Mr Former Rock Star. Lola had never seen Renia crying with rage. It frightened her. She tried to calm herself down. She didn't think that Renia really wished she had died in Auschwitz.

Lola thought that 'Auschwitz' was probably one of the first words she had learnt. She was a precocious baby, and already talking when she was ten months old, Renia always said. Auschwitz was probably a common subject in the DP camp where Lola was born. People had to talk about it. It was part of the biographical information that was being collected from survivors of Nazi death camps.

A few years later, most survivors would stop talking about Auschwitz. They would never stop thinking about it. And from time to time, the small explosive shards and fragments that belonged to that twisted, misshapen universe would erupt from them.

'Poor Ida, she wanted so much to have a child,' Renia would say every time their friends Ida and Yitzhak Stein left, after a visit. When Lola had once asked why, in that case, did Ida not have any children, Renia had said, in an almost inaudible voice, 'Because they did try to glue her womb shut.'

Lola always knew who 'they' referred to. The Gestapo, the SS *Obersturmbannführers* and SS *Sturmbannführers* and *Obersturmführers* and *kapos* who pulled Jews out of the barracks and rollcalls and work details to be killed or used for useless pseudo-medical experiments. Later she would read about the many German doctors who experimented with abandon at Auschwitz, including a Professor Dr Carl Clauberg who, under the guise of researching sterilisation devices, injected chemicals into the uteruses of many women in an attempt to glue the uteruses shut.

Lola felt bad. She couldn't believe Renia's response to the news that she was leaving the man who, Lola thought, Renia had possibly, initially, hoped she would not marry. She really hoped that her mother wasn't wishing she had died in Auschwitz.

Edek left the room. Lola thought that he was probably going off to read one of his detective-fiction books called *The Blood Soaked Barrel* or *Five Dead Wives* or *Terror Takes a Turn*. Or maybe Edek was looking for a piece of chocolate.

'It is an infatuation,' Renia said, as though the thought had suddenly occurred to her that Lola might be having an affair. 'It is not love. I was in love with somebody and I didn't leave your father.' Lola didn't want to hear any of that. She didn't want to hear how Renia had sacrificed her own happiness for Lola. Edek adored Renia. Why did Renia have to muddy the picture? The picture was already murky enough as it was.

'You was an example for us that a mixed marriage can work,' said Edek, who had returned with a trace of chocolate still on his lips.

'I'll try harder next time,' said Lola. There would be a next time. Lola knew that. She was leaving Mr Former Rock Star because she was in love with someone else. Really in love, she thought.

5

'You've got everything,' Patrice Pritchard said to Lola Bensky. Lola Bensky's chest constricted. Her ribs felt as though they'd clenched themselves, like fists, and were gripping her lungs. 'You've got everything,' Patrice Pritchard said, again. 'You look gorgeous, you've got a man who adores you, you've got great kids and you live in SoHo.'

Patrice, a senior editor at Oliver and Joseph, an international publishing conglomerate, was very thin, very blond and very earnest. And she was Lola's editor. 'Nobody has everything,' Lola said, in what she hoped was a more plaintive than terse tone. She tried to take a deep breath, but her chest wouldn't budge.

'And you're thin, too,' Patrice said, looking semi-pained. 'I work out every day for two hours so I can eat. I'm forty-three and I'm still waiting to meet the right man and have a family.'

'I'm not thin,' Lola said, in a reedy squeak. 'I'm not thin,' she tried to repeat as she attempted to clear her throat. Lola was fifty-one, almost fifty-two. She shouldn't be squeaking when she tried to speak.

The reason Lola now had a book editor was that she had written a book. She had written a book called *The Ultra-Private Detective Agency*. Lola didn't know why she had written the book. She didn't know anything about private detectives or private-detective agencies.

She had had a longing to write something other than a long magazine article. She had wanted to write without having to stop at three thousand or five thousand words. But why she chose to write this book bewildered her. She knew very little about detective fiction apart from having watched Edek absorbed in one detective-fiction book after another. *The Ultra-Private Detective Agency* had surprised Lola as much as it had surprised anyone who knew her.

Patrice Pritchard had acquired the book for a relatively small advance. It had already sold more than one hundred thousand copies. Lola had no idea who was buying it. Possibly people who didn't know much about detective fiction either.

Edek didn't like *The Ultra-Private Detective Agency.* 'Nothing happens in this book,' he said. Lola thought he was right. There were no murders and there was no blackmail. Edek liked a lot of murder and blackmail. The more murderers and blackmailers per chapter, the more Edek liked the book.

The Ultra-Private Detective Agency was focused on the more mundane problems of everyday life. The 52-year-old wife who kept disappearing on Wednesday mornings. The business partner who started dying his hair and rollerskating to work, decades after anyone else was on rollerskates. Or the husband who came home late three nights a week, puffy and puffing with allergies, yet was perfectly fine and on time for the other four nights.

The Ultra-Private Detective Agency also had a brisk business in divorce searches. They located the divorce records of clients' prospective new partners. Divorce records could tell you a lot about the person you were considering marrying. The arguments and accusations about money were extraordinarily revealing, as were the smaller details such as noisy eating, teeth-grinding or excessive flatulence. The agency also checked divorce files for evidence of drug-taking, alcoholism, child molestation or spousal abuse, which usually took the form of wife beating. Divorce records contained an avalanche of information.

The Ultra-Private Detective Agency employed two Jewish private detectives, Harry and Schlomo. They were both nervous of the weather. The television set in the back room of the company's East Village office was permanently tuned to the Weather Channel. Several times a day, one or the other of the two Jewish detectives checked the weather, and was alarmed by news of hurricanes, tornadoes or severe thunderstorms in any part of the country.

Schlomo carried a large umbrella with him at all times, regardless of the season. It was harder to trail someone inconspicuously if you were carrying a large umbrella in a heatwave, but Schlomo and his umbrella could not be parted. Schlomo was also a religious Jew. He wore a shabby, unintentionally shiny black suit, a black hat and long black *peyos*, side curls hanging down to his chin.

Like many Hassidic Jews and a large number of Chinese drivers, he drove like a maniac. He ignored all parking restrictions and road rules. He did sudden U-turns over double lines, drove the wrong way down one-way streets and made wild gestures with one arm out of the window of his battered van to warn other drivers of his intended manoeuvres. The warnings were both incomprehensible and too late. They usually came as the other driver was swerving to avoid oncoming traffic or crashing into Schlomo and his van.

In his everyday attire, Schlomo was in perfect disguise. No one ever suspected they were being followed by a middle-aged, untidy and anxious Orthodox Jew with a crooked black hat and overly long black side curls. Schlomo had painted a handwritten sign on the side of the van. *Brooklyn Academy Supplies. 68 Front Street, Brooklyn. Telephone 718-678-6786.*

'No one would be suspicious of a person who gives his name and address and phone number on his car,' Schlomo had said. Schlomo, who was born in America, spoke grammatically tortured English with a Yiddish accent. 'Where did you go to school? In Minsk? Or Pinsk?' his boss periodically asked him.

'In Brooklyn,' he always replied.

Schlomo was so inept that no one suspected him of anything. When he wasn't behind the wheel of a car, he elicited concern and sympathy from most people. Suspects he was following sometimes asked if they could help him. He had a lost look about him. He also had no sense of direction. He carried a hand-held global positioning device with him at all times, a waterproof GPS designed for hiking. With a waterproof GPS, Schlomo never had to worry about the device being damaged if it started to rain. He glanced at the device every one or two minutes while he walked. People often stopped to offer him help with directions.

Schlomo's wife also tried to help him. Every morning she put out his black suit, a clean shirt and fresh underwear and socks. She also packed his lunch, together with a printout of the weather forecast, and, in summer, sunglasses, into a black shoulder bag.

Schlomo's ineptitude, together with his harmless if not hopeless demeanour, proved to be advantageous. Suspects chatted to him freely, often revealing far more than the Ultra-Private Detective Agency needed to know. Husbands Schlomo was following confided in him. Schlomo often felt sorry for them. Feeling sorry for people was not part of the job description, Schlomo's boss had frequently reminded him as he handed over the photographs and recordings of the encounters.

The Ultra-Private Detective Agency was a three-man operation. Well, two men, Schlomo and Harry, and a woman, their boss, Petrushka Inge Maria Pagenstecker. Or Pimp, as Schlomo and Harry called her.

Schlomo's colleague, Harry, was also a licensed private investigator. Harry largely concentrated on Internet research. He seemed able to find any information he was looking for. He could do background checks on nannies, dog-walkers, babysitters, house cleaners, house sitters, blind dates and potential partners. Harry could check for evidence of a criminal record. He could find out if someone was being sued or was suing somebody. He could look up a person's driving record. He could investigate their finances and check for bankruptcies, bounced cheques, notices of defaults on loans, judgements against the person, and tax issues. If you wanted to know anything about your boyfriend or your best friend's ex-husband or your uncle's wife or your former violin teacher, Harry could find whatever you were looking for.

Harry was in charge of all divorce-file records investigations. He also put statistics together for the Ultra-Private Detective Agency. Because of Harry, the agency knew that they were extremely successful with marital surveillance cases. They caught the partners in ninety-eight per cent of the marital surveillance cases they handled. Harry thought they should advertise that fact. But Petrushka Inge Maria Pagenstecker didn't believe in advertising. She believed in word of mouth. 'Advertising is not private,' she would say. Neither Harry nor

Schlomo understood what she meant, but they rarely questioned or queried anything she said.

Harry pointed out that two-thirds of the Ultra-Private Detective Agency's clients were women. He also pointed out that when a man caught his wife cheating, in ninety-nine per cent of the cases the marriage would be over. However, if a woman caught her husband cheating, in fifty to sixty per cent of the cases the woman wanted to save the marriage. When male clients found out their wives were cheating on them, they became furious, Harry said. When women discovered that their husbands were unfaithful, they cried. Lola Bensky wasn't sure the Ultra-Private Detective Agency needed that sort of information, but Harry kept coming up with it.

Harry wasn't really suited to surveillance or other forms of fieldwork. He was not socially at ease. He was often tongue-tied and took an extremely long time to answer any questions. He was very thin. And always hungry. He didn't have the sort of constitution that could set up or monitor a phone or wiretap. However, in front of a computer screen, Harry metamorphosed into someone else. His fingers flew over the keyboard and he moved his mouse with the dexterity of a concert pianist and the speed of a racing-car driver.

While he worked, Harry could eat doughnuts, bagels with cream cheese, hot dogs and egg-salad sandwiches without pausing or breaking his concentration. Despite everything that he ate, Harry stayed thin. Schlomo was always trying to lose weight so he could hide more easily in narrow doorways. When Schlomo had first seen Harry, he had been thrilled. He had thought that Harry would be able to do any running or chasing that was necessary. But despite being very thin, Harry couldn't really run. It was just as well that the Ultra-Private Detective Agency didn't take on a lot of cases that involved running.

Lola Bensky thought that most Jews weren't really built or predisposed to be runners. There certainly wasn't a glut of Jewish Olympic track-and-field medallists. When Jews, regardless of their size, tried to put their bodies into motion, everything bumped into everything else in an unorchestrated and ungainly maze of elbows, knees, arms, legs, hips and stomachs.

Lola looked at Patrice Pritchard. They were in Balthazar, the eternally chic brasserie in Spring Street, SoHo. If this were happening in the Ultra-Private Detective Agency, Lola would have had Patrice distracted by having the waiter drop a carafe of water on their table, or having the man at the booth across the aisle throw up. As it was, she couldn't do anything. She had to keep listening to Patrice Pritchard, who had now moved on to the subject of Lola not only having a husband who adored her, but having also had a previous husband.

'I thought two husbands was a sign of failure,' Lola said.

'God, no,' said Patrice. 'It means you've been twice as successful.'

Lola started feeling a little dizzy. She wondered if she could surreptitiously get half of a twenty-milligram Inderal, a beta-blocker pill, out of her bag and put it in her mouth without Patrice Pritchard noticing. Half a beta-blocker usually stopped her heart from pounding, calmed her down, and diminished the dizziness.

Lola had the Inderal in a small, clear, round plastic container, which she always kept in her bag. She decided it would be impossible to find the pill without attracting Patrice Pritchard's attention. Anyway, it was only eleven a.m. and she didn't want to be swallowing pills this early in the day. She didn't want to be swallowing pills at all. She kept the Inderal on her for emergencies. She had just lived through three or four years of emergencies and couldn't quite believe that they seemed to be over.

The panic attacks she had experienced years earlier had come back with a vengeance. They had been accompanied by a two-year bout of agoraphobia. Agoraphobia was defined as an extreme or irrational fear of having panic-like symptoms, particularly in wide-open spaces or large crowds or uncontrolled social conditions. Lola had avoided shopping malls and parks and department stores and concert halls. She had chosen the narrowest streets in Manhattan she could find to get to wherever she was going and tried to avoid as many of the larger avenues as she could. She ran across those she couldn't avoid.

If she saw someone she knew while she was out, she couldn't stop and say hello. She couldn't stand and talk to anyone without feeling dizzy and as though she was about to fall over. Talking while standing up became impossible for her. In order to talk to anyone, she had to sit down. This made cocktail parties, which she had previously seen as merely tedious, untenable. Several times Lola had found herself at a cocktail party, face to face with people's waists. She was the only person in a crowd of thirty to forty people who was seated.

Lola had found the agoraphobia and the feeling that she was falling quite terrifying. She desperately hoped that the agoraphobia would never return. But there was no guarantee. Unlike the flu, agoraphobia was not something you could be vaccinated against. She had discovered there was a link between agoraphobia and people who have difficulty with spatial orientation. It had to do with the vestibular system, which contributed to balance and a sense of spatial orientation in most mammals. The vestibular system sent signals to the brain stem, which coordinated eye movement and posture and kept people upright. Lola thought that her vestibular system had definitely been sending the wrong messages to her brain stem.

Spatial orientation had always been a problem for Lola. If she approached a familiar street from a different direction, she had trouble working out where she was. Spatial relationships had never been Lola's forte, at the best of times. She found it hard to load a dishwasher. What went where didn't seem easy to discern.

A few years ago, Mrs Gorgeous, who was now twenty-three, had groaned and said, 'Anyone who can calculate calories at the speed of light can work out how to load a dishwasher!' Lola had been thrilled to tell Mrs Gorgeous about her dysfunctional vestibular system.

There were quite a few phobias Lola would have willingly taken on, in the place of agoraphobia. There was ablutophobia, the fear of washing, bathing or cleaning; or astraphobia, the fear of thunder and lightning; or hylophobia, the fear of trees, forests or wood; or pediophobia, the fear of dolls; or, the best of the lot, coulrophobia, the fear of clowns. Lola wasn't crazy about thunder or lightning or trees, forests, or woods, or even dolls. And she could easily have lived without clowns.

The second round of panic attacks and the agoraphobia that had accompanied them had appeared when Lola was forty-six, four years after she, her son, Mrs Gorgeous, the man she left Mr Former Rock Star for and his daughter had moved to New York. At forty-six, Lola had also experienced depression for the first time in her life. And with that depression came thoughts of sharp blades, bottles of pills, tall buildings and the lure of death.

It wasn't as though the years before that had been a breeze. Two years after she left Mr Former Rock Star, her weight had ballooned.

She was fatter than she'd ever been. She and the man she'd left Mr Former Rock Star for had had to do reconnaissance trips to restaurants to gauge whether Lola would fit into the chairs, before they could make a booking. Lola learned that chairs without sides, which were more comfortable for her, were not that common in restaurants.

Lola had also had an abortion. She had become pregnant the week after she'd left Mr Former Rock Star. She had decided that this would be a very untimely moment for a new baby to arrive, a decision she still regretted. And her mother had died. Poor Renia had gone from a bloated stomach that bothered her to metastasised pancreatic cancer and death in exactly four months. Renia had barely known what was happening. She had looked at herself in the mirror one day as Lola was helping her into the bath, and said, in a bewildered and shaky voice, 'What happened?' Lola understood Renia's bewilderment. In the mirror, Renia looked almost as skeletal as she must have looked in Auschwitz.

Lola had cried for weeks and weeks after Renia died. She didn't know she would be crying for Renia for the rest of her life. Lola missed her mother. She missed the mother she had and the mother she didn't have. She missed Renia's glamour and her fury. She missed her perfume. And she kept longing for a mother who could touch her, a mother who could comfort her. For years after Renia's death, Lola thought she saw Renia in the street, in stores, on public transport. She ran to the phone when it rang in the hope that it would be Renia on the other end of the line. She bought presents for Renia and only remembered after she paid for the presents that Renia was dead. Renia would need no more presents, would make no more phone calls and would never go for another walk.

Ten years after her mother's death, Lola found herself in a small, sparse post office in Havana. The post office was in one of the many streets in Havana, lined with crumbling, formerly beautiful homes whose skins and shells had the faded, pastel pallor of aged bridesmaids. Lola was trying, with her smattering of Spanish, to post a postcard to her mother. Minutes after the very helpful clerk had assured her that the postcard would reach its destination, Lola realised that no post office anywhere in the world could get anything to wherever it was that Renia was. She had forgotten that Renia was dead. She had been preoccupied with the thought that Renia would love to get a postcard from Havana.

Lola used to send Renia postcards every time she travelled. In the postcards, Lola could express all the expressions of love that seemed to get stuck in her gullet when she was in Renia's presence. Lola missed Renia. She didn't think she'd ever stop missing her. She was not sure which parts of Renia she missed. She had tried to think about it. It wasn't the long, cosy chats she'd had with Renia. Her chats with Renia were mostly brief. She didn't miss the things they did together. They didn't do much together. They didn't go to the movies together, they didn't go to the hairdressers together, they didn't even go for walks together. Occasionally, they went to the supermarket together, which, to Lola's surprise, had been an oddly nourishing experience every time.

Lola didn't think she would have been able to move to New York if Renia had still been alive. She didn't think she could have left her. Edek had made it easy for Lola to move to New York. He wanted her to go to New York. He saw America as the *goldene medina*, the land of opportunity. 'I will join you there later,' he'd said. 'You know your husband does very much want to go there,' he'd added.

Lola did know that her husband wanted to live there. He had dreamed of living in New York since he was a very poor, working-class teenager in the outer suburbs of Sydney. Although he was her husband, Lola rarely thought of him as her husband. She called him Sweetheart and thought of him as Mr Someone Else. It came from the endless explanations she'd had to give to her friends, her neighbours, her doctor, her dentist and almost everyone she knew, when she left Mr Former Rock Star. 'I'm in love with someone else,' she'd said, over and over again. Mr Someone Else loved her. And he loved Edek. Lola knew he'd been plotting with Edek to make sure Edek joined them in New York.

Lola decided not to take the Inderal. She felt too old to be popping pills. It felt unseemly, not to mention unsophisticated, to be furtively scavenging around in your handbag for pills. 'Do you think you are going to write more books about the Ultra-Private Detective Agency?' Patrice Pritchard said to Lola.

'I don't know,' Lola said. 'I have to finish *Schlomo in SoHo* before I can think about writing anything else.'

'That's a great title,' Patrice Pritchard said.

'I might change it,' said Lola.

'The readers love Pimp,' Patrice Pritchard said.

'I mostly think of Pimp as Petrushka Inge Maria Pagenstecker,' Lola said. She was feeling a bit mean for saying, after Patricia had admired the title of her new book, that she might change it. She had no intention of changing it. It had a nice ring to it. But something about Patrice made Lola want to be contrarian.

'They like Pimp, even though she screams all the time?' Lola said.

'Yes, they do,' said Patrice. 'I think that not enough women scream or speak up. Women talk at a very low decibel level, particularly in social situations when there are men around and in the workplace.'

'I quite like the way she screams,' Lola said. 'Particularly as I, myself, find it very hard to scream.'

It was such a relief for Lola to become Pimp. Pimp was very sure of her place in the world. Until she was one year old, Petrushka Inge Maria Pagenstecker had been Rachel Feinblatt. Her parents, Moishe and Fela Feinblatt, had had Rachel's name changed by deed poll to Petrushka Inge Maria Pagenstecker, in the hope of putting some distance between Rachel Feinblatt and her Jewishness. Pimp was dark-haired, tall and busty. Moishe and Fela Feinblatt had no idea how their daughter, who was five-foot-eleven, had turned out to be so tall. They were both exceptionally short. They were also bewildered by her ruddy complexion, her very large breasts, her choice of occupation and her confidence.

Pimp was a licensed private detective. She owned her own agency. She was forty-seven. She had been divorced three times and had three children, Esther, Elijah and Ezekiel. The three children were from her first marriage. Her first ex-husband, David Feingold, had agreed that the children could be called Feinblatt, which, as Pimp had pointed out to him, already contained half of his name. David Feingold was a very reasonable man, unlike Pimp's second and third ex-husbands, and Pimp appreciated that.

Pimp, when greeted with 'How are you?', unlike Lola, never paused to consider the actual question. She never wondered whether her kidneys were functioning well or whether her gastrointestinal tract was intact and unimpeded. Pimp's corporeal condition was something she hardly thought about. Twinges in her abdomen, aches in her legs or arms, or a pain, an inflammation or throb or cramp or stitch in any of her other body parts went uninterpreted and uninvestigated.

Lola tried to keep in check her anxieties about possible physical ailments. She knew her fear of illness or disease, or any bodily disorder, was linked to being the child of death-camp survivors. She tried to bear this in mind when she found herself panicking about her spleen or adrenal glands. Lola knew that terrible things could be done to bodies. She knew that in the male experimental section of Block 28 in Auschwitz, petroleum substances were injected and rubbed into the skin of prisoners' arms and legs. This caused huge abscesses, which contained a black liquid that reeked of petroleum. The Germans conducted experiments like this in an attempt to recognise any self-inflicted wounds among those Germans who were trying to avoid military service. The experiments were like a children's game with whimsical rules and nonsensical conclusions.

'Great,' Pimp always replied to anyone inquiring into her well-being. *Great* was a word Lola could never force out of her vocal chords. Lola thought very few things were great. Almost everything could be qualified.

Mr Someone Else, when asked how he was, often said, 'Fabulous'. His reply made Lola's anxiety levels soar. She felt compelled to offer up a prayer or touch wood or blink five times. She had no evidence that the blinking or the prayers or rushing for a piece of wood worked. But then, as she regularly told herself, she had very little evidence that they didn't.

Mr Someone Else said 'fabulous' with the joy of someone who savours his happiness. Feeling happy didn't bother him. Lola tempered her happiness. She let it surface in dribs and drabs so that it wouldn't be too noticeable to herself and to others. Outright joy was something that, despite three analysts on two continents and thousands of hours of analysts' couches, she felt she would never master. She was so much more at home with uncertainty and anguish.

Mr Someone Else woke up almost every morning feeling happy. Happy and peaceful. And grateful. Grateful for Lola, grateful for the three children, grateful to be living in New York and grateful to be alive. He was a painter. He painted beautiful and moving abstract images of mortality, and the fragility and poetry of what it meant to be human. Abstract images of life and its passages and pathways. Mr Someone Else worked well, he ate well, he emptied his bowels regularly and he slept well.

Lola had trouble sleeping. She thought she'd probably had trouble sleeping since she was a child. She often had nightmares. One of the recurring nightmares started when Lola was about seven. In these nightmares, she would be upright in a universe, hundreds of feet in the air. She would be walking and talking, in mid-air, in this elevated galaxy. It all looked normal, but hundreds of feet up in the air was not where Lola wanted to be. She would try to get herself back down to earth, but nothing she could do could budge her out of the sky and back onto solid ground. She used to wake up terrified. And began to dread going to bed at night. These and other recurring nightmares stayed with Lola for years. And so did the dread of going to bed.

In later years, Lola wondered what she had been doing up in the air. Was she up there with all the dead? She felt a familiarity with the dead. She felt she had memories of people she had never met. Cousins whose voices she'd never heard. An aunt with Lola's overly curly hair and her nose and high cheekbones and patterns of speech and wide feet. Was she with an uncle, who was pinching her cheeks and telling her that she looked like both of her grandmothers? She could see herself floating in these nocturnal journeys and outings, but couldn't quite make out who she was floating with.

'It was a little bit easier at night,' Renia used to say to her. Renia was talking about the death camp and how she lay on her bunk with her neighbours' ribs and wrists and ankles digging into her, and, wide awake, dreamt of her mother's thick potato soup and her honey cake. 'It was nearly like being with my mother, nearly like eating a meal,' she would say.

Lola had recently had dinner with an acquaintance, Rebecca Eisenhood, a lawyer whose mother had also been in Auschwitz. 'My mother is the happiest person I know,' Rebecca Eisenhood had said. 'My mother is always happy, always kind, always looking on the bright side. She wakes up cheerful and always cheers up everyone around her.' Lola had known, immediately, that there was no future in the friendship with Rebecca Eisenhood.

'She's the happiest person you know?' Lola said.

'Yes. She's happy all the time,' Rebecca said.

'There's something wrong with that,' Lola said.

'What?' said Rebecca. 'It's an inspiration.'

Lola thought Rebecca's mother's state was more distressing than inspirational. No one should be happy all the time.

'Your mother was in Auschwitz, wasn't she?' Lola said.

'Oh, yes,' Rebecca Eisenhood said, in an oddly jaunty tone of voice, as though a stay in Auschwitz was, like an expensive spa or Buddhist retreat, restorative and rejuvenating.

'Does your mother ever talk about what happened to her in Auschwitz?' Lola asked.

'Of course not,' Rebecca Eisenhood said. 'Why should she?'

Lola noticed that Rebecca Eisenhood, who had pale skin, pale hair and pale eyelashes, just picked at her food. Picked with miniscule little flicks of her fork. Actually she was prodding the food rather than picking at it, rearranging the carefully plated dish of falafel-crusted tilapia and roasted fiddlehead ferns and a quinoa couscous.

'I'm so full,' Rebecca Eisenhood said at the end of the meal. Lola looked at the rearranged plate. The tilapia was untouched, not one of the fiddlehead ferns was missing. About a dozen grains of quinoa seemed to have gone astray and landed scattered and disarrayed on the table.

Oh, God, there's something wrong with all of us, Lola thought. Something did seem out of whack with almost all the children of survivors of death camps she'd met. They were, too often, dour or excessively restrained or seemed blanketed by a fog.

No wonder it was a relief for Lola to become Pimp. Pimp wasn't dodging afflictions and impediments. Pimp didn't have a lot of doubt. She didn't have a lot of fear. She just did whatever she had to do. If she had to fly to the other side of the country, she got on a plane and flew there. She could sit in the middle of a crowded subway seat. She could stand in large crowds. She didn't examine her every move. She ate what she wanted to. She had no idea of the calorie value of an apple, a carrot, a boiled egg or a block of chocolate.

When Lola was Pimp, she felt calm. Rearranging and adjusting the small and large moments in Pimp's existence gave Lola a serenity. She put the words into sentences and phrases with a peacefulness she rarely felt. She shifted semicolons and quotation marks with the tranquillity of a Zen priest. There was a gratifying orderliness about ordering and reordering worlds and words. About placing and replacing vows, vowels and events.

Lola loved words. They were so reliable. Verbs and pronouns didn't suddenly decide they wouldn't speak to each other. Sentences stayed stable. Phrases and clauses didn't develop dislikes or become erratic. Any shocking revelations between vowels and consonants were mostly in Lola's control.

A single word could be so complete. Like the word 'plethora'. Plethora contained no absence. Lola felt filled with absence. Absence could be surprisingly filling. It seemed to take up a lot of space. Lola often wondered how something that wasn't there could be so present. There was the absence of people. The aunts, uncles, cousins she was meant to have grown up among. The grandparents she had never met but missed. There was the absence of answers and the absence of questions. Questions that were not answered and questions that were never asked. There was the absence of her mother. Her mother, who had so frequently felt absent in life, was, dead, very absent.

There were words that were weighted with absence. Lola couldn't say the word 'goodbye'. For Lola, the word contained a departure as rigidly and firmly final as death. 'See you, see you,' she would chorus when someone she loved, or even just cared about, said goodbye. The absence pierced Lola and left large gaps. Gaps that made her feel unsteady and unanchored. Surrounded by people who loved her, Lola felt alone and in peril.

Sometimes, when being touched by Mr Someone Else, or walking with her son or talking to Mrs Gorgeous, Lola felt whole. And at peace. A peace that infiltrated her bones and her brow. The same peacefulness she felt when she was assembling and disassembling words and paragraphs and chapters.

It was surprisingly satisfying to fit the pieces of a detective plot together. Like slotting the curved and irregular parts of a jigsaw puzzle into a clear picture. The details were all there. All visible. Nothing was missing. There were no loose threads and no ragged edges. It was soothing for Lola to unravel and uncover the cases that the Ultra-Private Detective Agency investigated. To decode and deconstruct the mysterious and the unsettling.

Lola used to think that psychoanalysis would do this for her. Locate and root out everything that was disturbing or disquieting. She used to think that analysis was the answer. She had a less idealised view now. She thought analysis could help, but it couldn't rebuild or reconstruct or even renovate some of the ingrained infrastructure of her psyche. She had thought that with the decades of analysis she'd had, she would be reborn. Instead, she was grappling with many of the same issues. With possibly more understanding and, now that the agoraphobia had subsided, more equilibrium. Still, there was so much she couldn't get rid of.

She still often woke up in the morning engulfed in fear. She had to get out of bed, walk around, brush her teeth and see that nothing had changed. That her teeth looked the same. That her hair and her eyes and her nose were still there. That she was in SoHo, New York. That it was just another ordinary day. And nothing ominous was on its way. Unlike Mr Someone Else, Lola never woke up unhurried and happy. She got out of bed as soon as she woke up, in an effort to shake off the half-light of the unconscious. She had to show herself that she was in her own home. That everything was the same as it had been yesterday and the day before.

Lola looked at Patrice Pritchard. She had no idea what Patrice had been saying. Lola had switched off, something she was trying to stop herself doing, and hadn't heard a word Patrice had said. Patrice was now talking about paperbacks and mass paperbacks and author demographics.

'Next month we'll start the publicity campaign for the paperback,' Patrice said. 'We're pitching you as the author of sensitive celebrity profiles.'

'Why do you have to say "celebrity"?' Lola said. 'I've interviewed a ton of people no one's ever heard of. A shoe-repair guy from Uzbekistan, identical-twin kidney transplant surgeons, a clown and a cardiothoracic surgeon, among others.'

'Why a cardiothoracic surgeon?' said Patrice Pritchard.

'Cardiothoracic surgery has always fascinated me,' Lola said. 'It requires brute strength and enormous sensitivity.'

'You are strange,' said Patrice Pritchard. 'I don't mean strange in a bad way,' she added. 'I mean you are a very sensitive person. And a sensitive writer.' Lola didn't mind being called strange. She didn't think it was offensive. She was a bit tired of being thought of as sensitive.

If she hadn't been thought of as a sensitive writer, she would never have met Mr Someone Else. She had been asked to do a profile of his dying wife, a poet. 'We need someone sensitive,' the newspaper editor had said. Lola had met Mr Someone Else, briefly. They had talked for two or three minutes when she had arrived to interview his wife. Lola knew that Mr Someone Else and his wife had had an unhappy marriage and had been separated when she had been diagnosed with breast cancer. He had gone back to her and nursed her through the two years of her illness. Two weeks after Lola's article had come out, Mr Someone Else's wife had died. She was thirty-eight. Mr Someone Else was thirty-two.

Lola saw him again a few weeks later, in a small bookshop in an inner suburb of Melbourne. He almost ran over to her. 'I was born to be with you,' he said. Lola was startled. Few people had greeted her that way. She started laughing. 'I've been dreaming about you my whole life,' he said. Lola didn't know what to say. She started to laugh again. Six weeks later they were together.

'I didn't mean to say that you are strange,' Patrice Pritchard said.

'I don't mind being thought of as strange,' Lola said.

'But I don't think of you as strange,' Patrice said. 'I think of you as very sensitive.'

Maybe her so-called sensitivity accounted for some of her phobias, Lola thought. Until she was in her mid-twenties, she had been fearless. She could do anything, go anywhere. Her third analyst had told her she had been counter-phobic. And now, here she was, almost fifty-two and placing endless restrictions on herself. She could only sit in an aisle seat at the cinema and at the theatre. She was unable to get on the subway. As soon as she started the descent below ground, her heart would begin to pound.

'The line we're going with for the paperback,' Patrice Pritchard said, 'is "Author of sensitive celebrity profiles creates hilariously sensitive private detectives."'

'Can you be hilariously sensitive?' said Lola.

'Of course you can,' said Patrice.

'Do you think they are sensitive?' Lola said.

'Of course they are sensitive,' said Patrice. 'Harry can barely speak or leave his computer. And poor Schlomo feels sorry for everyone, including the perps.'

Lola loved hearing Harry spoken about as though he were a real person. She thought of Harry and Schlomo as real people. She felt as though she knew them and their families well. She felt a sympathy for Schlomo's wife, as Schlomo, apart from being able to focus very sharply on how to switch lanes when he has driving, could be irritatingly absent-minded. And his fixation on the weather and the umbrella that was always affixed to him could drive Lola, who herself had more than a passing interest in the weather, mad.

'It's so fabulous to have you as an author,' Patrice Pritchard said. 'It has restored my faith in love and marriage and success.' Although Lola didn't quite understand what Patrice Pritchard meant, she felt that it was intended as a compliment. However, the wide-reaching implications of Lola's supposed achievements in terms of love, marriage and book sales had made Lola's chest feel tight again. When her chest constricted like this, Lola found it hard to take deep breaths. Her chest didn't seem to want to expand. As though it was cringing in horror, hunched and bent under the weight of that all-encompassing, ill-placed praise.

Patrice kissed Lola goodbye, twice. Once on each cheek. Lola was surprised. At their previous meetings, Patrice had offered her a quick, firm handshake. Maybe this new affection was derived from the imagined perfection Patrice had bestowed upon her. Lola was glad to be leaving. She hoped that outside, in the familiar carbon monoxide-tinged air, her chest might un-crush itself and expand.

Walking home, Lola looked at herself in the reflection of the window of Sur La Table, a kitchenware store on Spring Street. She definitely wasn't thin, she thought to herself. She wasn't fat, at least she wasn't fat in places that could easily be seen. Her thighs were still a bit chunky, but then very few people ever saw Lola's thighs.

She had lost weight slowly. All those hours on analysts' couches had finally removed some of her hunger. She had also been aided by becoming very anxious when she overate. She tried to stick to seventeen-hundred to eighteen-hundred calories a day when she was at home, and tried to make sure she enjoyed what she ate and didn't go overboard on any chocolate dessert when she ate out. Lola wondered if Renia would have been happy about Lola's weight loss. Or would it have removed a bond between them? Or worse, maybe the weight loss would have unnerved Renia? Lola sometimes thought that she steadied her own nerves by continuing to feel fat.

Lola inhaled deeply. Her chest had decompressed. Being outside had helped. Lola loved the smell of the streets in New York. The particular combination of food, cars and people. Lola loved New York. It had taken her a while to settle in. To acclimate to the fast speed and the direct speech employed by most New Yorkers. Now, she liked the lack of circumlocution. The lack of convoluted queries that circled and orbited the nature of the inquiry, winding and twisting and turning, and exasperating everyone on the way with a feigned politeness. Lola didn't miss sentences such as 'You wouldn't, by any chance, happen to know where I could find the subway?' instead of 'Where's the subway?'

The direct language in the city extended to its terminology. When

Lola had first heard that all the lofts in their building were being exterminated, she was bewildered. The notice seemed ordinary enough. *The exterminator will begin on the lower floors at eight a.m.*, the notice said. Lola watched a neighbour read the notice. He was Jewish and didn't seem at all panicked.

Lola had thought that 'extermination' only referred to the murder of Jews. She found out that it also included insects and rodents. The pest exterminator visited the building every month. It took Lola quite a few months not to feel alarmed at the thought of mass exterminations.

Lola knew that when she got home, Mr Someone Else would be in his studio painting to loud music. Probably Bob Dylan. Luckily, Lola's study was at the other end of the loft. And when she shut her study door, she effectively shut out Bob Dylan. Lola also knew that when Mr Someone Else saw her, he would put down his brushes and come over and kiss her. He never just kissed her once. He showered her with kisses until she either started laughing or wriggled out of his grip. Just like her mother.

Renia was always wriggling or, more accurately, wrenching herself out of Edek's grips or pinches or pats. Renia usually shook her head as she twisted herself out of Edek's grasp, as though she were far too busy for this sort of playfulness. When Edek came home after work, he always tried to grab Renia or pat her on the bum. He would also try to stroke her hair or hold her in his arms. He never succeeded. Renia always got away.

Edek had loved Renia for a long time. He had been smitten by her the first time they met. Renia was twelve, almost thirteen. Edek was nineteen, good-looking and wealthy. None of this swayed Renia. She didn't want a boyfriend. She didn't want to get married. She wanted to work hard and be a doctor, a paediatrician. Renia came top of every class she was in and tutored her fellow students in maths, science and history, four nights a week. Edek had had to work hard to inch his way into Renia's heart. And Hitler's arrival, several years later, had clinched the deal. Renia and Edek were married a few days before they and all the Jews of Lodz were forced to leave their homes and imprisoned in the ghetto.

Lola was almost home. She knew she had to clear up an argument Pimp was having with Schlomo. Pimp had already been very irritated that morning by Harry, who had remained in the Ultra-Private Detective Agency's small East Village office when Pimp and Schlomo had moved to SoHo. Harry had become very attached to the area and to the three delis where he bought the different components of his lunch every day. And Pimp had been unable to get out of the last year of the lease. Harry had cleared everything off the desk Pimp used when she was in the East Village office. When she had dropped in to do some work, she had been unable to find the documents she was looking for or her reading glasses.

'You don't have to be so anal,' Pimp had said to Harry.

Harry had been offended. 'I am not anal,' he said. 'I am fastidious. That's how we find who and what we are looking for.'

'You are beyond fastidious,' Pimp screamed. 'And being beyond fastidious is anal.'

Lola had been puzzled by why she was trying to differentiate between fastidious and anal. And had distracted herself by wondering if she could scream like Pimp. She thought her voice would probably seize up and come out as a small screech.

Pimp screamed at everyone. She regularly screamed at Schlomo.

'Why are you scrimming, scrimming, scrimming?' Schlomo would say to Pimp.

'I'm not scrimming. I'm screaming.' Pimp would shout. Schlomo's Yiddish accent drove her crazy.

Pimp's recent argument with Schlomo had been about equipment. Schlomo loved gadgets. He had decided he needed the Bionic Ear with Booster Kit he'd seen in a catalogue. The Bionic Ear with Booster Kit magnified faint or distant sounds, supposedly with remarkable clarity.

'You've already got that Parabolic Ear that you never use,' Pimp had said.

'The Parabolic Ear is good for sounds of nature up to a hundred yards away,' Schlomo said. 'There are no sounds of nature in SoHo.'

'Why did we buy it?' Pimp screamed.

'Don't scrim,' said Schlomo. 'We bought it because I thought it was good for voices. It doesn't work too good at all for voices.'

'Do you speak English at home with your wife?' Pimp said.

'Of course we speak English,' said Schlomo. 'Now you are acting offensive.'

'It should be *acting in an offensive manner* or *being offensive*,' said Pimp.

Schlomo shrugged. 'I need a Bionic Ear with Booster Kit,' he said. 'I was following the man whose wife says he is no longer interested in sex with her and I can tell you from the way he was looking at the woman he met that he is still very interested in sex. But I could not hear a word they were saying. If I want to hear what people are saying, I have to stand so close that they can smell me.'

'Do you smell?' said Pimp.

'Everybody does,' said Schlomo.

'You've got all this equipment you don't use,' Pimp said to Schlomo. 'What happened to the Memo Dictation Pen Recorder?'

'I thought I could pretend to write something when I was recording a suspect, but it didn't work out,' Schlomo said.

Lola sympathised with Pimp. Schlomo did have a lot of gadgets, none of which he appeared to use. He had ordered the Memo Dictation Pen Recorder and then discovered that he felt stupid waving a pen in the direction of someone standing in front of him. He had ordered a Wall Probe Microphone that could pick up even faint sounds through any solid surface before discovering that there was rarely a wall between him and the person he was following.

Harry thought that Schlomo was hopeless with equipment. 'Schlomo put the vehicle tracking device on his own car,' Harry had pointed out when the three of them were last together.

'Harry, I do not need your help,' Schlomo had said.

'Schlomo, you need somebody's help,' Pimp had said.

Lola needed to help Pimp solve the problem of Schlomo and the Sabbath. Schlomo observed the Sabbath. He left work early every Friday afternoon and was out of reach until after sunset on Saturday. Schlomo had to stop whatever he was doing on Friday afternoons and get home before sunset. Last Friday he had been minutes away from finding the identity of the blackmailer of the head of the New York chain of Best Ever Burger restaurants, when he'd had to pack up and rush home.

'Wouldn't God have been happier if we'd caught the blackmailer?' Pimp had said.

'No,' Schlomo had replied very firmly. This was the Ultra-Private Detective Agency's first case of blackmail. The owner of the Best Ever Burger chain was one of their richest clients. Lola had wondered if Pimp would be able to find a private detective who wanted to work on a sporadic basis on Friday afternoons and Saturdays.

Lola was in her study. She looked at the last page she had written. Schlomo had decided to take up yoga. Oh no, Lola thought. When had that happened? Then she remembered. It had happened at seven o'clock this morning. It was too late to change it now. Schlomo was already enrolled in the yoga school around the corner from Lola's loft.

6

Nobody was doing yoga when Lola Bensky was twenty. Not even the brand-new hippies at the Monterey International Pop Festival. The first person Lola Bensky saw when she walked into the Monterey County Fairgrounds was Jimi Hendrix. He was sitting on a folding chair outside the office building that functioned as the administrative centre of the Monterey International Pop Festival, a three-day festival billed as a weekend of music, love and flowers. Inside, Michelle Phillips of The Mamas and the Papas was working frantically, typing and answering the phones, and her husband John Phillips was still adjusting the concert schedule in his grey fur hat, which, despite the heat, he never seemed to remove.

Jimi Hendrix was doing something to the strings of his guitar. He was wearing a black hat with several silver brooches and badges pinned to the brim, a maroon jacket and a silk floral-patterned shirt. Large pink and green flowers were printed all over the cream silk. Around his neck were five necklaces of varying lengths. The shortest, a chunky silver necklace, sat snugly around his neck and the longest dropped to just above his waist, a few inches away from the bold silver chain belted around his jeans. He had two large silver rings on the last two fingers of his left hand.

Lola admired the way Jimi Hendrix dressed and decorated himself. At first glance, it looked as though he was wearing a technicolour mishmash of odds and ends. A hodgepodge of garments and adornments. But his outfits contained a surprising harmony, held together by his lean frame and a low-lying, slow-burning fervour.

Lola didn't want to disturb Jimi Hendrix. He seemed to be engrossed in his guitar strings. She thought he probably wouldn't remember her. She looked down and realised that she was wearing fishnet tights. Not the same pair that she'd had on when she'd seen him in London. But they were still fishnet tights. The net in this pair had more stretch and didn't dig into her over-abundance of flesh. With this pair, she didn't have to pad the inside of her thighs with tissues and worry about leaving traces of shredded tissue particles in her wake.

Jimi Hendrix looked up and saw Lola. He paused for a moment and then smiled. 'Hi,' he said. 'How are you doing? You never did come around and see me in my hair curlers.'

'No, I didn't,' said Lola. 'Although I was very interested in seeing where you placed the hair curlers if they weren't in straight lines.'

'I know exactly where to put hair curlers,' Jimi Hendrix said.

'That's what you said last time,' said Lola.

'Your hair is still straight but you've had it cut,' Jimi Hendrix said. Lola was very surprised. She found it hard to believe he'd noticed that her formerly long, ironed-straight hair was now short, straight hair. She had had a Mary Quant blunt-cut bob before she'd left London. She regretted it. Having a perky haircut made her feel a bit at odds with herself. She wasn't really the perky sort.

'It looks as though you've had it permed straight,' Jimi Hendrix said.

'How can you tell?' said Lola.

'I've had my hair permed straight before, and I recognise that very straight look,' he said.

Lola didn't think this was a good thing. If Jimi Hendrix could recognise permed-straight hair, then a lot of other people probably could, too. And the Monterey International Pop Festival, with its emphasis on love and peace and all things natural, was possibly not the place to turn up wearing artificially permed hair.

'I shouldn't have had it straightened,' Lola said.

'It's fine,' said Jimi Hendrix.

Lola consoled herself by thinking that few people were as knowledgeable about hair as Jimi Hendrix. What was she doing, anyway, Lola thought, talking to Jimi Hendrix about permed hair and bad haircuts?

'You are a groovy chick, man,' Jimi Hendrix said. Lola laughed. 'You don't think you're a groovy chick, do you?' he said.

'Not really,' said Lola. She had never thought of herself as a chick or as groovy. Chicks, especially groovy chicks, had long blond hair, slim hips and bare, shapely legs. They weren't covering the pudginess of their thighs and calves with lace or fishnet tights. Groovy chicks could also dance in rhythm and with abandon, on the dance floor or on the beach, and were not, on the whole, Jewish. Lola would have had to undergo a divine transformation to be categorised as a groovy chick. She would have had to reconfigure history, alter her genes, and catch malaria to lose weight.

'You are a cool chick,' Jimi Hendrix said. 'I'm being serious.' He looked at her. 'You've got a very pretty face. I don't measure girls by their appearance,' he said. 'Some people go for appearance. I don't.'

Lola felt embarrassed. Was he telling her what she knew was the truth, that she was too fat to be attractive? She didn't think so. His face looked too earnest to be saying anything hurtful.

'Looks might make you want to be with a girl for a second or two, but that's all,' Jimi Hendrix said. 'There are other things that girls have to offer besides their looks. I don't know exactly what, but you can feel little things about a person that aren't as obvious as looks.'

'I agree with you,' Lola said. 'Choosing a person on the basis of their looks is a pretty superficial choice.'

'But you still don't think you're a groovy chick, do you?' he said.

'No,' said Lola.

A pale-haired guy with a headband made out of feathers came up to Jimi Hendrix. 'Hey, man, I met you in Buffalo a few years ago,' he said. 'You come from Buffalo, don't you?'

'No,' said Jimi Hendrix. 'I'm from Seattle, Washington. I was in Buffalo for a couple of months, but I left. I was too cold there.'

Lola wondered what made Jimi Hendrix so unfailingly polite. Too many of the men in the rock world were arrogant. The rock stars, the road managers, the assistants. It seemed that just being in the orbit of a celebrity could induce a disdain for anyone outside that small cosmos.

'Wasn't it just as cold in Seattle?' said the feathered-headband man.

'No,' said Jimi Hendrix. 'Seattle has a different kind of cold. Seattle has a nice coldness. It doesn't cut into you the way the coldness in Buffalo does.'

'My father used to say that about Poland,' Lola said. 'He said he never felt the cold in Poland. He said it was a good cold. The sort of cold that didn't get into your bones. I think maybe he didn't feel the cold because he felt at home there.'

'Maybe,' said Jimi Hendrix.

Mr Feathered Headband wandered away, probably less than capti-
vated about what Edek felt about the cold in Poland. Lola tugged at the
sides of her purple and white dress. She was sure that last month this
dress hadn't been that tight. She had just sent Renia a postcard saying
that she was on a diet. She figured out that she had about ten days before
the postcard arrived to start the diet. That way she wouldn't be lying.

The fairground was beginning to fill up. People were streaming in.
Nobody paid much attention to Jimi Hendrix. Despite his hit records
in England, few people in America had heard of Jimi Hendrix. The
band, The Jimi Hendrix Experience, had never been on American
television, they had had very little exposure on American radio and
hardly any press.

'Nice to see you, again,' Jimi Hendrix said to Lola.

'Nice to see you, too,' said Lola. She waved to him as she walked
off and then felt stupid. Her wave was the prolonged wave of a small
child. She looked back. Jimi Hendrix was waving and smiling.

The Monterey International Pop Festival was planned as a com-
ing together, with love, of people from all over the world. Bands from
America, England, South Africa and India were booked to appear.
It was the first large festival to include bands from all over America.
Many of the bands, despite their fame, had never met each other.

The festival program exhorted everyone to be happy, be free, wear
flowers, bring bells and have a festival. Lola thought that the thousands of people who had attended the festival had listened.

She had never seen a crowd of people looking so happy. Person after
person was smiling. Large smiles that radiated a sense of optimism and
a sense of brotherhood. Lola had never seen a crowd of people so at

ease with each other. Trees and cars and vans and babies and young children and large and small dogs were festooned with signs saying 'Love' and 'Peace'. And then there were the flowers. There were flowers everywhere. Almost everyone had flowers. Flowers in their hair, around their necks, attached to their garments or their sunglasses or painted onto their faces.

And the clothes. The clothes were wild. Lola was mesmerised by the clothes. She watched a woman in a purple paisley jacket, with matching purple paisley shoes, share a sandwich with her dog. The dog was wearing a purple paisley vest. There were men in psychedelic shirts and girls in long floral dresses. Others were in T-shirts and shorts or tweed jackets with leather patches or military trousers and jackets emblazoned with gold bands and embroidered emblems. Several young women had short summer dresses with black tights and black knee-high boots. There was no uniform. And no sense of uniformity apart from the palpable, almost concrete feeling of goodwill.

Music was being played over the sound system. Couples were dancing on the grass. Others were walking or sitting or eating. Eating fresh fruit. Lola had never seen so many people eating fruit. Everyone seemed to have an apple or an orange or a piece of watermelon. As though fruit were a symbol of a fresh start.

Lola felt as though she had landed on another planet. Was she witnessing the beginning of a revolution? She knew that it was possible for the world to change overnight. For Renia, the future had changed. Overnight. It had spun on its axis and cracked and crazed and fractured. It was split into pieces with fissures and chinks and splinters. Overnight, everything had changed. One minute Renia was a beautiful and studious teenager. The next minute she was, like all the other Jews of Lodz, a bedraggled prisoner, imprisoned in a universe bereft of sustenance of almost every sort.

Lola was offered an orange by a young man in a Black Watch tartan kilt and a Black Watch tartan headband around his head. He took the orange out of the back of an old station wagon that was filled with boxes of oranges. 'Thank you,' said Lola.

'You're so welcome,' he said, and bowed with a flourish.

The congregation of Temple Beth El had set up a store where you could buy pastrami sandwiches. There was a soul-food stand and the Monterey Kiwanis, part of an international foundation that helped children in need, were cooking fresh corn on the cob and serving it, hot, on a stick. In other parts of the fairground you could buy macrobiotic food, popcorn or posters or brooches or pins and paper dresses.

There were a lot of policemen at the festival. The police in their shiny blue helmets were also smiling. Quite a few of them had flowers tucked into their helmet straps. Lola didn't think she'd even try to describe this scene in her postcard to Renia.

She saw Brian Jones wandering around, almost ethereal in his blondness and draped in a pink cape with what looked like more than one patterned silk scarf around his neck and a patterned silk shirt. Lola knew that Brian Jones loved clothes. He was often dressed in layers of satin and lace and necklaces and frills. His flamboyant style had made him a fashion icon of sorts in England. He looked as though he was in a semi-dream. Partly removed from everything around him. Lola was due to interview him in less than an hour. She had heard that he was hypersensitive, a bit jumpy and often stoned. She had been told he took a lot of Mandrax, a sedative and muscle relaxant similar in effect to barbiturates, along with a stash of other drugs.

Lola had seen some childhood photographs of Brian Jones. He hadn't looked like a happy child. His mother was a piano teacher and his father an aeronautical engineer who also played the piano and led the church choir. Despite his middle-class upbringing, Brian Jones already looked lost.

The fact that he used a lot of drugs and also drank heavily seemed to have already had a bad effect on his health. He had been hospitalised for 'health problems' several times. Lola thought the alcohol and the drugs probably exacerbated his detached, anti-social tendencies.

There was another even more bothering side to Brian Jones. Lola had heard that he sometimes beat up his girlfriend, Anita Pallenberg. Anita Pallenberg had often been seen with bruises on her arms. Quite a few people seemed to know. No one appeared too bothered. Lola wondered why it was a criminal offence to beat up someone in the street, when beating up your wife or your girlfriend was viewed as part of ordinary everyday life, as merely a domestic spat or disagreement.

Three months before the Monterey International Pop Festival, Anita Pallenberg, who had been with Brian Jones for two years, left him for Keith Richards. She left when Brian Jones was hospitalised in Morocco while the three of them were travelling together.

Brian Jones was on time. They sat down side by side on a bench under a tree, not far from the festival's office. Lola looked at Brian Jones. His hair was as bouffant and bouncy as it always was. Lola had heard that Anita Pallenberg used to do Brian Jones's hair and make-up. His hair didn't look as though it was missing Anita Pallenberg's touch. He looked a bit pale, but maybe it wasn't a lack of make-up, maybe he always looked pale.

'This festival is already pretty exciting, isn't it?' Lola said to Brian Jones. 'Do you think it is going to be quite an extraordinary event?' Brian Jones looked at her. He opened his mouth. Nothing came out. Lola waited.

'Three days. Three days,' he said.

'Yes,' said Lola. 'It is a three-day festival. What made you want to fly over for it?'

'Jimi,' he said. 'Community.'

Lola thought about it. Did he mean he came over to see Jimi Hendrix and the local community? Lola was used to interpreting and translating seemingly incomprehensible sentences. Her parents' English always needed interpretations and adjustments.

'Jimi Hendrix is great,' Lola said.

'Best world,' Brian Jones said slowly.

'This community is the best in the world?' Lola said. Brian Jones looked even more bewildered. 'Jimi Hendrix is the best in the world?' Lola said. Brian Jones just stared at her. *Thinks Jimi Hendrix is the best guitar player in the world*, Lola wrote in her notebook.

'I think,' Brian Jones said. 'I think,' he repeated.

He thinks, Lola wrote, and waited.

She looked up at him. He was slowly listing to his right. He was almost leaning against Lola. She tried to prop him back to an upright position. 'Community,' he said. 'Form a community.'

'In Monterey?' she said. He didn't answer. 'You mean you think the people at the festival will form a community?' Lola said.

Brian Jones blinked. Lola thought that must be what he meant. *Brian Jones feels that the people who come here will, after spending three days together at the Monterey International Pop Festival, have formed a community*, Lola wrote in her notebook.

'I think I understand what you're saying,' Lola said to Brian Jones. 'And I think you're right, I think a community, maybe even living in different parts of the world, will be formed.' He didn't answer Lola. His eyes were closed. He appeared to be asleep. She peered at him. He was so out of it – so unaware of anything around him. Lola examined his face, at close range. His skin was smooth. It had an almost innocent flawlessness about it.

Even passed out, every part of Brian Jones's ensemble was impeccable. His scarves were draped with casual perfection. His cape with its fur-trimmed collar still contained a romantic aura. And each of his many pieces of jewellery was polished and in place.

The mess, Lola had heard, was in his home. Apparently there were clothes and underwear everywhere and piles of dirty dishes and stale food and grooming accoutrements on every surface. Mick Jagger, Lola had been told, supposedly found it intolerable to visit. Lola could believe that. She didn't think Mick Jagger liked too much mess.

Lola gingerly shook Brian Jones. He opened his eyes. 'Do you think the world is changing?' Lola said. 'Is this a social revolution?'

'Change?' Brian Jones said, looking straight at Lola. 'I don't think so,' he said, slowly, while he tried to put his hand into the pocket of his satin trousers.

'No,' he said in a slurred voice.

Lola suddenly realised that Brian Jones thought she was asking for money. She was horrified. 'I don't want change,' she said.

'Change?' he said as his eyes rolled into the back of his head.

'I was asking you, if you thought, looking around here, that the world might be changing,' Lola said, before giving up on the rest of her sentence.

Brian Jones was leaning back on the bench. He seemed to be in a coma, or asleep. She tried to prod him again. He didn't move. She pushed him slightly towards her, so she could keep him propped up until someone came to collect him. She hoped, as he'd flown over from England for the concert, that he would revive before the concert began.

Lola felt quite disconcerted by Brian Jones passing out. 'He's stoned,' the guys who came to pick him up said. 'How do you know he's not having a heart attack or a stroke?' Lola said.

'He's stoned,' the guys carrying Brian Jones off said to Lola, again. Lola walked back to the main area of the fairground. A man with a yellow pork-pie hat smiled at her. She smiled back. A girl with cherries around her ears, carrying a bowl of raw carrots, offered Lola a carrot. She took one. Something was happening. Something was changing. There was a happiness in the air that felt almost contagious.

In front of the stage were hundreds of rows of folding chairs. Quite a few of the seven thousand seats were already filled. Lola had a press pass. This meant that she could sit in the front four or five rows of seats. She squeezed past some people and sat down just to the left of the middle of the row.

Lola looked to her left. To her horror, she was sitting two seats away from Mama Cass. She had nothing against Mama Cass, but she didn't want to sit that close to someone who was so fat. Few people were that fat. It was the sort of fat that made people turn around and stare. Lola very much hoped that she was not as fat as Mama Cass.

She felt bad about wanting to change seats. She knew that it didn't make her any more or any less fat to be sitting next to another fat person. Lola looked at Mama Cass. Mama Cass was smiling. It was a beautiful smile. The smile of someone who was utterly at peace. There was no hint of aggravation or discontent in her smile. Mama Cass's smile was at odds with her body, which looked overgrown, over-wrought and uncomfortable. It took up a lot of space and preceded her whenever she turned in her seat.

Lola felt sad. She didn't know why she should feel sad. Mama Cass didn't look at all sad. She looked transcendentally happy. Her head, tilted to one side, rested on the shoulder of a very good-looking blond man. Lola thought Mama Cass must be more at peace with her body than Lola was with hers. Lola looked at Mama Cass's upper arms and prayed that her own arms were not anywhere near as fat.

Lola took another look at the blond man. She remembered that he was Mama Cass's new boyfriend, Lee Kiefer. Lee Kiefer had the good looks of a movie star. He was tall and had taut, chiselled, symmetrical features. He was tanned, lean and muscled. They looked like a strange couple as Mama Cass's features had been rearranged by the fat. Her face had acquired extra dimensions and added planes and chins.

Lola almost wanted to cry. She felt sad for Mama Cass. And sad for herself. She really must start a diet, she thought. She already had a new diet plotted out. It involved peaches, apricots, cantaloupe and eggs. The diet was based on having one peach, one apricot, one egg and half a cantaloupe, five times a day. That totalled fifteen hundred calories a day, which usually meant a weight loss of two pounds a week.

The diet could be varied. She could have two peaches, two apri-cots, two eggs and a whole cantaloupe twice a day plus one peach, one apricot, one egg and half a cantaloupe once a day. There was a lot of eating involved for a relatively small number of calories, which, Lola thought, along with being easy to remember, could be the key to a successful diet.

Maybe she should also exercise, she thought. She had tried exercising once, when she was seventeen. She had ridden round and round in circles on her bicycle in Renia and Edek's small backyard in St Kilda, Melbourne. Riding round and round had made her hungry as well as dizzy.

Lola caught a whiff of cannabis in the air. People were passing a joint along in the row in front of her. Lola got out her notebook. *Start the Peach, Apricot, Cantaloupe and Egg Diet,* she wrote to herself. Somebody sat down in the seat on Lola's right. Lola glanced up at them. She looked again. It was Janis Joplin. Lola thought she had seen Janis Joplin walking around earlier. Janis Joplin smiled at her and said, 'Hi.' It was a cheerful, enthusiastic, almost girlish 'Hi'. A 'Hi' that seemed in marked contrast to her looks. There was very little that looked girlish about Janis Joplin. She had flat, badly pockmarked skin, and untamed dry hair with stringy split ends. Lola felt sorry for her. It must be hard to live with skin that was so marked. At least she isn't fat, Lola thought.

'Hi,' Lola said. 'I'm Lola Bensky. I'm a journalist. I write for *Rock-Out,* a newspaper based in Melbourne, Australia.'

'Oh man, Australia, that's groovy,' Janis Joplin said.

Lola instinctively liked Janis Joplin. There was an earnestness about her. And an intensity. Lola turned to her. 'Could I ask you a weird question?' Lola said.

'Sure,' said Janis Joplin. 'I like weird questions.'

'Do you think I'm as big as Mama Cass, who's sitting two seats to my left?'

Janis Joplin leaned over and surreptitiously eyed Mama Cass.

She looked at Mama Cass for what felt to Lola like a long time, then turned to Lola and said, 'Hell no,' in a voice that Lola feared was loud enough for Mama Cass to hear, 'She's much bigger.'

'Are you sure?' Lola said in a whisper.

'Of course I'm sure,' Janis Joplin said. 'I'm trying not to bullshit myself, I'm trying to be real, so I wouldn't try to bullshit you.'

'That's a relief,' Lola said. 'Her size freaks me out a bit.'

'I understand,' Janis Joplin said. 'I was fat when I was a teenager and it isolated me even more. It didn't help that my face was also constantly covered in big red pimples. I used to get called "pig" or "freak". It all happened almost overnight when I was fourteen. I didn't get any tits, but I gained weight and got acne. I wasn't exactly Miss Popularity before then. I was already different. I read books and I painted and I didn't hate niggers.'

Lola knew that she had been right to like Janis Joplin. 'I had a school friend,' she said to Janis Joplin, 'who was very thin. We'd go to the beach together when we were about fourteen or fifteen. Other kids would see us and start chanting, "Fat and Skinny went to war. Fat got shot and Skinny swore." Did you have that little ditty in America?'

'I've never heard it before,' said Janis Joplin.

'I wasn't even fat then,' said Lola.

'Are you still thinking about whether or not you're as fat as Mama Cass?' Janis Joplin said.

'Not really,' Lola said. 'Although the thought still does bother me.'

'Well, you're not,' said Janis Joplin. 'I know what it's like to obsess about something like that. I obsess about my skin. It's so ugly.'

'It's not ugly,' Lola said. 'And you're not ugly.' What she was saying was true. Janis Joplin had an attractiveness that had nothing to do with having blemish-free skin or being perfectly groomed. She was someone it was easy to be drawn to. It was partly her truthfulness and her openness and a sense that she cared. Janis Joplin wasn't the sort of person, Lola thought, for whom life was one big ice-cream cake.

'Neither are you,' said Janis Joplin.

'A few people have said I could be very pretty if I lost weight,' Lola said.

'Fuck them,' said Janis Joplin.

'My mother is obsessed with my weight,' Lola said.

'Fuck her, too,' said Janis Joplin.

'My mother isn't bothered by the word "fuck",' Lola said. 'I say "fuck" in front of her all the time. It doesn't bother her. Her English isn't good enough to know that it's quite a crude word.' Lola paused. 'My mother hates people who are fat,' she said to Janis Joplin. 'She was in a Nazi death camp and the only people who were fat in there were some Nazis and the few prisoners who were doing something that was helpful to the Nazis.'

'Are you Jewish?' said Janis Joplin.

'Very,' said Lola.

'My two best friends at school, Karleen and Arlene, were Jewish.'

'Really?' said Lola.

'I practically lived at Karleen Bennett's house,' Janis Joplin said. 'Her parents liked me. Nothing about me was acceptable and still isn't to my mother. She was always telling me to be like everyone else. She wanted me to wear skirts and white shirts and bobby socks. She wanted me to be anything but what I was. So I spent all the time I could at Karleen's place. I even went to temple with them.'

'Are there many Jewish people in Port Arthur?' Lola said. She knew that Janis Joplin was born in Port Arthur, Texas.

'Hardly any. People were suspicious of anyone Jewish. I think being Jewish is very cool,' said Janis Joplin, looking quite thrilled that Lola was Jewish.

Lola was not at all sure that it was thrilling to be Jewish, but she didn't want to start a conversation at the Monterey International Pop Festival about the endless catastrophes and tragedies that had befallen Jews solely because they were Jewish.

'You went to temple?' Lola said to Janis Joplin.

'Yes,' said Janis Joplin. 'I loved it. We'd go with Karleen's parents and her grandmother.'

'I wasn't allowed to go to synagogue because neither of my parents believed in God, not after what they'd experienced,' Lola said.

Janis Joplin was quiet. 'I've always hated discrimination,' she said. 'When I spoke up in high school and said I was in favour of integration, everyone thought that I had gone crazy. At my high school, Thomas Jefferson High School in Port Arthur, just being good at English or reading books or doing art could get you beaten up. I got such shit for doing art.'

'We had boys that beat up other kids when I was at primary school,' Lola said. 'I was terrified most of the time I was there, which was from the time I was six till I was ten.'

'What did your parents do about it?' said Janis Joplin.

'Nothing,' said Lola. 'I didn't tell them. I didn't think it would help.'

'It must have been hard to talk to a mother who'd been through all that,' Janis Joplin said.

'My father was also imprisoned in a Nazi death camp,' she said.

Janis Joplin looked sad. Lola felt bothered. She didn't like the knack she seemed to have developed for making people sad. It seemed to be almost unavoidable if both your parents had been in Nazi death camps. Lola thought she definitely would have had a more cheery range of life stories to exchange if her parents had been trapeze artists or weightlifters.

'A journalist friend who saw you perform in New York told me you were sensational,' Lola said to Janis Joplin. Janis Joplin clapped her hands together like a child and beamed. 'Did he?' she said. 'That's so cool. We played in New York in March. He must be a groovy cat.'

'He is a she,' Lola said.

'Well, that's even better,' said Janis Joplin.

'Really?' said Lola.

'Yes,' said Janis Joplin. 'I find women are more honest. And men still think all of us chicks are supposed to get married and have a brood of children and shut up.'

Lola tried to think about what Janis Joplin had just said. She wondered if that was what men expected of women. She thought it probably was what women expected of women. She didn't think that most of the girls or women she knew thought of themselves as becoming brain surgeons or nuclear physicists. Lola herself mostly thought about how to lose weight. Needing to lose as much weight as she needed to lose was a time-consuming occupation.

Mama Cass passed a large tray of watermelon slices along the row. Lola and Janis Joplin each took a slice. 'Thank you,' they called out to Mama Cass.

'You could never say "fuck" in my house,' Janis Joplin said to Lola. 'My mother would have been furious. She used to call me a harlot without me uttering any obscenities. The first time she said it, Karleen and I had to look it up in the dictionary as I couldn't believe my mother would call me that.' She paused. 'She had no reason to say that to me,' she added.

'My father used to call me a prostitute if I came home after ten p.m.,' Lola said. 'I used to think that maybe the word prostitute didn't sound so bad, in Polish, and he didn't know how hurtful it was. I was so virginal and so offended.'

'Me, too,' said Janis Joplin.

'Your mother sounds pretty awful,' Lola said.

'She is very controlling,' Janis Joplin said. 'And cold. Nothing I can do is right. She still wants me to wear demure skirts and put my hair up in a bun.'

'My mother isn't cold or detached,' Lola said. 'She just isn't there. You can see her but she's absent. She's not there. I think she'd probably like to be present, but she can't be. The only time that she's there is when she's telling me to lose weight.'

'Well that's an incentive to stay fat, isn't it?' said Janis Joplin.

'I guess so,' said Lola. She hadn't thought of that.

'You don't mind that I called you fat, do you?' Janis Joplin said.

'I am fat,' Lola said. 'I sometimes think that I must be too fat for my mother to kiss. She never kisses me. And rarely touches me. Sometimes I think that maybe it has got nothing to do with my being fat, I think that maybe she was just touched too much.'

A bowl of raw peeled carrots was being passed along the row. Lola was pleased to see the carrots. They cut short the conversation about Renia having been touched too much. Lola had already refused the neatly rolled joints that had been shared around and the box of white pills. She felt she had to say yes to the carrots. She took a carrot. Janis Joplin shook her head and said no to the carrots. She reached down into her bag and pulled out a bottle of Southern Comfort. She took a swig out of the bottle. Lola must have looked shocked because Janis Joplin laughed, and said, 'I always make sure my purse is big enough to hold a book and a bottle.'

Lola had never seen anyone drink whiskey from a bottle. She hadn't seen many people drinking whiskey. Janis Joplin took another few swigs. Lola didn't think doing that could be good for Janis Joplin. It looked like a lot of whiskey to be swigging down.

'Is that good for you?' she said to Janis Joplin.

'Hell, yes,' said Janis Joplin. 'Very good. Do you want some?'

'Not really,' said Lola. 'I don't like alcohol. I prefer chocolate.' Janis Joplin laughed. She had a strange laugh. It was almost like a cackle. And almost like a giggle.

'You don't drink anything?' Janis Joplin said.

'No,' said Lola. 'I don't drink at all.'

'Do you take speed?' said Janis Joplin.

'No,' said Lola.

'What do you do?' said Janis Joplin. 'When all you want to do is sit around and mope?'

'I don't know,' said Lola. She didn't really sit around and mope, she thought. There was quite a bit of moping in Lola's future, but Lola didn't yet know that.

'I'm usually pretty busy,' Lola said to Janis Joplin. 'I do my interviews, arrange more interviews, write the articles and then I plan diets.'

'Good heavens,' said Janis Joplin. 'You plan diets?' Lola was startled at Janis Joplin's response. Not at the fact that Janis Joplin was surprised

that Lola planned diets. Lola was surprised at the words Janis Joplin
had used. 'Good heavens.' It was such a prim expression. There was
nothing prim about Janis Joplin.

'Yes,' said Lola. 'I plan diets all the time.'

'Speed could help you with your diet,' Janis Joplin said. 'It really
peps me up.'

'I think I just need to eat less,' said Lola.

'Speed can meet a lot of your needs,' said Janis Joplin.

'I took it once when I was in high school,' Lola said. 'I couldn't
sleep for three days.' Lola tried to think about whether she'd eaten any
less after the speed, but she couldn't remember.

'Have you tried heroin?' said Janis Joplin.

'No,' said Lola. 'Do you use heroin?'

'Only when I can afford it, and that's not very often,' Janis Joplin said.

'Do you mope a lot?' said Lola.

'Sometimes,' said Janis Joplin. 'Now I've got George, I mope less.'

'Who is George?' Lola said.

'My dog,' said Janis Joplin. 'He's part German shepherd and part
English shepherd. He was already called George when I got him,
when he was a puppy. I didn't want to confuse him, so I kept the name.'

'What do you mope about?' said Lola.

'A feeling of emptiness, a feeling of loneliness, a feeling that I'm
not good enough,' Janis Joplin said.

'Not good enough at what?' said Lola.

'Not good enough at anything,' said Janis Joplin.

Lola felt sad. She recognised something about the sadness Janis
Joplin was talking about, the loneliness Janis Joplin was talking
about. It would take Lola decades to feel her own loneliness. She

didn't know she was lonely. She knew she was fat. And she knew she was hungry.

'I feel a lot,' said Janis Joplin. 'And when you feel that much you have really horrible downs. Really bad downs. If I didn't have my music I might have done myself in. When I'm on stage, singing, I feel good. I feel great. I got turned on to Otis Redding by a friend and saw how Otis really goes into the music. After that I got more and more into the music. When Otis Redding was on at the Fillmore, in San Francisco, for three nights, I went every night. I got there early every single night to make sure I could see. I got there so early they hadn't even opened the building.' When she was talking about Otis Redding, Janis Joplin's face still had traces of the flush of excitement she must have felt when she was watching him perform.

'What do you think about when you're singing?' Lola said.

'I'm not thinking much when I sing,' Janis Joplin said. 'I just try to feel. Being on stage and singing is about trying to get those things that are inside you out. The things that don't make for polite conversation.'

Lola thought that just about everything in her life was made up of things that didn't make for polite conversation. Her fishnet tights and the way they dug into her thighs, her diets and the mess of her mother picking at another person's vomit and having things done to her by dogs. Lola was glad that Janis Joplin's dog George was only half German shepherd.

Janis Joplin looked at Lola. 'I sometimes think I should just put my hair up in a bun, wear make-up and go back to Port Arthur,' she said.

'Really?' said Lola.

'No,' said Janis Joplin. 'I tried just over a year ago, and it definitely didn't work.'

A very tall, dark-haired girl a couple of rows in front of Lola and Janis Joplin was taking photographs. She turned around and took a photograph of Janis Joplin. Janis Joplin smiled at her, and looked at her for a long time.

'Boy, am I turned on by her,' Janis Joplin said to Lola. Lola was surprised. She hardly knew anyone who was openly homosexual. She also knew hardly any girls or women who talked about feeling sexually aroused. The girls Lola knew talked mostly about love.

Lola must have looked surprised because Janis Joplin laughed. 'I get turned on by chicks,' she said, 'and by dudes. I think it's normal to be turned on by a person – not by their gender.'

'It does make sense,' said Lola, although she wasn't sure that it really did.

Many years later a friend would tell Lola that she herself could never have been a rock journalist. 'My sexuality would have gotten in the way,' she said.

Lola had stared at her. 'All I cared about was my Olivetti portable typewriter, my tape recorder and getting the best story I could,' Lola said. But afterwards, she had worried for hours about where her sexuality was.

'My sexual tastes are very broad,' Janis Joplin said. Lola was stunned. She had never thought of taste as being sexual. Taste, Lola thought, involved food. Chocolate cake. Cheesecake. Poppy-seed strudel. Not men or women.

'What are your sexual tastes?' said Janis Joplin. 'Do you make out with chicks?' Lola felt she could hardly tell Janis Joplin she was reeling from the thought of tastes being sexual.

'Not really,' she said. 'But then I'm not doing a whole lot of making out. I did some making out with girls when I was about thirteen or four-teen,' Lola said.

'Everyone does that,' said Janis Joplin.

Lola thought Janis Joplin seemed very sure of herself when she was talking about sex. She spoke about sex with freedom and an air of authority. As though it was just another everyday subject that every-one thought about. Maybe it was, Lola thought.

'I think I am more myself when I am with chicks,' Janis Joplin said. 'I probably feel more at ease. But then I'm turned on by so many dudes. I like fucking.' Lola had heard that when Janis Joplin had been asked by someone she knew why she didn't snort heroin rather than shoot up she had barked, 'Why jerk off when you can fuck?'

'I'm looking forward to hearing you sing tomorrow,' Lola said.

'I'm so nervous about it,' said Janis Joplin, tapping her foot. 'This is the biggest audience we've ever played to. What if they hate me?'

'This is not Port Arthur,' said Lola.

'It's definitely not Port Arthur,' said Janis Joplin as a shirtless man with about twenty rows of beads around his neck and a daisy chain around his head stepped over them to get to his seat.

'And it's not Melbourne,' said Lola. They both laughed.

A tall guy with long straight hair called out and beckoned to Janis Joplin. 'That's Sam Andrew, one of the band,' Janis Joplin said to Lola. 'He's a great guitarist.' Lola recognised Sam Andrew from photo-graphs of Big Brother and the Holding Company. 'I'm coming,' Janis Joplin mouthed to Sam Andrew. She got up.

'I'm so glad that we sat next to each other,' Janis Joplin said to Lola. 'Me too,' said Lola.

Lola looked around. She saw Brian Jones sitting cross-legged in an aisle, in the dirt. He was clearly waiting for the concert to start. The arena was totally packed. Lola thought that Brian Jones probably hadn't been able to find a seat. He looked comfortable and happy. Lola was relieved to see him awake. And alive.

The first band to play was The Association. Lola hadn't liked their previous hits 'Along Comes Mary' and 'Cherish'. The Association was playing their hit record 'Windy'. Lola was irritated by 'Windy'. She thought it was a tedious song with tepid lyrics. Lyrics about a character called Windy having stormy eyes and wings that fly. 'Windy' couldn't have been less interesting if it had been about stomach pains and flatulence, she thought.

Lola mostly watched the audience and made notes. There was peacefulness in the air, and joy. Lola had never seen mass happiness. She thought that most people probably hadn't. Most people had seen photographs of people in pain or in shock or in fear, but there were not many instances she could think of that contained an image of a lot of people radiating happiness. It wasn't the happiness of a victorious crowd at a football match or a soccer game. That sort of happiness involved someone else's defeat. This happiness, to Lola, looked like a pure happiness. Maybe she was witnessing a revolution? Maybe the world really was about to change. Maybe people would no longer be estranged from each other. Maybe everyone would be linked and joined and connected.

It was dark by the time Eric Burdon and The Animals started playing. Lola had heard them before. She liked Eric Burdon. There was a grittiness to Eric Burdon. It was in his voice, in his singing and in his person. Eric Burdon was short and solid and had a depth to him, Lola thought. He had belted out The Rolling Stones' 'Paint it Black' until you felt you were enveloped by some of that blackness, some of that pain. Lola looked at Brian Jones. He was applauding wildly.

Simon and Garfunkel took the stage. They looked young and innocent. Maybe it was because of their clean-cut, more fresh-faced appearance and the sweetness of their music, Lola thought. They were singing 'Homeward Bound'. Lola tried not to think about why she was going to go home to Australia in a few months and she tried not to think about what the future Mr Former Rock Star might be doing.

It was one-thirty a.m. by the time the night was over. People were moving to the camping area near the arena of the football field at the Monterey Peninsula College, which was close by. There were sleeping bags everywhere. The aroma of pot drifted through the air.

Lola went back to her motel room, not far from the fairground. A group of people, mostly musicians, were standing around in the grounds of the motel, talking and drinking and smoking. Lola went straight to her room. She'd been lucky to get a motel room. She'd heard that every motel and hotel within a thirty-minute radius of the fairground was completely booked out.

The room had a king-sized bed. Lola had never slept in a king-sized bed. She looked at a series of knobs on the bedhead and discovered that for ten cents, she could make the bed vibrate for ten minutes. America, Lola thought, was just extraordinary. It had non-fat ice-cream, chubby-teen sections in department stores and vibrating beds. She put ten cents into the slot on the bedhead and lay down. The bed began to rumble and shake. Lola didn't like it. She started to feel sick. She had to get up and wait for the bed to stop vibrating before she could sit down again.

That night she dreamt about a woman who was walking very, very slowly. The woman was covered in layers of rags with ripped edges. Her clothes were so torn it looked as though she was wearing rows of stained and ragged fringed trimming. She looked hypnotised or drugged. But Lola knew the woman was in a daze. A daze of hunger and a daze of shock. She had short dark-brown hair and large dark-brown eyes. Lola could see that the woman must once have been very pretty. The woman stopped briefly. She tried to say something to Lola but the words fell out of her mouth in a jumbled and scrambled manner and it had been impossible for Lola to piece the fragments of sentences and separated letters together. The woman moved on. She walked past an emaciated child who was squatting in a doorway. Lola had tried to pick up the small boy and he had disintegrated in her arms like confetti. The woman had kept walking. Lola had tried to catch up to her, but she couldn't. Every time Lola got close, the woman appeared a few steps out of Lola's reach.

Lola woke up in a sweat. She looked around her. She was in Monterey, California, in a king-sized bed that could vibrate for ten minutes for ten cents. There was no short-haired, dark-eyed woman and no small skeletal boy. Lola got in the shower. She needed to wash off that dream. It felt as though it was still stuck to her skin.

Decades later, Lola would almost stop in her tracks when, watching a documentary filmed in the Warsaw Ghetto, Lola would see that woman with her slow, only partly-alive walk and her shocked, dazed face, walking on one of the squalid, over-crowded streets. In the film, the woman walked past a small hollow-cheeked boy squatting in a doorway. Lola would not be able to sleep for the next few nights trying to work out how you could dream about people you'd never seen.

Lola stood in the shower in the bathroom of her Monterey motel room for more than twenty minutes before she felt cleansed of her dream. She got dressed and went straight to the fairgrounds. Mama Cass was sitting in almost the same seat. There was an empty seat two seats down. She said hello to Mama Cass as she squeezed past her.

Mama Cass, Lola knew, was born Ellen Naomi Cohen. No one who was called Ellen Naomi Cohen could be anything other than Jewish. Lola contemplated mentioning to Mama Cass that she, too, was Jewish. She decided against it. Meeting another Jew was no big deal for American Jews. They didn't treat you as though you were a relative or an old friend. Being a fellow Jew seemed almost inconsequential. It wasn't like that in Melbourne. In Melbourne it was a big deal. You were embraced. If you were under thirty you got your cheeks pinched, your weight and appearance commented on, and, if you were single, your potential in the marriage market evaluated. When one Jew met another Jew there was an instant connection. A connection that Lola sometimes, in Melbourne, felt was constricting, yet here in America she found herself missing. Lola decided to introduce herself to Mama Cass anyway. She emphasised the word Bensky, but the friendly expression on Mama Cass's face remained the same.

Lola was half-watching Canned Heat, on the stage. She didn't think the band was very inspiring and decided that the readers of *Rock-Out* could live without a report on Canned Heat. Lola was waiting for Janis Joplin to perform. She very much hoped that Janis Joplin would do well. She knew Janis Joplin would feel terrible if she didn't. Canned Heat finished their set.

Some stagehands rearranged the equipment, and then suddenly there was Janis Joplin fronting Big Brother and the Holding Company. Janis Joplin was wearing jeans and a top. She looked raw and unadorned. It took her less than one minute to stamp her foot down and take control of the stage. By the time she got to 'Ball and Chain' you could feel that Janis Joplin had seized every one of the seven thousand people in the audience. There was hardly any movement in the arena.

Janis Joplin began the song very slowly, singing about sitting at her window just looking at the rain. A minute later, her soul was pouring out with every note. Shaking her head and stamping one leg, she was half-singing, half-crying, with her eyes closed and her face twisted and contorted, she cried out, asking herself, the audience, God, anyone, why love had to be like a ball and chain.

The pain in her face and in her voice as she lingered over the word 'pain' later in the song, was almost painful to watch. Lola could see that Janis Joplin was lost. Lost in her wounds and injuries and aches. You could almost touch the lacerations and inflammations of her heart. Lola didn't know how Janis Joplin was going to emerge from that immersion.

Lola looked at Mama Cass. Mama Cass was open-mouthed in astonishment. 'Wow,' she kept saying. When Janis Joplin sang the very last note, the audience erupted with wild applause. Slowly Janis Joplin started to smile. She looked happy. She bowed and began to walk off the stage. Halfway across the stage, the walk turned into a skip and then a jump. The arena, on that Saturday afternoon, felt as though it had been set alight.

Lola saw Janis Joplin later in the day. Janis Joplin ran up to her. 'Was I good? Was I good?' she said.

'You were fabulous,' Lola said. Lola knew that a lot of people must have already said the same thing to Janis Joplin, but Janis Joplin, despite her excitement, looked as though she couldn't quite believe what had happened.

'They've asked us to go on again tomorrow,' Janis Joplin said. 'Isn't that groovy?' She suddenly clasped her head. 'Oh, Jesus, what am I going to wear?' she said, and looked quite anxious as she asked the question.

Lola wished she could miraculously come up with something wonderful that Janis Joplin could wear.

Lola used to frequently have a fantasy in which she made Renia beautiful clothes. She would make Renia exquisitely constructed tailored suits, and evening dresses with lace and Lurex inserts. In her head, Lola designed and made outfits for Renia for every season. Shorts and tops and cotton dresses for summer, cocktail dresses for more formal occasions, and suits and skirts for when Renia went into the city. The truth was that Lola couldn't even sew on a button. The dressmaking fantasies were as soothing to Lola as her car-crash daydreams. In the fantasies, Renia would shine with excitement at all her new clothes and glow like the adored youngest child she once was. Lola partly felt she was rescuing Renia from her sadness with beautiful clothes. Lola thought that the preoccupation of trying to rescue their parents from the past could easily eat away at the lives of children of survivors.

'I have a beautiful old Singer sewing machine that I bought in a second-hand shop,' Janis Joplin said.

'One of the ones with gold filigree on the black machine?' said Lola.

'Yes,' said Janis Joplin. 'Aren't they beautiful? Do you sew, too?'

'No,' said Lola. 'I wish I could.'

'The first thing I made on the sewing machine was a blue velvet dress to wear on stage,' said Janis Joplin. 'I also made a dress out of a Madras bedspread.'

Lola was impressed that Janis Joplin could sew. It was such a domestic thing to be able to do. Janis Joplin, with her rough edges and grazed and bruised parts, didn't look like a picture of domesticity.

'I'll have to think about what to wear,' Janis Joplin said.

'That was heavy, man,' Mama Cass called out to Janis Joplin. Mama Cass stood up and clapped in Janis Joplin's direction. Janis Joplin grinned and beamed.

Jefferson Airplane was performing. Hundreds of people had joined the band onstage and were dancing. Grace Slick's strong voice rang out over the arena. The light show that engulfed the group gave Grace Slick's long pale-blue dress an incantational, otherworldly lustre. The group played 'The Ballad of You and Me and Pooneil'. Marty Balin sang the song's poignant refrain, in which he wondered whether the moon would still hang in the sky if he died, over and over again. They were haunting lines. But Lola knew that the moon would still hang in the sky. The moon seemed to keep hanging in there, regardless of whatever else was happening.

Thinking of the moon still hanging in the sky made Lola feel sad and hungry. She decided to go and get something to eat. She had two apples and a boiled egg in her bag, but she didn't feel like eating the boiled egg or the apples. She bought a pastrami sandwich and an orange.

She got back to her seat just as Otis Redding, in an impeccably tailored bluish-green suit, stepped on to the stage fully charged. The audience roared in applause. Otis Redding danced and shook and sang. He moved with small, lightning-quick, high-speed steps and taps and nods. Every nerve in his body, every part of his heart was present and pumping. He started off with 'Shake' and never stopped his high-octane, high-voltage performance. His energy and his intensity were contagious. He looked as though he was having a very good time.

There was a maturity about Otis Redding, Lola thought. He looked as though he knew exactly who he was and what he was doing. There was nothing scruffy or unfinished about him. There was no long hair, no moustache, no embroidered anything. His maturity stood out in a rock world where everyone was trying to look youthful and radical.

Otis Redding was twenty-five. He was serious. Serious about his work. And serious about his life. He'd met his wife, Zelma, when he was eighteen, and they were married when Otis Redding was twenty. They had four children and lived in a two-storey brick home on a 300-acre farm in Round Oak, Georgia.

Otis Redding wrote many of his own songs. He owned his own record label and he used the money he made to invest in real estate, and stocks and bonds. He also had his own plane, a twin-engine Beechcraft.

Lola was very impressed by Otis Redding's business acumen. She herself had just under a hundred dollars in the bank and didn't know anything about stocks and bonds or where and how or why you bought them.

Otis Redding had big ideas. He thought that music could be a unifying force and bring different races and cultures together. He had a white manager and a racially mixed band. Otis Redding's appearance in Monterey in front of a very large, largely white audience was a breakthrough for a black artist.

Otis closed his set with 'Try a Little Tenderness'. He began the song very, very slowly, every syllable saturated with tenderness, then he sped up and revved up until he himself was almost a blur and the audience was in a frenzy.

It was Sunday afternoon and Ravi Shankar was about to start playing the sitar. He sat on the stage adjusting a few strings. Before he began playing, he explained to the audience that the work he was going to play was very spiritual, and he asked that no photographs be taken. He also thanked the audience, in advance, for not smoking. 'I love you all,' he said. 'And how grateful I am for your love of me.'

In India, music concerts could last for over ten hours. Four or five hours was not an uncommon length of time for a concert. In Monterey, Ravi Shankar played for three hours. The audience was transfixed, mesmerised. Lola was restless, fidgety and bored. Three hours of sitar playing was a long time. She shifted in her seat, looked at her watch and studied the audience. She felt a little guilty for not being able to partake in this exchange of love.

Years later, to Lola's horror, she saw herself in the outtakes of D.A. Pennebaker's documentary of the Monterey International Pop Festival. The audience was still, engrossed and transported. And there was Lola. Looking to her right and to her left unmoved by Ravi Shankar.

Lola was utterly alert later that night when Janis Joplin and Big Brother and the Holding Company took the stage again. Janis Joplin had bought a new outfit. She was wearing a tunic top made out of a gold lamé knitted fabric and matching gold lamé knitted bell-bottom pants. She wore delicate, pointed-toe, slip-on shoes with a low heel. She had what looked like pancake make-up on her face, which Lola thought she didn't need. It emphasised the marks on her skin. Although Lola knew that no one watching Janis Joplin sing would be examining her skin.

Again, Janis Joplin began 'Ball and Chain' slowly. Two minutes later, all of her intensity was evident. On stage, Janis Joplin changed into someone else. Someone who had no girlishness, no awkwardness, no gaiety. On stage, she turned into someone who was charged with pain. Filled with longing. Someone with a lot of love. And a heart that had been tilted. In the middle of the pain and the longing was a piercing sexuality. It punctured and penetrated every syllable she sang. The audience went crazy. Something about Janis Joplin's pain and her ability to open herself up, to feel so much, moved Lola deeply. But Janis Joplin's burning sexuality disturbed her. Lola thought she probably envied Janis Joplin, her ability to be so in touch with that part of herself. It was the opposite of plotting diets.

While The Group With No Name and then Buffalo Springfield played, Lola made notes to herself. Notes about trying to think more about her sexuality. Although when she'd filled less than a page of her notebook, she realised she wasn't at all sure how to even begin to put this plan into action. And it wasn't something you could easily ask other people's advice about.

Seeing Pete Townshend brought Lola back to earth. She stopped thinking about herself or the more carnal, libidinous aspects of Janis Joplin. She looked at Pete Townshend on stage with the rest of The Who and could still feel the discomfort of him yelling at her. The group was dressed as though they were dandies from another century. A cascade of white frills ran down the front of Pete Townshend's shirt.

His jacket looked as though it was made from patterned satin-brocade upholstery fabric. A dandy was defined as 'a man unduly concerned with a stylish and fashionable appearance'. Lola didn't know why the description fitted Pete Townshend so well. Probably because of the wilful arrogance of his expression.

Roger Daltrey wore a gold floral cape fastened around his neck. Long black fringing hung from the edges of the cape. He looked like a capricious prince from the hinterlands of Czechoslovakia. Halfway through the first song, Keith Moon, The Who's drummer, already looked demented. He shook his head ferociously to the beat, his mouth was wide open in a huge O, his face was almost a blur, and his hair was flying everywhere. Lola didn't know how his head could survive all that banging and crashing and nodding.

'This is where it all ends,' John Entwistle, the bass player, said to the audience before the band launched into 'My Generation', with its stuttering and stammering and angry repetitive utterings. Roger Daltrey sang. In a firm, fervent voice, he declared his hope that he would die before he got old, again and again, before swinging his handheld microphone in a wide and carefree circle over his head.

Pete Townshend upped the action. He swung his guitar around and slammed it into the floor, repeatedly. Lola saw a few of the young men in the audience beginning to look anxious. Pete Townshend continued to smash his guitar into everything he could see. The rest of the band kept playing. A nervous stagehand dashed onto the stage and removed a microphone and a microphone stand. More and more parts were flying off the guitar. Roger Daltrey was whirling round and round, his fringed cape following him, until Pete Townshend walked off the stage. Roger Daltrey, almost meekly, stopped whirling and followed him, like an obedient, younger, shorter brother.

Keith Moon kept drumming for another half a minute before he kicked his whole drum kit over with his feet. Smoke billowed around the stage from a smoke bomb Pete Townshend had lit. It looked as though an amplifier had exploded. The smashing and breaking and wrecking had been carried out with remarkable detachment. There was no anger, no passion, no outrage, no feeling and, Lola thought, no meaning. Lola had seen The Who perform before and had been just as puzzled by what they were doing.

She thought it was a mistake for the group to have John Entwistle walk up to the microphone and say, 'This is where it all ends.' Not much was ending, she thought. Was the ending a broken guitar and some possibly dented drums? People who had known real endings would know this was just a performance. Lola thought the statement, which was clearly meant to sound portentous, had simply sounded pretentious.

Lola hoped her reception to The Who wasn't clouded by Pete Townsend's rudeness. She didn't think it was. There was something disturbing about the detachment and sterility of the vandalism. 'In England they've reached a dead end in destruction,' Lola heard Brian Jones say to someone. That was the sort of quote from Brian Jones Lola had been hoping for.

Lola decided to give The Grateful Dead a miss. A short walk, she thought, would do her good. She needed to clear her head. She walked over to the Temple Beth El stand and bought herself a pastrami sandwich on rye bread. She'd never had pastrami, a highly seasoned, smoked and thinly sliced beef, before Monterey. In New York the Jewish delis she'd been to had all served hot pastrami sandwiches. She'd never seen pastrami in Melbourne.

Lola looked at her sandwich. It was a big sandwich. She thought there were probably about fifteen to twenty slices of pastrami in the sandwich. They were paper thin, but there were a lot of them. She thought that this sandwich probably contained well over five hundred calories. She could have had five or six apples for that. Or five or six boiled eggs. Or four ounces of chocolate.

Lola got back in time for Jimi Hendrix. Brian Jones, looking clear-eyed and fresh, introduced Jimi Hendrix as 'The most exciting guitar player I've ever heard.' Jimi Hendrix came onstage. He was smiling and looked happy to be there. He was wearing very tight red trousers and a bright yellow shirt with ruffles down the front and around the cuffs. A metal belt with a medallion hanging from the buckle and a brightly coloured scarf were tied around his waist. He wore a black-and-white vest over the yellow shirt. Somehow the outfit, like all of Jimi Hendrix's outfits, worked. Jimi looked as wild as his clothes. Only his smile was wide and slow.

Just before he started playing, he looked down at his guitar with unadulterated tenderness. The sort of tenderness you mostly saw in movies. Lola noticed that Jimi Hendrix had gum in his mouth. She had no idea how he could chew gum and sing. But he did. He played 'Wild Thing'. He sang as his guitar wailed alongside him. He looked as though he was hardly touching the guitar, as though it were just another part of his body as easy to move and manipulate as his fingers or toes or tongue. In between notes he chewed his gum with a palpable sensuality. Every chew looked like a sexual manoeuvre. 'Sock it to me one more time,' he sang, elongating the S until that formerly innocent S resembled a prolonged seduction.

'Wild Thing,' he sang, while he played his guitar behind his back and above his head, and his guitar whined and cried and strutted and sang. Jimi Hendrix walked and squatted and twisted and, without warning, bent down and somersaulted over the stage, all the while playing his guitar. Lola felt he could brush his teeth, eat a meal, do anything and never let go of a note on his guitar.

In the middle of a chorus of 'Wild Thing' he played a few bars of 'Strangers in the Night' with one hand while he held his other arm up in the air, in front of his face, as though he were shielding himself from something. Maybe his own passion? Or maybe he was having a brief shy moment.

'Wild Thing,' he sang, as he humped his guitar against an amplifier before walking to the front of the stage and dropping to his knees. He put the guitar on the floor and played it, kneeling and with one hand, while his body jerked and throbbed to the music. You could almost hear the audience gasping.

With the rest of the band still playing, Jimi held up both of his hands, looked at the guitar lying on the stage and beckoned it to him. But the guitar didn't move. It remained on stage. Jimi kept trying. He was communing with his guitar. Summoning it to him. As though the guitar could feel the connection between them as powerfully as he did. Was he trying to see if it would respond without being caressed, Lola wondered. Jimi played the instrument again, with one hand, while his pelvis and his trunk thrusted and quivered and rocked. This was a love scene as torrid and tempestuous as any Lola had seen.

Jimi Hendrix stood up. He was holding a small can of lighter fluid in his hand. He started squirting the lighter fluid onto the guitar. The fluid squirted out in a thin line as though Jimi was urinating or ejaculating. Jimi knelt down and kissed the guitar in a prayer-like movement. He lit a match and threw it onto the guitar. The guitar was alight. Jimi, still on his knees, and with his hands cupped, beckoned the fire to rise. It looked like a religious rite. A climax to a complex ritual of worship. A burning and a returning to the earth.

Jimi Hendrix sprayed the remainder of the lighter fluid onto the guitar. He then picked it up and started wildly smashing it against the floor until it was in pieces. The audience looked stunned before bursting into feverish applause.

There was a short break, too short, Lola thought, before The Mamas and the Papas came onto the stage. The Mamas and the Papas with their clear voices and lilting melodies had a Californian wholesomeness about them. Mama Cass introduced one of their big hits, 'California Dreamin''. 'We're gonna do this song because we like it and because it is responsible for our great wealth,' she said, laughing.

Mama Cass looked at ease on the stage. Her voice was strong and unencumbered. There was no hint that this voice might have had to struggle through a lot of fat. Maybe, Lola thought, vocal chords were completely detached from any excess weight their owners carried. Mama Cass was wearing a voluminous dress with short, wide sleeves. Gathered just below the bust, it contained yards and yards of fabric. Lola felt pained looking at all the fabric it took to cover Mama Cass's body.

Mamas Cass's voice soared and floated. She swayed from side to side to the music. Her body's separate parts, which were too big to move in unison, followed a few seconds behind the beat. Lola wanted to cry. She felt sad seeing how much of herself Mama Cass had to haul and heave for every move.

Michelle Phillips was moving effortlessly. At one point she looked adoringly at Denny Doherty as he sang a couple of solo lines. Michelle had been in love with Denny. Mama Cass was still in love with Denny. Mama Cass had been in love with Denny for a long time. Denny flirted with Mama Cass, but for Denny there was no real intention beyond the flirting, Lola had been told.

Denny and Michelle had had an affair. Michelle had tried to tell her husband John Phillips that she found Denny very attractive but John had dismissed as ridiculous the notion that anything could happen between Michelle and Denny.

Mama Cass had wept when she had been told about the affair between Michelle and Denny. It had been Denny who told her. He also told John. John and Michelle had separated, temporarily. John had moved out and shared a house with Denny, who had sort of apologised to him. John and Michelle had briefly reconciled, but it didn't last. Michelle got fired from the group. John had composed the letter telling her she was out of the group and Denny and Mama Cass had also signed it. Three months later Michelle was asked to rejoin.

John and Michelle got back together, again, too. They were together now, and the strains of 'California Dreamin'' and 'Monday, Monday' and 'Dream A Little Dream of Me' could be heard all over the Monterey County Fairground, where people were coming together, with love, to be happy, be free and wear flowers.

Lola caught a plane from Monterey to Los Angeles. She had interviews arranged with The Mamas and the Papas and Sonny and Cher.

She was also hoping to interview The Byrds. The plane was a very small plane. It was a short flight but Lola really didn't like small planes. They felt tinny, to her. Like large saucepans or stockpots rattling through the troposphere.

She had been on a small plane once before, in Melbourne. All the passengers had had to be weighed on industrial scales before anyone was allowed to board. Lola had been horrified at the thought of being put on the scales in front of all the other passengers. She'd been even more horrified at the thought that she might be too heavy to be allowed to board.

'I haven't got any luggage,' she'd said, in an effort to appear lighter to the man doing the weighing. 'Please don't tell me what I weigh,' she'd added.

'The plane isn't full,' he'd said. Lola took that to mean that if the plane had been full, she might not have made it onto the flight. To her relief, no one was told they had to be weighed for this flight from Monterey to Los Angeles.

The only other passengers on this very small plane were Eric Burdon and the Animals and Ravi Shankar. Ravi Shankar was very quiet. And not overly friendly to Lola. She wondered if he could possibly have known that she was impatient and agitated when he was playing. He looked very spiritual, the sort of person who might know things without having to have actually witnessed them. The sort of person who might have a sixth sense. Lola decided that she didn't really believe in sixth senses and that Ravi Shankar was either tired or just wanted to be private. She adjusted her sunglasses. She was wearing a new pair of sunglasses she'd bought in Monterey. She thought they made her look interesting. She kept them on in the plane despite the fact that the interior of the plane was already quite dimly lit.

Before the plane had even reached its cruising altitude, Eric Burdon was fast asleep. He clearly wasn't made nervous by small planes, Lola thought. Lola was sitting next to John Weider, The Animals' lead guitarist and violinist. John Weider was Lola's age. He had been in bands since he was very young. He played with Steve Marriott and the Moments before Steve Marriott and half The Moments went on to form The Small Faces. 'I don't like small planes,' Lola said to John Weider. 'They make me nervous.'

'Are you Jewish?' John Weider said.

Lola laughed. 'Do you think I'm Jewish because I'm nervous?' she said.

'Maybe,' he said.

'I'm very Jewish,' she said.

'I'm Jewish, too,' John Weider said.

'I thought so,' Lola said. 'Because of the violin.'

'I studied classical violin for nine years from the time I was seven till I was sixteen,' he said. 'I also took up the guitar and the bass.'

John Weider had a large Afro hairstyle. She thought his hair was probably naturally curly, even though he came from England where more and more men were perming curls into their hair. Jews tended to have curly hair, Lola had noticed. Mama Cass, Linda Eastman and Lillian Roxon seemed to be exceptions to that rule.

Lola was about to ask John Weider if his parents minded him being in a rock band, when the plane lurched violently to the right. Lola gripped her seat. No one else looked alarmed. Ravi Shankar had the same peaceful expression on his face as he'd had when he was playing the sitar. Eric Burdon was still asleep. The plane felt as though it was bumping into solid pockets of air. Lola felt a bit sick. She hoped her sunglasses hid her queasiness.

'Please make sure your seatbelts are on and firmly fastened,' the captain said. 'This turbulence will be over in about two minutes and we will be landing in Los Angeles very soon after that.' Lola looked at Ravi Shankar. He did look a little green now, she thought. She smiled at him. He smiled back.

She wondered if she had enough time to ask John Weider how his parents felt about him being in a rock band. She looked out of the window. They were just about to land.

7

Mama Cass was holding a large, highly polished, bright-green Granny Smith apple. Lola, who was there to interview The Mamas and the Papas, wondered why Mama Cass was carrying an apple. Maybe she, like Lola, was planning to go on a diet. Mama Cass had just arrived in her new yellow Aston Martin at the Bel Air, Los Angeles, a house that John and Michelle Phillips shared. Denny Doherty wasn't there yet. Maybe he was still in his Laurel Canyon home that had once belonged to the actress Mary Astor.

John and Michelle's spectacular house on Bel Air Road had been owned by Jeanette MacDonald, who had starred in many Hollywood musicals with Nelson Eddy and Maurice Chevalier. The house was on two-and-a-half acres of carefully planted and manicured and terraced gardens. There were trees and shrubs and flowers and a grapevine and a rose arbour and a fountain. A path led from the house to the swimming pool, which had curved instead of straight edges. Next to the pool was a small version of the main house. It had a living room, a fireplace, a bedroom, a bathroom and a kitchen. There were also stables that Jeanette MacDonald's husband had built to house their horses. To go with the house, John and Michelle had a 1932 Rolls-Royce

Tourer, a 1932 Rolls-Royce Limousine and a 1957 Rolls-Royce Silver Door Coupé.

Lola found the house and the cars a little overwhelming. But then Lola found Los Angeles a little overwhelming. There was too much of it and everything was a long way from everything else. The cornflakes and the milk in the supermarket only came in giant sizes. There were sixteen-year-olds driving very large cars. And the police were nowhere near as nice as they were in New York. Their guns and their expressions looked menacing.

Lola had rented a second-hand Volkswagen. Two days ago, she had been pulled over by a policeman on Wilshire Boulevard while she had been trying to navigate several unnamed streets and eerily similar roads. He had asked for her ID. 'In Australia we don't have to carry ID,' she said.

'You're not in Australia any more, Miss,' he said. 'I could arrest you on the spot.'

Lola didn't want to be arrested a second time. Her arrest for shoplifting, when she was ten, had not been a picnic. Lola didn't think that Renia and Edek would take the news of another arrest any better than they'd taken the previous arrest.

'I promise I'll carry my passport with me everywhere I go, Officer,' she said. She had learned to address all policemen as 'Officer' from Edek, who was an impatient driver and was continually being caught for exceeding the speed limit. 'I'm sorry, Officer' was always the first thing Edek said. He often repeated it several times. Being apologetic to policemen was always a good thing, Edek said.

Edek had had his own run-in with police. It had been with the American Military Police, in Feldafing, the camp for displaced people not far from Munich, where Edek and Renia were still sleeping in barracks and still desperately trying to get out of Germany, after the war. Edek had been wheeling and dealing, on a very small scale, on the black market. He had collected and sold cigarettes and coffee rations given to him by the Red Cross in an effort to buy Renia some butter. He finally had a pound of butter for Renia, when he was stopped by an American military policeman.

'I should arrest you for having more butter than your rations entitle you to,' the American military policeman had said.

'I'm very sorry, Officer,' Edek said. He still barely weighed a hundred-and-twenty pounds. The American military policeman grinned at him.

'I'll let you go if you eat the butter,' he said.

'Now, Officer?' Edek said.

'Yes, now,' he said.

'Yes, Officer,' said Edek. He ate the pound of butter. He was sick with abdominal pains and diarrhoea for a week.

'I'm really sorry, Officer,' Lola said to the policeman who'd pulled her over. 'And thank you for explaining the situation to me.'

The cop nodded. 'Don't forget, this is America,' he said.

Lola drove off, slowly. She was going to the Ambassador Hotel, where she was staying. She had chosen the 500-room Ambassador Hotel from a hotel directory at the airport because it was expensive and, in her admittedly limited experience, she felt that expensive hotels, unlike their cheaper counterparts, would not ask for a deposit. Lola had no money. Or, more accurately, she couldn't find the money that she had. If finding which bank her salary from *Rock-Out* had been transferred to was difficult in London and New York, it was impossible in

Los Angeles. You could drive around Los Angeles for a year and you might still not find the right bank.

Lola had been stunned when she had first seen the Ambassador Hotel. It was huge. It occupied twenty-three-and-a-half acres at 3400 Wilshire Boulevard. The hotel's Cocoanut Grove nightclub featured entertainers like Frank Sinatra, Barbra Streisand, Judy Garland, Louis Armstrong, Nat King Cole, Bing Crosby, Lena Horne, Little Richard, Liberace and Liza Minnelli. Marilyn Monroe had begun her career as a client of the modelling agency that had its office just next to the swimming pool at the Ambassador Hotel.

Diana Ross and The Supremes were staying on the same floor of the hotel as Lola. They were performing at the Cocoanut Grove. Lola was bothered by the spelling of Cocoanut. It was cocoa and coconut. Not cocoanut. She knew the hotel was owned by the Schine family. It sounded like a Jewish name. Lola wondered if they were Jews who could not yet spell well. That was before she discovered that G. David Schine, the president of the Ambassador Hotel, was the son of J. Myer Schine. The family had established a number of successful business ventures in hotels, real estate and movie theatres. Lola knew that if the Schine family had done that well, they probably knew how to spell.

Earlier in the day, Lola had passed Diana Ross in the corridor outside her room. Apart from being startlingly beautiful, Diana Ross was very slender and light-footed. She looked as though her feet, in her high stiletto heels, hardly touched the carpeted floor when she walked. She walked with the delicacy and grace of an antelope. Lola felt like an elephant.

To Lola's relief, no one at the Ambassador Hotel had asked her for a deposit. All the staff had been very friendly. Lola thought the friendliness must come with the extra dollars. No one at the Horwood Hotel in New York had ever been anything but surly or grumpy.

Lola was checking out of the Ambassador the next day. She had finally located her money and rented a small studio apartment. The apartment was on Sunset Strip, on Sunset Boulevard, diagonally across the road from the Whisky a Go Go.

John Phillips looked a bit agitated that his fellow Papa, Denny Doherty, still hadn't turned up. John, who was born John Edmund Andrew Phillips, a name that sounded to Lola as though he were part of Britain's royal family, did have a slightly patrician air about him. Maybe that was because he was older than Lola. John Phillips, who was thirty-one, was eleven years older than Lola and nine years older than Michelle. John Phillips had given Lola a tour of the house when she had first arrived. He was charming, but Lola had felt wary of his charm. Lola thought he was a little condescending to Michelle. Someone had told her that John's response to Michelle about her affair with Denny had been, 'Don't fuck with my tenor.'

John's tenor, John had decided, was clearly not going to show up. Lola thought that that might be a good thing given the convoluted romantic interconnections between Denny and Mama Cass and Michelle and Denny and Michelle and John. Although Lola knew that Michelle was now pregnant with John's child, Lola thought that the possibly still-raw entanglements might have complicated things. She had been told that Denny had been trying to drink Michelle out of his life. But maybe complications like this were a part of everyday life in this part of the world. This was Los Angeles and movie stars and celebrities did wild things, which were reported with gusto by gossip columnists and lapped up by the public.

John Phillips wandered off and left Lola with Michelle and Mama Cass. Mama Cass was wearing a floral-print cotton dress that was gathered below the bust and came to just above her knees. Mama Cass's legs, Lola noticed, were not that fat. Her ankles and calves looked an almost normal size.

Mama Cass was still holding her Granny Smith apple. She put it on the table in front of her. They were sitting in what Lola thought must be the sunroom or part of the kitchen. Lola wondered if Michelle felt awkward sitting with two fat women. She didn't look awkward. She'd given Mama Cass a big kiss when Mama Cass had arrived. There was something unexpectedly sweet about Michelle Phillips, Lola thought. Michelle had brought Lola a drink and made sure there was enough space on the table for Lola's tape recorder and her notebook.

'Do the two of you get on well together?' Lola said.

'We do,' said Michelle. 'We've always – or almost always – been close.'

'Michelle is a really good person,' Mama Cass said. 'And looking the way she does, she could easily be a bitch and everyone would still fall in love with her. But she's not a bitch. She's very beautiful and she's a good person and a very good friend.'

'We're all beautiful in a different way,' said Michelle.

'That's lame,' said Mama Cass. 'You can't be beautiful if you're fat. No one sees your beauty.'

'Maybe that's an asset,' Lola said. 'You have to try harder.'

'Being fat is never an asset,' said Mama Cass. Mama Cass was probably right, Lola thought. Being fat was probably never an asset. And it took up a lot of time. She was sure Michelle Phillips had never spent even one minute planning a diet.

'Cass is brilliantly clever,' Michelle said. 'She had an IQ of 165 when she was still a child.'

'We joke,' said Mama Cass, 'that she's the body and I'm the brain.'

'She is the brain,' said Michelle. 'She does all the talking when we are on stage because she does it so well. And she's so funny. I don't feel comfortable talking on stage and I don't do it well. I'm comfortable with the fact that Cass talks on stage and John talks to the press. He's good at that.'

John certainly was good at that, Lola thought. He'd given Lola a blow-by-blow account of all of their successes, every album and each single. He'd also explained how unique they were as a group and how he had trained Mama Cass not to belt out songs, but to 'blend, blend, blend' her voice with Michelle's.

Michelle Phillips did seem comfortable in herself. She sat and walked with the air and ease of someone who was at home with her arms and chest and pelvic bones and feet. When Michelle met John Phillips, he was married with two children. He divorced his wife and married Michelle, who was eighteen. Lola wondered how Michelle could still look radiant and at peace with herself after losing her mother when she was young, and growing up with a constantly unravelling series of four stepmothers and half-a-dozen changes of location.

Mama Cass bit into her apple. Lola was surprised that Mama Cass had brought her own apple. Although she shouldn't be surprised. Lola understood the necessity of making sure you had the right food when you were on a specific diet. And maybe John and Michelle didn't have much fruit in the house. Lola couldn't see any. Renia always had fruit in the house. Even when they were very poor. She always had a bowl of apples, oranges, mandarins and bananas on the table. And, when they were in season, a bowl of cherries. Renia saw fruit as a symbol of wealth. In Renia's terms, if you could afford fruit, you were definitely not starving.

John and Michelle Phillips had other symbols of wealth. The cars, the Limoges porcelain, the Venetian glass and the drugs. An open container of assorted pills was in the living room. It was placed there as though it were a bowl of nuts or sweets for guests to snack on. John had offered Lola some. He hadn't said what they were. Maybe, Lola thought, you were supposed to be so familiar with what everyone was taking that you knew what you were being offered.

'No thanks,' she'd said to John Phillips. 'I'm already a disappointment to my parents because I'm fat and I'm not a lawyer. I think it might kill them if I started taking drugs.'

'That's so cute,' John Phillips had said. Lola didn't know which part was cute – the part about her being a disappointment, or the part about her killing her parents.

'Anyway, I don't like being out of control,' she'd added.

'This isn't being out of control,' John Phillips said. 'It's an expansion of your control.'

'I'm on a diet,' Mama Cass said to Lola.

'I wish people didn't make so much of Cass's size,' said Michelle. 'Every line that's written about us mentions Cass's size.'

'When people describe me they don't say I'm smart, which I am, they say I'm fat,' said Mama Cass. 'Everyone mentions Michelle's looks, too.'

'Maybe that's just part of being female,' said Lola. 'Guys can be thin or short or fat or covered in acne and it doesn't seem to matter. It's not reported.'

'That's true, and probably always will be,' said Mama Cass.

'I wish people would concentrate on Cass's voice,' Michelle said.

'Maybe they will when I've lost weight,' said Mama Cass. 'I've decided that now I'm a mother, I'm going to lose weight.'

Mama Cass had given birth to a daughter a few months before the Monterey International Pop Festival. No one other than Mama Cass knew who the father was. 'I was surprised to find myself pregnant,' said Mama Cass. 'I'd been told that at my size my chances of conceiving were very slim.' She laughed. 'My chances of conception were the only slim part of me. When the doctor told me I was unlikely to get pregnant again I knew straightaway that I was going to have this baby'.

Lola couldn't understand why a woman's size would affect her ability to get pregnant. The sperm only had to travel up one of the two fallopian tubes and fertilise an egg. And, after a while, the fertilised egg moved on to the womb. Lola thought Mama Cass's fallopian tubes or her womb weren't where her fat was stored. Still, it seemed to be a commonly held belief.

'My mother has been telling me for years that fat girls don't find it easy to get pregnant,' said Lola.

'Do you mean your mother wanted you to get pregnant?' said Michelle, looking worried.

'No. Not at all,' said Lola. 'She was absolutely sure I wouldn't be having sex. Her remark about me having trouble getting pregnant was usually preceded by how fat girls don't get boyfriends and no one wants to marry them.'

'That's probably true, unless you're rich or famous,' said Mama Cass. 'Do you have a boyfriend?'

'Sort of,' said Lola. 'But I think he'd prefer someone slimmer.'

'Dump him,' said Mama Cass.

'I'm not rich or famous enough,' said Lola. Her answer was supposed to be a joke, but when it came out, it didn't sound at all funny.

Michelle left the room. Lola wondered if the conversation had become too focused on fat.

'Did you feel well when you were pregnant?' Lola asked Mama Cass. She wasn't sure why she wanted to know. Maybe she was just checking out what a pregnancy for a fat person would be like. She didn't think she was asking the question for the readers of *Rock-Out*.

'I felt great,' said Mama Cass. 'I took acid five times when I was pregnant.'

Lola knew she would definitely not be mentioning this fact in *Rock-Out*.

'I did the things I always did,' said Mama Cass. 'I worked, I recorded, I went out, I had lots of friends over.'

'You took acid five times when you were pregnant?' Lola said.

'Yes,' said Mama Cass. 'Five times. I don't feel I hurt my daughter in any way. I think you know instinctively what you can do. I just continued doing what I was doing before I was pregnant.'

Lola wondered if Mama Cass had continued smoking joints and snorting cocaine. Probably, she thought. Mama Cass was very emphatic about not having changed any part of her life.

'I gave birth to a very healthy little girl,' Mama Cass said.

'I know,' said Lola. 'I've heard she's beautiful.'

Mama Cass shifted around in her chair. 'Does being fat disturb you?' she said to Lola. 'You're not as fat as I am. I know that.'

'I'm very fat,' said Lola.

'Not as fat as I am,' said Mama Cass.

'You've just had a baby,' Lola said. She couldn't believe she was arguing with Mama Cass about who was fatter than whom.

'You're very kind,' said Mama Cass. 'I was this big before I got pregnant.'

'Does being fat disturb you?' Mama Cass said again.

'It must disturb me,' said Lola. 'I'm always planning a diet, or going on a diet, or breaking a diet. The fact that I'm fat drives my mother crazy. She plans all sorts of remedies for me. And issues all sorts of threats. And enlists her friends to harangue me about being fat.'

'Being fat sets you apart,' said Mama Cass. 'You know you're not like everyone else.'

'It does shut you out,' said Lola.

'So does being famous,' said Mama Cass. 'When you're famous, you really don't get to know people any more. Everyone wants you to like them, to be their best friend, so they show you the best parts of themselves and you don't ever see who they really are.'

Renia was always emphasising how you couldn't ever really know who people were. 'You will never know what people are capable of doing,' she would say. Lola knew that Renia knew. And that she, herself, never would know. Lola often wished she could erase that knowledge from Renia's memory. She wished she could just wish it away. It was depressing to Lola that wishes didn't work.

'At least I don't get perfect strangers taunting me,' Mama Cass said. 'When I worked as a waitress I'd have people call out things like, "Hey, Fatty, you forgot our orders – or did you eat them all yourself?"'

'It sounds funny now,' said Lola. 'But I know it can't have been funny then.'

'I was a thin child and not a very good eater until my sister was born when I was seven,' Mama Cass said. 'I'd been an only child for seven years and I think sharing my parents wasn't easy for me. I think I thought that I would please my parents by eating well. And I just didn't stop. By the time I was seventeen, I weighed 180 pounds. Also, my grandmother who'd lived in poverty in Poland loved feeding every-one,' Mama Cass said. 'But no one else got fat.'

'My parents are from Poland,' Lola said. 'From Lodz.'

'Were you born there?' said Mama Cass.

'No,' said Lola. 'I was born in Germany. But I'm not German,' she added. 'I was born after the war.'

'Were your parents in a camp?' said Mama Cass.

'Yes, they were in Auschwitz,' Lola said.

'I'm sorry,' said Mama Cass.

'So am I,' said Lola.

'My parents took in refugees from Poland and Germany and Russia during the war,' said Mama Cass.

'The refugees must have got out just in time before it became impossible to leave,' said Lola.

'They did,' said Mama Cass. 'Most of them never saw their families again. I picked up Polish, German and Russian by listening to them.'

Lola wondered if Mama Cass had also picked up Yiddish. There was something comforting about Yiddish, Lola thought. It was the language of a time when Renia had probably been happy and still had her parents and her siblings, and still thought that she was going to become a paediatrician.

Lola had her favourite Yiddish words, which she sometimes repeated to herself. They were *Fardrayt* and *Farblondjet*, both of which meant confused, disoriented, not sound of mind. And *Faflekt*, which meant stained or dirtied, and *Narish*, which just meant stupid or foolish. If you said them together it sounded fabulous. *Fardrayt, Faflekt un Narish*, confused, stained and foolish. The words always made her laugh. She decided not to ask Mama Cass if she could speak Yiddish. Too much of the conversation had already been about being fat or being Jewish.

'My grandfather, my mother's father, was a tailor and a cantor in Poland,' Mama Cass said.

'So he could sing, too,' said Lola.

'He had a beautiful voice,' said Mama Cass. 'Everyone in the family was musical. We sang and harmonised together. My father's father, who came from Russia, would teach each of us our harmony parts and then he would conduct the whole family. I remember singing harmony when I was three or four years old.'

That sounded like a blissfully idyllic picture of family life to Lola. Renia and Edek would have thought she was crazy if she'd suggested they all sing together. Lola tried to imagine the three of them singing together. Even in her imagination she couldn't even place them all in the same room, let alone have them burst into song. Renia was always darting about. She could never stand still. She was always moving, cooking, polishing, scrubbing, cleaning. And Edek, when he wasn't working or driving the car, was sitting in his armchair buried in the plot of one of his luridly bloody books of detective fiction. Singing would have seemed like an act of lunacy.

'Did you complain when your sister was born?' Lola asked Mama Cass.

'No,' said Mama Cass. 'It wouldn't have occurred to me. We didn't talk about feelings. We were very close. My parents were committed socialists and we discussed politics a lot, but not feelings. Feelings were something that were supposed to be kept to yourself.'

Maybe the Cohen family life wasn't quite as idyllic as it seemed, despite the singing, Lola thought. 'Were your parents upset when you said you wanted to go into show business?' said Lola.

'They weren't pleased,' said Mama Cass. 'But they knew I was crazy about Broadway musicals and they let me move from Baltimore, where I'd grown up, to New York.

'I narrowly missed out on getting the part of Miss Marmelstein in the musical *I Can Get It for You Wholesale*,' said Mama Cass. 'The part went to Barbra Streisand, who was as unknown as I was. I was too fat. Although Barbra Streisand, whose looks are not the standard acceptable version of female beauty, was an unconventional choice. I would have been an even more unconventional choice.'

'Wow,' said Lola.

'I'm still annoyed,' said Mama Cass.

'Your parents must have been impressed that you almost got the part,' Lola said.

'Not really,' said Mama Cass. 'I was working as a hat-check girl and they thought I'd never make any money. My father was the second youngest of eleven children. Several of his brothers became doctors but my father wanted to be an opera singer, and when that didn't work out he began the first of a series of catering business ventures. He went bankrupt ten times when I was young. He didn't live long enough to see how rich I was going to be. He died, after a car accident. He was forty-two.'

'That's so sad,' said Lola.

'It is sad,' said Mama Cass. 'My father was a very charming, very easygoing man. He knew I wanted to be famous and he didn't ever say to me that that would be impossible.'

'Did you always want to be famous?' Lola said.

'Yes,' said Mama Cass, nodding her head with enthusiasm, the excitement of her early dreams still evident on her face. 'I wanted to wear fabulous evening gowns and be on a stage.'

'I wanted to be thin,' said Lola. She felt embarrassed at the narrow scope of her ambition.

'I used to tell people that I was going to be the most famous fat girl who ever lived,' Mama Cass said. 'And I am.'

She was right, Lola thought. Lola couldn't think of another fat female who was as famous as Mama Cass.

'I'm fat and I'm famous,' said Mama Cass. 'I weighed myself after I had my daughter and I weighed three hundred pounds. What do you weigh?'

'I don't know,' said Lola. 'I'm too nervous to weigh myself. I gauge whether I'm putting on weight or not by how tight or loose my clothes are. They're getting tighter at the moment.'

'It's not easy being fat,' Mama Cass said. 'John thought I was too fat to be in the group. The three of them were skinny and then there was me. Not even my fingers are skinny.' She paused. 'But then he heard my voice,' she said. There was something odd about the way she said that, Lola thought.

'John and I are both Virgos,' Mama Cass said. 'That could have been part of the problem, too.'

'I'm a Virgo, too,' said Lola. 'Not that I believe in astrology.'

'I don't either,' said Mama Cass. 'I don't think that was part of the problem. When you're fat, people find it easier to be rude to you, unless, of course, you're rich and famous.'

'I know that,' said Lola. 'Someone stopped me in the street in New York to ask me why I was fat.'

Mama Cass laughed. 'That's one of the things I like about New York,' she said. 'People are so much more direct. They're direct about everything. Your clothes, your hair, your politics. John is direct. He tells me I should have my own record label, which I could call Fat Records. The ads, he points out to me, could read *Another obese release from Fat*. I know that's funny, but it's not really funny. He also keeps saying that my eyes are really close together.'

'Your eyes don't look any closer together than anyone else's eyes,' said Lola.

'I don't really care what he says,' said Mama Cass. 'I'm used to it.' Mama Cass looked a bit tired. As though all the slurs and slights and jokes had taken a toll.

'What sort of diet are you on?' Lola asked Mama Cass.

'I haven't been on it for long,' Mama Cass said. 'I fast for four days of the week, usually Monday to Thursday. I have nothing but water. On the other three days I have a cup of cottage cheese in the morning and steak and green vegetables or an apple for dinner.'

'That's a very strict diet,' said Lola.

'I plan to include some more food, gradually,' said Mama Cass. 'But I want to stick to a thousand calories a day.'

'I could talk calories with you for days,' said Lola. 'I'm a walking encyclopaedia of calorie values. It's a bit sad.'

'I'm tired of being fat,' said Mama Cass. 'I'm tired of having my friends tell me that every man I go out with is only interested in my fame or my money.' Mama Cass did look tired. 'It's as though most people I know who think I am great to hang out with and have fun with think that I am too fat for anyone to want to be my lover or to fall in love with me,' Mama Cass said.

'I'm sure that's not true,' said Lola.

In Monterey, Lola had only seen the side of Mama Cass that was cheerful, generous, enthusiastic and excited. Lola felt bad. She thought she must have brought out Mama Cass's sadness.

The studio apartment Lola had rented had a small courtyard near the front of the building. Half-a-dozen people were sitting in the courtyard smoking joints. To Lola, it seemed as though everyone in LA was smoking pot. Well, maybe not everyone. The people working in the nine banks she'd been to in an effort to locate her money didn't look as though they were smoking pot. But here, on Sunset Strip, the air was dense with marijuana. Lola went into the apartment to write a postcard to Renia.

Roger Daltrey's line from The Who's 'My Generation' about hoping to die before he got old was going round and round in Lola's head. She couldn't get rid of it. She tried humming 'Humpty Dumpty', a previously irritating tune that had stayed in her head for days but which she thought would be preferable to thinking about dying before she got old. It didn't work.

Lola had had enough of death. She had grown up with the dead ricocheting around her head. She didn't want The Who's lyric to join the chorus. What if there was a God and he took the lyric seriously? Lola didn't want to die. Especially before she got old.

Renia wanted to die after the war. She had tried to kill herself. She had walked to the middle of a bridge, somewhere in Germany, and tried to jump off. She couldn't swim. She knew she would drown pretty quickly. She knew her parents and brothers and sisters were dead. Drowning didn't seem a bad option. But she couldn't jump, she told Lola, until she found out whether Edek was alive.

Lola was sure that Renia often wished she had died. 'Why did I live?' Renia used to say to Lola when Lola was small. 'Why did I live and they died?'

'I don't know,' Lola would sometimes say.

'I also don't know,' was always Renia's answer.

Renia, Lola knew, felt bad about surviving when everyone in her family died. 'You should feel proud that they didn't kill you, too,' Lola had said to Renia when Lola was about thirteen. Renia had exploded.

'I should be proud that I watched my sister and my father being murdered?' she had half-screamed. 'There is nothing to be proud of. What should I be proud of? That I could see thousands of bodies being burned in big pits, outside, when the crematoriums were too full to burn any more bodies? Should I be proud that I saw children sitting on the ground with gangrene in their legs, arms, toes and fingers? Gangrene that was caused by doctors for lunatic experiments?

'Should I be proud that the Americans and the British couldn't be bothered bombing the railway lines into Auschwitz?' said Renia. 'Especially before the Hungarians arrived. The Hungarians were in good condition, not skeletons like us. They would have survived.

Beautiful mothers and beautiful children walking to the gas. Because nobody cared. Is that something to be proud of?'

'You should be proud that you didn't die,' Lola had said, quietly.

'That is nothing to be proud of,' Renia had retorted.

Renia, Lola knew, felt she had to atone for not having died. She would never be free of that atonement. It would be as imprisoning as any prison. Renia ate her meals, mostly made from scraps and leftovers, by herself, sitting facing the sink. She ate with her back to the table, after Edek and Lola had finished their meals.

Renia rarely laughed. She rarely felt joy. She felt fear and shame in abundance. Lola felt that Renia didn't want her dead mother or father or any of her dead brothers or sisters to think she had had a moment's happiness in being the one who was left alive.

It wasn't that Renia looked miserable, Lola thought. She just looked alone, aloof and a little out of reach. Renia had looked a little sad when Lola had boarded her flight out of Australia. Lola had been startled by that. She usually only saw Renia agitated by her. Agitated by what Lola was eating. And by what Lola wasn't eating.

Lola sat on the bed in her Sunset Boulevard studio apartment and began to write a postcard to Renia. Lola had found a postcard of the giant Hollywood sign perched on top of Mount Lee, the tallest peak in Los Angeles. The sign was 450-feet long and the letters were forty-five feet high. The sign had thousands of light bulbs, and every day a large number of them had to be changed by a caretaker who lived in a house behind one of the Ls. Lola thought Renia would find the Hollywood sign interesting. Renia liked going to Hollywood movies, although she often missed the beginning and the end of the movie as she would only put on her glasses when the cinema was totally dark and she would take them off again well before the lights came back on.

Lola couldn't understand why Renia did this, as her glasses were beautiful cat's-eye glasses with small fake rubies embedded in the frames. But Renia didn't want to be spotted wearing glasses. She came from the old school of 'Men don't make passes at women in glasses.' The truth was plenty of men made passes at Renia. Renia exuded glamour. And the glamour and the admiring looks did give Renia some pleasure.

In her postcard, Lola told her mother about the sixteen-year-olds driving huge cars, Cadillacs and Pontiacs and Chevrolets. She described the size of the cornflake packets and the huge cartons of milk. She was going to write about the enormous buckets of ice-cream, but decided against it. 'I have a very small fridge in my room,' she wrote. 'It is so small it can hardly hold anything except some milk and a few apples.' Lola hoped that that would placate Renia and not have her imagining that Lola was drinking gallons of milk or wolfing down giant boxes of cornflakes.

Cher was sitting in the living room of her house. She was wearing a one-piece pantsuit that looked as though it must have been stitched on to her. There was no room at all between Cher and the pantsuit. It followed the contours of her body, which had no ripples or bulges or bumps. Everything about Cher looked smooth. Her hair was smooth, thick and lustrous. Lola thought that each individual hair was probably shiny and incandescent. Cher's arms and what Lola could see of her legs were perfectly toned and polished. Lola wondered how anybody could have a body that unmarked, unscarred, unscraped or grazed.

Cher looked pleased to see Lola. So did Sonny. 'Hi, we saw you in London, didn't we?' said Sonny.

'Yes,' said Lola. She looked around her. Sonny and Cher's house looked very large. 'This is a beautiful house,' she said. She hoped Sonny would offer to show her around, but he didn't. Lola wondered if either of them remembered the diamante-lined false eyelashes Cher had borrowed from Lola. Lola thought they probably had no recollection of the eyelashes. Dozens of pairs of false eyelashes must have passed through Cher's hands or been glued to her eyelids since then. Lola decided not to bring up the diamante-lined lashes. They suddenly seemed inconsequential. She didn't think that having her false eyelashes back was going to help her to lose weight or write better articles.

'Your pantsuit looks gorgeous on you,' Lola said to Cher.

'Thank you,' said Cher.

'Our wardrobe is our most expensive overhead,' Sonny said. 'We spend about two thousand dollars a month on clothes.' Lola was shocked. That was a lot of money to spend on clothes every month. Sonny and Cher were spending almost half of what the average person would earn in a year on clothes every month.

'The clothes you saw in London have been put into storage,' Sonny said. 'New clothes are being made continually.' The clothes Sonny was referring to were the seven suitcases and several wardrobes crammed with clothes Sonny had shown Lola. 'We have our own seamstress who works for us full-time,' Sonny said. 'Cher designs our clothes. Her clothes and my clothes.'

'How can you come up with all these different ideas for outfits?' Lola said to Cher.

'Cher has this marvellous talent for designing,' said Sonny. 'She'll get an idea and within three minutes she has sketched another outfit. I wish I could write songs like that.'

Cher smiled modestly and took Sonny's hand. He put his arm around her.

'Did you enjoy London?' Lola said to Cher.

'I bought Cher this ring in London,' said Sonny. Lola remembered seeing the ring, in London. It was enormous. It was so big, it looked fake. 'It's a twenty-carat diamond-and-sapphire ring,' said Sonny. 'I bought it for Cher's twentieth birthday.

'We owe a lot of our success to London,' Sonny said. 'We were getting nowhere. Our clothes and everything about us were just too weird for Americans. The Rolling Stones told us that if we wanted to make it, we had to go to England. So we did. When we tried to check into the London Hilton Hotel, they told us that we didn't have a reservation. I knew it was because of the way we looked. I was upset. There was a bit of a commotion in the lobby. Two photographers were there and took photographs. Later that day we were on the front page of the *Daily Telegraph.*'

'And we were famous,' said Cher.

'Thousands of people turned up at our store appearance,' said Sonny. 'And "I Got You Babe" came out and replaced The Beatles at the top of the charts.'

'It all happened so fast,' said Cher.

'When we came back from that trip to London the news had spread, and everything was happening for us here in America,' said Sonny.

'We went from having to be so careful with our money to being able to go shopping for anything we wanted,' said Cher. 'I couldn't get used to it,' she said. 'I wanted to buy extra things for when the money ran out and we were poor again.'

'What do you do when you're not working?' said Lola. She hadn't addressed the question to anyone in particular.

'We like to go out on hill hikes or ride our motorcycles,' Sonny said.

'I am terrified of motorbikes,' Lola said. 'When I was about eight, a man riding a motorbike crashed into our house. He was so smashed up.'

There was a silence. Lola wished she hadn't said that. It was hardly an uplifting thing to say.

'Poor guy,' said Cher. 'Was he okay?'

'He didn't look okay to me,' Lola said, and immediately chided herself. She should have said that he was fine.

Sonny was frowning. Maybe Sonny's frown had nothing to do with Lola or the man who'd crashed his motorbike into the Benskys' house. Lola had heard that Sonny was unfaithful to Cher, and that Sonny's most recent infidelity had been with his new secretary – and Cher had caught them mid-act. Maybe that was partly responsible for Sonny's frown.

Lola asked Cher if they had a lot of friends in LA. 'We do not involve ourselves intimately with other pop stars,' Sonny said. Lola restrained herself from asking if he saved his intimate involvements for his secretaries. Something about Sonny was starting to annoy her. 'We're only closely related to about five or six people, and they are mostly business associates,' Sonny said. Sonny's language, Lola was learning, could meander and be a bit obscure. *They don't socialise with pop stars. Only have a handful of people they're close to. Mostly business associates*, she wrote in her notebook.

'We don't go out much,' said Sonny. 'We enjoy each other's company tremendously. I think the main things essential for personal happiness are doing things that you enjoy doing and, in our case, having each other.'

The phone rang. Sonny took the phone and walked into another room.

'I'm in awe of Sonny,' said Cher. 'He calms me down.'

'Calms you down about what?' said Lola.

'Calms me down about being on stage,' said Cher. 'I couldn't appear on stage without him.'

'What are you frightened of?' said Lola

'I get a shut-up, locked-in feeling on stage. I feel trapped. I then panic about what would happen if I needed to get off stage in the middle of a performance. But with Sonny there, I'm okay.'

Lola was surprised to hear Cher speaking like that. She'd thought that with Cher's looks, her beautiful face and perfect and perfectly slender body, Cher would feel embraced by the world. Not scared or frightened of being trapped. 'Did you always feel that way about singing?' said Lola.

'Yes,' said Cher. 'I was terrified to even sing backup on other people's records. I rely on Sonny for everything, really,' said Cher.

'You've been with Sonny since you were sixteen, haven't you?' said Lola.

'Yes,' said Cher.

'He's twelve years older than you. Does that age difference matter to you?' said Lola.

'I like it,' said Cher. 'Sonny makes me feel very safe.'

'Has being so successful and so famous helped you with your fears onstage?' said Lola.

'I think it has,' said Cher. 'But it's really Sonny who's made me feel better.' Lola was getting a bit tired of hearing how wonderful and wonderfully protective Sonny was. Something about Sonny seemed too slick to her, too opportunistic, too chauvinistic.

'I'm also terrified of flying,' said Cher. 'Sonny used to have to talk to me for hours sometimes before I could get on a plane. I'm better now. I take sleeping pills and knock myself out for the entire trip.'

'You don't look like a person who's terrified of anything,' said Lola. 'You look so perfectly beautiful.'

'Thank you. That's very nice of you,' said Cher.

'This is a fabulous house,' said Lola.

'It is, isn't it?' said Cher. 'I feel lucky to be able to live like this. We have a woman who comes and cooks on weekdays. I'm not really the housewifely type. The woman can't come on the weekends so I have to cook and make the beds. Sonny calls them my womanly duties.' Lola felt glad that she hadn't brought up the diamante-lined false eyelashes. Something was making her feel sorry for Cher.

'I think we look a little alike,' said Cher, looking at Lola. Sonny came back into the room. He hovered around Cher as though he were nervous of what she had been saying. 'Do you think we look alike, Son?' said Cher, looking at Lola.

'Other people have said that,' said Lola. 'But I always reply that I'm twice Cher's size.'

'I can see the resemblance,' said Cher. 'Can you, Son?'

'No,' he said, looking perplexed. 'I can't see any resemblance at all.'

'It's okay,' said Lola to Cher. 'You don't have to worry about looking like me. You look nothing like me.'

'You sure don't,' said Sonny.

Lola was sitting at one of the tables close to the stage at the Whisky a Go Go. Lola thought the DJ, who played records in between sets by live bands, had the volume up way too high. She put her hands over her ears and watched the two go-go dancers, who were dancing from cages suspended from the ceiling. Lola didn't know how anyone could dance in a cage, let alone one suspended from a ceiling. Being up in the air didn't seem to bother either one of the girls dancing in the cages. Both of them wore very brief outfits. Lola wondered whether, if she hadn't been fat, she too would have been able to bare her body like that. She wasn't sure. She was so used to covering herself up that she couldn't imagine having a body that she wanted to show off.

The dancers looked a little bored, Lola thought. Their dancing, which looked more free-form than choreographed, didn't seem to require a lot of precision or skill. It was basically a series of repetitive, uncomplicated movements with their arms and legs and sometimes their heads. Still, there was something mesmerising about having girls dance in midair. It must be linked to the thrill, Lola thought, of watching trapeze artists or highwire performers.

Lola was early. The Whisky a Go Go wasn't crowded yet, but Lola knew it would be. She had come to see Sam and Dave, whose string of hits included 'Soul Man', 'Soothe Me' and 'Hold On, I'm Comin''. Lola was hoping to get a short interview with Sam and Dave, or at least one of them. She knew they'd just arrived back from a tour of Europe with Otis Redding.

Lola was feeling disconcerted after her interview with Sonny and Cher. She had written about Sonny and Cher's beautiful and beautifully furnished house, and Cher's designing skills and her bell-bottom trousers, which were now being copied around the world. But she felt bothered. She wondered if Cher minded Sonny answering almost all of the questions, including the ones specifically addressed to Cher. And she wondered whether Cher minded Sonny fucking other women.

Lola came out of these thoughts about Cher to see Jimi Hendrix waving to her. He was talking to someone on the other side of the stage. Lola knew that Jimi Hendrix, who was still almost unknown in LA, was also on at the Whisky a Go Go that night.

The Whisky a Go Go, although it was only a few years old, was known as a place where stars who were about to be discovered, as well as those who had already been discovered, performed. The Doors had been the house band at the Whisky a Go Go until one night when Jim Morrison, supposedly high on acid and alcohol, began a meandering, semi-improvised, rambling rendition of 'The End'. Thirty-five minutes later, Jim Morrison got to a line about wanting to fuck his mother all night. And that was that. The Whiskey's management didn't want their club closed. They stopped the show and fired the band.

After Monterey, Jimi Hendrix may still have been relatively unknown by the general public in Los Angeles, but the cognoscenti at the heart of the rock world in LA was all over him. She had heard he was staying at Peter Tork's estate in Laurel Canyon. Lola had met Peter Tork when she'd interviewed The Monkees. Peter Tork, who was short and slight and had a very deep voice, was quiet and quietly intelligent. Jimi was in good company in Laurel Canyon. Among his neighbours were Brian Wilson, Judy Collins, Joni Mitchell, Mama Cass, David Crosby, Stephen Stills, Graham Nash, Mike Bloomfield and Carole King.

Jimi Hendrix came over to Lola. 'Hi,' he said. 'I wasn't even surprised when I saw you.'

Lola laughed. 'I'm not stalking you,' she said.

'I know you haven't come to LA to see my hair curlers,' said Jimi Hendrix.

'No,' said Lola. 'I've come here to interview a few people.'

'You're very serious, aren't you?' he said.

'I don't know,' said Lola. 'I don't feel very serious.' She didn't think she was very serious. Planning diets was not a serious occupation or hobby. And she didn't seem serious about starting the diets.

'You are a serious chick,' said Jimi Hendrix. 'Where were you staying in Monterey? I didn't see you after the first day.'

'I had a motel room quite close to the fairgrounds,' said Lola.

'You're also an organised chick, aren't you?' he said.

'I think I am organised,' she said. Lola laughed and looked at Jimi Hendrix. 'I doubt if you were walking around Monterey looking for me,' she said.

'No, I wasn't,' said Jimi Hendrix. 'I just noticed I didn't see you around.'

'You had plenty to occupy you at Monterey,' said Lola. 'You were a sensation.'

'It was groovy,' he said.

'I think it was more than groovy,' said Lola.

'I'll sit down with you for a few minutes, if you don't mind,' said Jimi Hendrix, 'and then I have to go and get ready. We're on first before Sam and Dave.'

'I've heard they're very good,' said Lola.

'Their nickname is Double Dynamite,' said Jimi Hendrix. 'They're very, very good.'

'Even Double Dynamite could have a hard time following you,' said Lola.

'Your mother and father being in Nazi death camps is probably what made you serious,' said Jimi Hendrix.

'You remember that?' said Lola.

'It's not something you hear about every day,' said Jimi Hendrix. 'Of course I remember.'

'I think I'm organised because my parents' lives were so disordered, disarranged and deranged,' said Lola. 'In the death camps, the rules changed from minute to minute. Everything was unpredictable. My mother said you never knew what to expect.' Renia hadn't actually said that directly to Lola. Renia used to mutter it to herself.

'Any minute was another selection, another rollcall, another *kapo* coming to check up on you if you took more than one minute in the toilet block, even if you had diarrhoea or were vomiting,' Renia used to say to herself. Lola knew by the time she was four and at kindergarten that the selections were for the gas. She didn't know what the gas was, but she knew it wasn't good. When Lola started school and discovered that there was a rollcall first thing in the morning, she had fled and tried to hide.

'I can see why you would want to avoid anything unpredictable,' said Jimi Hendrix.

'I can see why I book motel rooms well in advance and make sure I never run out of recording tape,' said Lola.

'I like to go with the flow,' said Jimi Hendrix. 'I like to shoot the breeze.'

'I don't shoot anything,' said Lola.

'I think I know that, man,' Jimi Hendrix said. 'And it's probably a good thing. Some of the stuff that's on the streets is no good.'

'But you use it, don't you?' said Lola.

'Everyone does,' said Jimi Hendrix.

Jimi was looking at a woman sitting at a table on the other side of the room. The woman had long, tangled, curly black hair and was wearing a long black dress.

'She looks like she works voodoo roots,' said Jimi Hendrix.

'Voodoo?' said Lola.

'Yeah, voodoo,' said Jimi Hendrix. 'Some people can work voodoo roots. They can put something in your food or put a hair in your shoe. Voodoo stuff. Someone worked voodoo roots on me, but she must have been half-hearted because I was only sick in the hospital for two or three days.'

'You were in hospital because someone worked some sort of voodoo on you?' said Lola.

'Yeah,' said Jimi Hendrix. 'It was a while ago.'

'I don't believe in voodoo,' said Lola.

'You should,' said Jimi Hendrix. 'It's very powerful. You have to be careful. Human beings die too easily.'

There was a long silence. Lola knew how easily human beings could die. She thought she'd probably known that all her life. What she would discover, decades later, was that it wasn't that easy to live.

'I nearly died of fright last week,' Lola said to Jimi Hendrix. 'I was driving and I was pulled over by a cop with a gun and a threatening expression. He said he could arrest me for driving without any ID. In Australia the police don't carry guns, so being that close to a gun and a cop with a menacing expression was bothering enough.'

'You should try being black in America, man,' Jimi Hendrix said. 'You can get pulled over, worked over and sent to jail for anything.'

'That must be very frightening,' Lola said.

'It is, man,' said Jimi Hendrix. 'It really is.'

Lola felt she had to change the subject. She seemed to have an ability to enable any conversation to take a morose or sombre turn. Even Mickey Mouse would probably become surly and ungregarious after talking to her, she decided.

'You must be happy about Monterey,' Lola said to Jimi Hendrix. 'Everyone said it was your big breakthrough in America.'

'I am happy,' said Jimi Hendrix. 'I'll be very happy if it means that we can spend more money on making our records. I want to be able to get the things I see and feel into the music. I want to make money to make the music better. It's not that I have no other value for money. Of course I value money. But I want to make money so I don't have to do albums that are made in a very short time because there's not enough money to do them properly.

'You can always do things better,' said Jimi Hendrix. 'Sometimes when I finish recording something, I've got a hundred completely new ideas and I'd like to go back and record it differently. You can do that if you've got money. I hate one-dimensional sounds. I like a really deep sound, when you've got all the depth of your thoughts and your feelings in the sound.'

'I think you're going to have enough money to record records in whatever way you want to record them,' said Lola.

'Thank you for saying that,' Jimi Hendrix said.

'My father would have answered me with "From your mouth to God's ear,"' Lola said. 'It's an old Yiddish saying.'

'I like that,' said Jimi Hendrix. 'From your mouth to God's ear.' He looked at Lola. 'You still thinking about the death camps a lot?' he said.

'Do I think about them a lot?' said Lola.

'I think so,' said Jimi Hendrix. 'I would, too,' he added. Lola thought about it. She didn't think she thought about death camps that much. She spent far more time planning diets.

'I hear you're staying with Peter Tork,' Lola said.

'Yes,' said Jimi Hendrix. 'That house has one or two thousand rooms and a cute yellow puppy and balconies from which you can see Seattle and Piccadilly Circus.' Lola saw Noel Redding wave to Jimi. 'Time to go,' said Jimi. 'It was nice talking to you.'

The Whisky a Go Go was full now. There were a lot of celebrities there. Mama Cass was sitting next to Jim Morrison. Jim Morrison looked as petulant as he had in New York. The Jimi Hendrix Experience began to play. Lola looked around her. Jimi Hendrix was having the same effect on the audience here as he had had in Monterey. People looked both astonished and electrified.

Somewhere in the middle of 'Purple Haze' Lola drifted into a reverie. She was driving her Volkswagen, somewhere in Laurel Canyon, when she noticed a car wedged against a tree at a strange angle, as though it had skidded to a stop. She noticed the windshield was cracked and somebody was slumped against the steering wheel. Lola panicked. Because she was in her rented Volkswagen in Los Angeles

and not in her second-hand pink Valiant in Melbourne, she didn't
have a first-aid kit on her. She had no bandages, no antiseptic, no rubber gloves, no tweezers, no thermometer and no sterile gauze pads.
Luckily, she had a flashlight with fresh batteries. Lola parked the
Volkswagen well over to the side of the road. She knew that the first
rule in responding to a car accident was to put your own vehicle out of
the way of oncoming traffic.

Lola ran over and looked inside the damaged car. She got quite a
shock. The person slumped against the wheel was Jimi Hendrix. He
had facial contusions and lacerations. The car door was jammed. Lola
found a rock and, with a crowbar-like motion, jimmied open the door.
Jimi Hendrix was still breathing. She listened to his breathing to see
if she could hear any sort of gurgling noise. A gurgling noise could
indicate the possibility of blood and other secretions in the nose and
mouth. A man came up to the car. 'Call an ambulance, please,' Lola
said to the man.

'I already have,' he said. 'Let's get him out of the car.'

'Don't touch him,' said Lola. 'It's very risky to move a person with
a head injury, in case they have a broken neck.' Jimi Hendrix started
groaning. 'You're okay,' Lola said to him. 'Just stay as you are. An ambulance is on the way.'

'We've got to get him out of the car and lie him down,' the man said.

'If he's got a broken neck and we move him, we've got a good
chance of making him an instant paraplegic,' Lola said.

'You sure you know what you're doing?' said the man.

'I know what I'm doing,' Lola said.

She turned to Jimi Hendrix. 'You're going to be all right, Jimi,' she
said. 'Don't worry.'

'I don't like leaving him in the car slumped over the steering wheel,' said the man.

'If he was unconscious and started to choke on his secretions, we'd have to risk taking him out of the car and lying him on his side so we could clear his airways,' Lola said to the man. 'But he's not choking and he's not unconscious, he is just in a daze. The ambulance should be here any minute.'

'I saw the whole thing,' said the man. 'He swerved to avoid a yellow puppy dog and hit the tree.'

The ambulance arrived. 'You did the right thing, Miss,' the ambulance driver said to Lola. 'You didn't risk moving him. That could have been dangerous.'

Jimi Hendrix opened his eyes, looked at Lola and said, 'Thank you.'

'The ambulance is here,' Lola said. 'You're going to be fine. But please don't swerve to avoid any dogs, it can be very dangerous.'

Lola came out of this potentially fatal drama in Laurel Canyon to hear The Jimi Hendrix Experience playing their last number. Jimi was covered in sweat. He looked completely intact and unharmed. Lola didn't know why she had to go into a car-rescue fantasy about Jimi Hendrix. He didn't need rescuing. He seemed perfectly capable of looking after himself.

Lola had managed to arrange a brief interview with Sam and Dave. She went backstage. They were expecting her. 'We've only got five minutes,' an assistant said to Lola. Lola set up her tape recorder.

'You've just come back from a very successful tour of Europe with Otis Redding,' she said. 'Was there a difference between performing in America and performing in Europe?'

'The audiences are great in both places,' said Dave Prater, 'but the

big difference is that in Europe and London there are no coloured restaurants, no coloured hotels, no coloured entrances, no coloured water
fountains. At the hotel we were treated just like the rest of the guests.
Coming from America, which still has a lot of segregated parts, that
was like another world.'

'Yes,' said Sam. 'It was something else.'

Lola was shocked at the thought that separate hotels or restaurants
or drinking fountains still existed. 'Do you still feel that it's largely a
white person's world in America?' said Lola.

'Of course it is,' said Dave. 'A lot of people love our music but they
don't love a lot of us.'

'You've got two more minutes,' the assistant said.

'How were the European audiences?' said Lola.

'They were so great,' said Sam. 'In London, at the Hammersmith
Odeon, they were stomping and stamping their feet on the balcony
and I thought the balcony floor might cave in.'

'They could feel our soul,' said Sam. 'The soul part of soul music
is your soul. You sing the lyrics but what you put into the singing is
your soul.'

'Thank you very much,' Lola said to Sam and Dave.

She went back to her table. People were still talking about Jimi
Hendrix. She hoped Sam and Dave didn't have a hard time following
Jimi Hendrix. Lola saw a girl who reminded her of Lillian Roxon's friend
Linda Eastman, but it wasn't Linda. Lola had called Lillian Roxon from
a payphone in the courtyard of her apartment complex last night.

'I definitely prefer New York to LA,' Lola had said to Lillian.

'So do I,' said Lillian. 'There's no city in the world that matches
New York.'

Lola realised that it had not been smart of her to bring up New York. Lillian was bound to suggest, again, that she come to New York instead of going back to Australia.

'Are you still going back to Australia?' Lillian said.

'Yes, I think so,' said Lola.

'Please don't,' said Lillian. 'You can't go back just for that schmuck.'

'He's not a schmuck,' said Lola. 'Schmuck', a frequently used Yiddish word, meant an idiot, a hapless idiot. Literally translated, 'schmuck' meant penis and could also be used in the sense of prick, as in, *he's a prick*.

'He is a schmuck,' said Lillian. 'He's fucking someone else and that makes him a schmuck. You can move in with me. I know you'll do well here. The people you're interviewing who aren't already world-famous are going to be world-famous. They'll know you and, I'm sure, trust you, so you'll be in a very good position to do great interviews. What are you going to do in Melbourne, anyway?'

'I don't know,' said Lola. 'I'll keep working at *Rock-Out*.'

'I bet you'll get married and have three children,' said Lillian. 'You're way too young to do that. I'll introduce you to a couple of magazine editors. You'll do really well. Come to New York. Please.'

'I'm not sure I can,' said Lola.

'Why?' said Lillian.

'I don't really know,' said Lola. She wished she knew why she was going home to Australia. It just seemed like it was something she had to do. Maybe she was worried that she'd never find another boyfriend. And that would mean she'd never get married and always be on her own. Lola had felt bad after she'd hung up from Lillian.

Sam and Dave were about to start. Backed by a slew of saxophones and an almost all-black band – apart from the white guitarist and white bass player. Sam and Dave ran onto the stage. From the first note, the music almost lifted people out of their seats. Lola understood why Sam Moore and Dave Prater were nicknamed Double Dynamite.

They danced and moved and sang in unison and at high speed. There was a gospel-tinged euphoria about them and their music. Sam and Dave's music could make you want to go to church. It could make you want to believe. It could make you want to pray. It could lift you out of a cloud.

'Hold On, I'm Comin',' they sang. There was a preacher-like ecstasy to their voices and their movements and gestures. Their voices separated and reunited. They moved together side by side and then around each other, as though each were part of the other. Their souls as well as their vocal chords and legs and arms seemed to be in accord and agreement.

It must have been the music that fused them. Offstage, Sam and Dave didn't speak. Didn't say a word to each other. They hadn't spoken to each other for a long time and wouldn't speak to each other for many, many more years.

8

'Would you like a Maine lobster and cold-water shrimp cake, rolled in Japanese-style Panko crumbs?' the waiter holding the tray of lobster and shrimp cakes said to Lola Bensky.

'Cold-water shrimp?' Lola said. 'Don't all shrimp and fish live in cold water? They would boil, or at least blanch, in hot water.'

The waiter took a deep breath. 'Like lobster and crabs, there are cold-water shrimp and warm-water shrimp,' he said. 'Cold-water crustaceans and fish come from cold-water oceans like the Atlantic and the Arctic, and warm-water crustaceans and fish come from warm-water oceans like the Pacific and the Indian.'

Lola was dazzled. First, she hadn't even known there were cold-water and warm-water oceans. It was the sort of information that she felt, at sixty-three, she should somehow have managed to acquire. And second, this waiter knew his fish. A decade ago, few waiters or other food-industry personnel could have told you very much about a dish or its components. Now, each ingredient and herb and spice had its own pedigree, provenance and history. Now it was not just people in the food business who were interested in food. More and more ordinary people were becoming food experts. Food was having its moment. Food was the new stock market.

Fifteen years ago people were talking about their therapists. A decade ago, the conversation was all about Internet start-ups. And then food took over. Culinary terms appeared in every second sentence. Terms like *sous-vide*, semifreddo, *au jus*, deglaze and *confit*. No one could just say lunch or dinner. It had to be a chicken salad *au jus* or lamb *sous-vide* or deglazed pork shoulder or leg.

How things had slipped from the psychological significance of missing three sessions with your therapist to exactly how your chicken was cooked was a little incomprehensible to Lola. Being knowledgeable about food now made you more socially desirable than a brain surgeon. Or maybe not. In New York everyone liked to know a medical specialist.

The waiter with the lobster and shrimp cakes came past Lola again. Lola took the last Maine lobster and sweet cold-water shrimp cake rolled in Japanese-style Panko crumbs. 'You know a lot about shrimp,' Lola said to the waiter.

Lola was on the Upper East Side at a fundraising dinner for the New York Public Library or the New York City Ballet or maybe it was another New York cultural institution. Lola couldn't remember. The dinner was at the home of Phyllis-Elissa and Elwood Earlwood, who owned several of Mr Someone Else's paintings. They were important art collectors.

Phyllis-Elissa was never just called Phyllis, it was always Phyllis-Elissa. Lola, who had an inbuilt and irrational dislike of very rich people, quite liked Phyllis-Elissa. Phyllis-Elissa had a warmth about her. She was confident and direct. And she was fat. Not hugely fat. But fat. It was unusual in very wealthy circles for a woman to be fat. Fat women were under-represented in the world of the very rich. There were quite a few very fat, very rich men, but very few very rich, fat women.

Phyllis-Elissa didn't seem to mind being fat. She didn't try to wear more flattering clothes. Her buttons often gaped and her clothes looked too tight. Tonight she was wearing a black, vintage, beaded 1940s dress. Her bust was straining to get out in the gaps between the shiny, quartz-like multi-faceted buttons. The cellulite in Phyllis-Elissa's thighs and hips was bumping against the *crepe de Chine* fabric of her dress. Lola admired Phyllis-Elissa for being at ease enough with her size to be able to display it without any firming undergarments or other slimming tricks.

Phyllis-Elissa and Elwood Earlwood's Fifth Avenue apartment was, Lola thought, very beautiful. It looked as though it had been built in the 1920s. The apartment was very big. One of the living rooms, which faced Fifth Avenue, was fifty-five feet long. But even at that size and with three Picassos, two Dalís and several de Koonings and Rothkos on the walls, the room looked lived-in and comfortable. The library, which had large, overstuffed sofas and armchairs and a wall-to-wall series of Matisse etchings, had the cosiness of a regular family den. There also must have been six or seven bathrooms. Lola, who had been drinking a lot of mineral water, had already used three.

Lola estimated there were about fifty or sixty people at this fund-raising dinner. Most of the guests were slim. Many looked like dancers or ex-dancers. Maybe the dinner was for a dance company. Lola was no longer fat herself, although she didn't like to state it so blatantly in case the fat somehow leaped back and adhered itself to her. Lola hadn't been fat for at least two decades.

Lola still felt fat. She couldn't stop feeling fat. Feeling fat, she thought, must in some way be a comfort to her. Otherwise, why would she cling to it? Why would she still feel so attached to her fat? If she put on four or five pounds, she panicked and felt huge. Maybe that panic was comforting, too. The panic about how fat she was could immerse her for days in a reassuringly familiar universe of anxiety.

At sixty-three, Lola still wished she could be really thin. She had been able to get there a few times and become thin enough to be able to see that she was thin, but she couldn't maintain that weight. She inevitably started to eat more. One extra Weight Watchers ice-cream bar, one extra apple, one extra tub of low-fat cottage cheese and she had added another three- to four-hundred calories to her daily intake and a couple of inches to her hips.

But she was happy to be sixty-three and standing up with a glass in her hand, talking, like everyone else. She could now stand and talk. For hours, if she wanted to. She could, with a degree of trepidation and a little anxiety, travel by subway. She could also sit anywhere in the theatre or cinema, except possibly in an upper level – particularly if it had a deep, downward slope.

Lola knew she still had anxieties she juggled and struggled against, but on the whole she was okay, she thought. She felt lucky to still be so in love with Mr Someone Else and to have children who liked her. Or who, mostly, liked her. Her children were grown up. All three had chosen partners who adored them. And didn't bore them.

At Mrs Gorgeous's wedding and, later, at her son's wedding, Lola had been lifted up in the air, in a chair. She had laughed like a child as four men had hoisted her and the chair in the air and carried her around the room as the band played '*Chosen Kale Mazel Tov.*' Lola had felt exactly the way she used to feel when she was riding on top of the elephant at the Melbourne Zoo. She had felt on top of the world. She wished Renia could have been there. Could have seen how beautiful Mrs Gorgeous looked. Could have seen Lola on top of the world.

Lola was talking to a choreographer Phyllis-Elissa had introduced her to. She had never met a choreographer before.

'You must really have to know the body and how it works to be a choreographer,' Lola said to him. Unlike a writer, Lola thought, a choreographer couldn't ignore their body while they pondered whether overwrought or overexcited or overstated best expressed what they were trying to say.

'Yes, you do, down to the smallest movement like how each finger can flex and extend and abduct and adduct,' he said, demonstrating the four movements. Lola was impressed.

'Do you know that apart from the genitals, fingertips have the highest concentration of touch receptors and thermo receptors of any part of the skin?' Lola said. 'It means that they're very sensitive to temperature, vibration, pressure, moisture and texture.'

'No, I didn't,' said the choreographer, and laughed. Lola was relieved that he had laughed. She had no idea what had possessed her to talk about genitals to a perfect stranger. She thought that it must be an overly-enthusiastic need to contribute to the anatomical dialogue.

'Have you always been thin?' The choreographer said to Lola.

Lola started stuttering and spilled some of her mineral water down the front of her dress. 'No,' she said, firmly. 'Anyway, I'm not thin,' she added.

'You look thin to me,' he said.

'Well, I'm not,' she said, patting her hips and thighs to emphasise their size.

Lola was flushed. Being called thin unnerved her. Being called fat never used to unnerve her. But then nothing much did. For years. Until almost everything began to unnerve her.

A small but audible murmur spread through the room. Lola looked up. Another guest had arrived. To Lola's surprise, the newly arrived guest was Mick Jagger. You could feel the added frisson in the room. Even for a blasé New York crowd, Mick Jagger was a big deal.

Lola was happy to see Mick Jagger. Mick Jagger looked good. He was wearing a shiny plum-coloured jacket and the skinniest stove-pipe trousers in a tan, grey and dark-red tartan, with black sneakers and fluorescent green socks. He looked remarkably like himself. A lot of people, more than forty years later, only retained a glimmer of who they were. But Mick Jagger was still Mick Jagger. His hair was more or less the same. He didn't look as though he'd lost any of it. His body looked lean and taut. Lola was happy to see Mick Jagger looking so good. He looked prosperous. And happy. He was with L'Wren Scott, the former model and stylist who was a very successful fashion designer. Mick Jagger, Lola had read in the *New York Times*, referred to L'Wren Scott as the person he was kind of dating, although they'd been together for ten years.

L'Wren Scott was very striking. At six-foot-three in her bare feet, she towered over Mick Jagger and most of the other people in the room. She was dressed entirely in black. A long black dress, black tights, black shoes. Her long, almost waist-length hair was as black as her clothes. And her face was as pale as a face could be and still exude a healthy glow.

Mick Jagger was often photographed sitting in the front few rows at L'Wren Scott's fashion shows looking very proud. But then Lola thought that Mick Jagger had probably been very supportive of the most important women in his life. Lola had heard that when Marianne Faithful was learning the script of Chekhov's *The Three Sisters*, Mick Jagger had helped her by playing the roles of the other sisters. And that he had helped Jerry Hall choose her modelling photographs.

Either Mick Jagger or L'Wren Scott must have had an interest in the ballet or the library or whatever cause this fundraising was supporting to be here tonight, Lola thought. She wished she could remember what the cause was.

Phyllis-Elissa came over to Lola. 'I want you to meet Mick Jagger,' she said, taking Lola by the hand and leading her to where Mick Jagger was standing. 'Mick, I want you to meet Lola Bensky, the wonderful, very talented author of the international bestseller *Schlomo in SoHo*,' Phyllis-Elissa said.

'Hi,' said Mick Jagger, and shook Lola's hand. 'Nice to meet you.'

'*Schlomo in SoHo* was a sensation in Europe,' Phyllis-Elissa said.

'Not really *Europe*,' Lola said. 'Just Germany, Austria and Switzerland.'

'That's Europe,' said Phyllis-Elissa.

New Yorkers had a tendency to use superlatives when introducing people, as though the greatness of the guest or friend or acquaintance added to their own lustre. Phyllis-Elissa, with her Picassos and Matisses, didn't really need any more lustre, Lola thought, especially not lustre added by Lola or Schlomo. 'Germany, Austria and Switzerland is definitely Europe,' Mick Jagger said.

'It's part of Europe,' said Lola, and wished she had been more gracious, or at least less pedantic.

'Lola lives in a fabulous loft in SoHo with her painter husband, whose work you can see in our apartment,' Phyllis-Elissa said.

'It's not really a fabulous loft,' said Lola. 'It's a nice loft. We were lucky, we bought it over twenty years ago.' Why was she downgrading her loft, Lola thought. Did she not want to appear rich? Mick Jagger's fortune, she had heard, was estimated to be over three-hundred-million dollars. Why was she embarrassed at owning a loft in SoHo, which they had bought when SoHo was nowhere near as chic or choked with designer labels.

Mick Jagger looked at Lola carefully and a faint frown appeared on his face. Lola thought it was probably because he'd never heard of *Schlomo in SoHo* and could have been puzzled by who or what Schlomo was.

'Are you Australian?' Mick Jagger said to Lola.

'Yes,' she said. 'But I've lived here for over twenty years.'

'She's very well known in Australia, too,' Phyllis-Elissa said. Phyllis-Elissa, Lola thought, was worse than Edek. Edek, who had been living in New York for more than a decade, told everyone he met that his daughter was a famous writer. If the person looked blank when he mentioned Lola's name, Edek decided that they were stupid.

Edek, who was ninety-three, still lived on his own, in an apartment on the Lower East Side. He loved his apartment, he loved New York and New York hot dogs and hot chocolate. And he was happy. Edek was happier than Lola had ever known him to be. He was almost always in a good mood and when Lola asked him how he was, he always replied, 'As good as gold.'

Lola and Edek met two or three times a week at Caffe Dante on MacDougal Street. Lola had a chamomile tea with lemon and Edek had two scoops of chocolate gelato and two cups of hot chocolate.

Lola didn't understand where Edek's calm had come from. It had appeared when he was about eighty-five. Lola was glad that Edek had lived long enough to feel peaceful. And happy. She wondered if Renia, if she'd lived to eighty-five, would have also started to calm down. Lola didn't think so. Lola couldn't imagine Renia being eighty-five. She couldn't imagine Renia without her high heels, her firm thighs, her strapless bras and mascara'd lashes. She certainly couldn't imagine Renia calm. Calm, Renia would have been someone else. She wouldn't have been Renia.

'You grew up in Australia, did you?' Mick Jagger said to Lola.

'I lived there from the time I was two to when I was forty-two,' she said.

'You're giving your age away,' Phyllis-Elissa said.

'I'm sixty-three,' said Lola.

'I'm even older than that,' said Mick Jagger.

'You look fabulous,' Phyllis-Elissa said to Mick Jagger.

Mick Jagger, Lola thought, still looked as though something was bothering him. He was probably still puzzled about Schlomo, she thought. He couldn't possibly have recognised Lola, or remembered meeting her. He must have met thousands of people in his life. Besides which Lola was half the size and three times the age she had been then. Phyllis-Elissa took Mick Jagger's arm. 'You must read *Schlomo in SoHo,*' Lola heard her saying as she led him away.

Lola's mobile phone beeped. She took it out of her bag. It was a text message from Edek. *I did buy you sunglasses. They are very good.*

Dad. Lola dreaded seeing the sunglasses. She knew that Edek would only have bought them if they were an extraordinary bargain. Like two pairs for a dollar. Edek loved a bargain.

Less than a minute later another text message from Edek appeared. *I did buy one pair for myself.* Edek could text, email and Skype. He could send attachments, print photographs and find information online. This sometimes drove Lola mad. He would forward get-rich-quick schemes to her and text, sometimes daily, to ask her about book sales.

The Internet, with all its possibilities, excited Edek as much as the magicians, hypnotists, comedians and strippers at the Tivoli Theatre in Melbourne used to. The fact that Edek could misspell words and still be understood by his computer thrilled him to his core. He had recently, flushed with excitement, told Lola that he thought Skype was a true miracle. Lola had no idea who Edek was Skyping. She was just glad it wasn't her.

Three years ago, Lola had taken Edek to Germany with her on her second book tour there. In Germany Edek had sent her text messages from his US cell phone whenever they'd been apart for more than half an hour. More often than not the texts said things like, *Wurst very good.* He had sent the text messages from the room of his hotel when she was in the room next door and text messages from the lobby of the hotel to ask her if she was coming down for breakfast. The bill for all this international texting had been exorbitant.

Still, Lola had been pleased to get all the texts. She had worried about Edek being in Germany. The last time he'd been in Germany, over five decades ago, he had been a ragged and frayed human remnant of a death camp, living in a displaced persons' camp.

On the first day of Lola's book tour, Edek had developed a

stomach-ache. Edek never got stomach-aches. He had a cast-iron constitution. He could eat cornflakes and smoked mackerel and sausages for breakfast, with no ill effect. Or two slices of cheesecake followed by a piece of chocolate cake and a cappuccino. Lola discovered it was the sound of German being spoken in the streets that gave Edek the stomach-ache. 'In the *Lager* if you did hear German you did try to look invisible,' he had said to Lola.

Before they'd left New York, Lola had explained to Edek that things had changed in Germany. The people speaking German were not the same Germans. Lola had seen from her first book tour of Germany that she and the Germans born after the war were tied together by the same small piece of history. They shared a bond, the children of the victims and the children of the perpetrators. They had so much in common. They grew up with a past that was omnipresent. And incomprehensible. So much of that past didn't make sense. Much of it was hidden, half-told, hinted at. Knotted and cramped, garbled, scattered articles and particles of sentences and pronouns that slipped out of someone's mouth.

The children of the perpetrators grew up not knowing, half-suspecting, half-imagining, half-horrified and half-terrified. They felt the same fear and the same guilt as the children of the victims. Lola had talked to many Germans her own age and younger. She recognised their guilt. And she recognised their shame.

Edek had calmed down and his stomach-ache had abated. He chatted, in German, to cab drivers and hotel doormen and told anyone sitting next to him at the book readings that Lola was his daughter and was making a very good living from her books, even though she knew nothing at all about private detectives.

Lola looked around for Mr Someone Else. She saw that he was being introduced to Mick Jagger. She wondered what he would think of Mick Jagger. It was hard not to like Mick Jagger. He didn't do anything unlikable. He seemed very even-keeled. As though he never exploded and was never out of control. He looked as though he kept a firm grip on every aspect of his life and the empire that was The Rolling Stones. Lola had heard that Mick Jagger kept a close eye on all financial matters relating to The Rolling Stones and understood and oversaw every detail of their concert tours, from the lighting to the backdrops to the way the curtains would go down and hit the floor.

It made Lola surprisingly happy to see Mick Jagger looking so good. He looked healthy and fit. He probably ate whatever he wanted to – or maybe he was still not eating much meat and avoiding milk and a lot of starchy foods, like potatoes. Mick Jagger's metabolism was probably wired to be thin, Lola thought. She wondered whether she was right in thinking that Jews were predisposed to being fat. There didn't seem to be a lot of angular, Jewish long-distance runners.

Lola knew that Mick Jagger worked out strenuously. He had to be in shape for the concert tours The Rolling Stones were still doing. They were still filling arenas all around the world. The tours were very lucrative. Lola had heard that even when Mick Jagger wasn't touring, he worked out for forty minutes every other day. Lola worked out, too. Six mornings a week she huffed and puffed her way through one hour and seven minutes, at 3.6 miles an hour on an incline of nine per cent, on a treadmill. She didn't understand why she'd chosen to make it one hour and seven minutes, but she was rigid about the one hour and the seven minutes.

She was so rigid that she wouldn't get off the treadmill ten seconds earlier than the full one hour and seven minutes. She couldn't get off earlier, even if she had a good idea for something Schlomo or Harry could do or say. She couldn't get off the treadmill even if she had a ream of dialogue coming out of Pimp's mouth. She would try to memorise the ideas or the dialogue. She would repeat them over and over again in her head until the one hour and seven minutes were up.

Lola had started exercising when she moved to New York. She had bought a Nordic Track, a machine that simulated cross-country skiing, and in her loft in SoHo she cross-country skied to 'Dancing in the Street'. Twenty repetitions of 'Dancing in the Street' took approximately one hour. It took Lola years to realise that she preferred to ski in silence.

Mr Someone Else was now talking to L'Wren Scott. L'Wren Scott made everyone else look short. Mr Someone Else, who was six feet tall, looked almost squat next to the statuesque Ms Scott. Lola wondered how Renia would feel about a daughter who was six-foot-three. Renia had thought that Lola, at five-foot-nine, was way too tall. When Lola was at high school everyone wanted to be petite or at least average. Now everyone wanted to be tall. Women who were not naturally blessed with height were walking around on eight-inch heels. Lola admired L'Wren Scott. She didn't slouch like a lot of tall women. She had very good posture. And was very graceful.

Lola's posture was not bearing up. She wanted to sit down. She had spent all day with Pimp and Schlomo. Lola had been working on her new book, the third in the series. When Lola had left Pimp, Pimp was screaming into the phone, 'Petrushka, Petrushka. Not Patricia, not Leticia, not Pamela – Petrushka.' Schlomo had had his hands over his ears. Since he'd taken up yoga, he couldn't stand loud noise. And Pimp was loud. 'Petrushka Inge Maria Pagenstecker,' she shouted. She spelled Pagenstecker out with an exaggerated and laborious emphasis on each letter, 'P-A-G-E-N-S-T-E-C-K-E-R. If you can say Häagen Dazs,' Pimp screamed, 'you can say Pagenstecker.' Lola thought that Pimp had confused the issue. Häagen Dazs had nothing to do with Pagenstecker.

'Can you please not shout,' Schlomo had said to Pimp.

'Since you've taken up yoga you think that you are on a higher plane than the rest of us, like a rabbi or a priest,' said Pimp. 'You're not. You're a private detective who spends too much time standing on his head.'

'A headstand is very good for the heart,' Schlomo said. 'It gives the heart a rest. The heart has to work against gravity all day.'

'You believe in God, Schlomo,' Pimp said. 'If God thought the heart couldn't cope with gravity, we'd all be walking around, upside down, on our hands.'

Schlomo's newly developed devotion to yoga bothered Pimp. It had taken her by surprise. An overweight, untidy Orthodox Jew wasn't the sort of person you would think of as likely to become a yoga fanatic. Schlomo went to yoga classes three times a week. Before his first class, he'd asked the women in his class if they wouldn't mind dressing modestly, with no low-cut necklines and no high-cut shorts. All eight of the women had agreed.

Schlomo was very popular with his fellow yoga students. One of the women in the class had become a client of the Ultra-Private Detective Agency. The woman suspected that her husband, a pilot, had another wife, and another family, somewhere in America.

'There are too many things that don't make sense in our lives,' the woman had said to Schlomo. 'And I've been too scared to find out what they might mean.'

'Leave it to me,' Schlomo had said to her. 'We run a very private and a very ultra detective agency.' He had said this even though Pimp had explained to him, more than once, that 'ultra' was a prefix and couldn't be used without an adjective.

Harry was doing the initial research on the pilot from their East Village office. So far, Harry had uncovered another wife in Houston who had three children, and a wife in New Orleans who was six months' pregnant.

'I think your friend is going to need more than yoga when we get to the bottom of this investigation,' Harry said to Schlomo. 'There is a lot that is still missing. Like how is he doing this on a pilot's salary?'

Schlomo decided not to say anything to his friend at the yoga class until a few more details had emerged and they could all meet at the office when Pimp was there. Pimp was surprisingly good at helping clients receive bad news. Other people's bad news soothed Pimp. She stopped screaming. And was very clear-headed and comforting.

Schlomo was sure that yoga would help his friend, the pilot's wife, whatever the outcome of the investigation. Yoga had definitely helped him. He couldn't explain exactly how it had helped him, but he knew it had helped. He did yoga at home every night. He stood on his head, with his *yarmulke* fixed firmly in place with four clips. He also did shoulder stands and arm balances, which he felt strengthened his connection to his intuition. Schlomo's intuition, however, hadn't developed enough to intuit the weather. He still scrutinised the weather forecasts. He studied the beach and ocean temperatures and knew odd things like that, on the whole, the water would be ten to fifteen degrees cooler than the surrounding land.

Lola wished she could rid Schlomo of his obsession with tides and the weather, but she couldn't. Schlomo's wife aided and abetted him. She called him, often at inopportune moments, to warn him about any imminent bad weather. She had called him this morning to talk about a squall in Nevada when Schlomo had had to hang up. Harry had needed to talk to him.

'We've made progress on the husband of your yoga friend,' Harry had said. 'I've found ten bank accounts he has opened, in different states. They are all in his own name. And they are all flush with cash.'

'Something is going on,' said Schlomo.

'We're going to have to tail the pilot if his wife wants to find out any more,' Pimp had said to Schlomo.

'Tail him across America?' said Schlomo.

'Yes,' said Pimp. There are kosher hotels everywhere. You'll be fine. And don't even think of bringing up the fact that you'll miss your yoga classes.'

Patrice Pritchard had called Lola in the middle of these developments. 'I'm sorry to bother you,' Patrice Pritchard had said to Lola, 'but we really need to decide the title of the new book. We want to include it in the list of our upcoming Fall publications.'

'I think I'm going to call it *Petrushka Inge Maria Pagenstecker*,' said Lola. 'It's either that or *Schlomo's Poses*.'

'I think *Schlomo's Poses* is a better title,' said Patrice Pritchard.

'I think I prefer *Petrushka Inge Maria Pagenstecker*,' Lola said.

'Let's see what the people in the office think,' said Patrice, 'and I'll get back to you.'

'I have another question,' Lola said. 'There's a line in the middle of the publishing information in the front pages of the other two books.

It gives the author's year of birth and then there's a dash. The space after the dash always looks ominous. It's a blank date of death space. And looks as though it's sitting there waiting for someone to fill it in. Do I have to have that line?'

'I'll look into it,' said Patrice. 'I don't think that's going to be a problem.'

'Thank you,' said Lola.

Lola had done a little more work before she'd had to stop and get ready for Phyllis-Elissa and Elwood Earlwood's fundraising dinner. Lola had left Pimp in the office with a bad headache and Schlomo boarding a flight to Wyoming with a yoga mat in his luggage.

The guests were about to be seated. Phyllis-Elissa and Elwood were urging people to take their seats. Lola hoped she wouldn't be seated too far from Mr Someone Else. She could sometimes lose herself in a crowd of strangers. When she was with Mr Someone Else, it was easier for her to remember who she was.

Lola looked at Mick Jagger. He was talking animatedly to L'Wren Scott. They had a natural ease between them. They looked like two people who enjoyed each other's company. L'Wren Scott, it seemed to Lola, was clearly her own person. She wasn't known as Mick Jagger's girlfriend. She was known as a talented and very successful fashion designer whose clothes were admired for their flawless construction, sensual silhouettes and sumptuous fabrics. Madonna, Michelle Obama, Angelina Jolie and Carla Bruni-Sarkozy had all been seen wearing L'Wren Scott's designs.

Lola found it oddly reassuring to see Mick Jagger and L'Wren Scott so engrossed in their conversation. He looked happy. She found it very reassuring that Mick Jagger was happy. She found it was reassuring that Mick Jagger was alive. So many of the others had died.

Three years and three months after Jimi Hendrix's performance at the Monterey International Pop Festival, Jimi Hendrix was dead. He was twenty-seven. Two weeks earlier he had told an interviewer, in Denmark, that he wasn't sure he'd live to see his twenty-eighth birthday. He died three years after Lola had last seen him at the Whiskey a Go Go, in Los Angeles. How had he gone from being engaged and engaging and amused and amusing and polite and thoughtful, to being exhausted and strung-out and then dead? What had changed? Just about everything, Lola thought. He had achieved enormous fame, and with that came management issues that Jimi Hendrix was ill-equipped to deal with. Jimi Hendrix, Lola thought, was probably too trusting and too honest. As his stress and his anxiety increased, he became careless. Careless with drugs. Careless with his life. He mixed drugs and alcohol with a reckless abandon. He started to look shaky on stage and off. Lola wondered what had happened to the calm young man with the slow smile. Too much, she thought. The night before he died, Jimi Hendrix had had trouble sleeping. He took nine sleeping pills that belonged to his girlfriend, over six times the recommended dose for a person of Jimi's size. He had also taken amphetamines earlier in the day. He was dressed and covered in vomit when he was found. The coroner's report said that death was due to asphyxiation in his own vomit.

After the autopsy, Jimi's body was sent to a funeral home where they got rid of his vomit-covered clothes and dressed him in a large flannel shirt, to be flown back to Seattle. Jimi, who chose his clothes and accoutrements with such care, would have been appalled, Lola thought.

Janis Joplin was also dead. She had died two weeks and two days after Jimi Hendrix. Janis Joplin was twenty-seven. Her body was discovered at the Landmark Motor Hotel, in Los Angeles. Janis Joplin had been staying there while recording her new album, in a nearby recording studio. Alone in her hotel room after a recording session, Janis Joplin had injected herself with heroin. According to reports Janis Joplin had skin-popped the heroin instead of injecting it directly into a vein. This had given her enough time to go into the hotel lobby to change five dollars so she could buy a packet of cigarettes.

Back in her room, she sat on the bed, put the packet of cigarettes beside the bed and suddenly fell forward, hitting her head on the bedside table. For eighteen hours Janis Joplin's body lay wedged between the bed and the bedside table. Rigor mortis had set in by the time she was discovered. When she was found, she was wearing a short blouse and a pair of panties. Her lips were bloodied and her nose was broken. She was still clutching the four dollars and fifty cents change from the cigarettes in one of her hands. Her psychedelically-painted Porsche was still outside in the parking lot.

A few days before she died, Janis Joplin signed a revision of her will. She had changed a few details. There was now more money involved. And Janis Joplin felt more kindly towards her parents. Janis Joplin left half her estate to her parents and a quarter each to her sister and her brother. She also left two-and-a-half thousand dollars to throw a wake in the event of her death. Lola thought it was strange for a 27-year-old to be thinking about a party after her death. There was a difference between working out who should inherit your estate and planning a wake for yourself, Lola thought. Planning a wake seemed to make the death feel more imminent and, possibly, more anticipated. Three days after planning the wake, Janis Joplin was dead.

Brian Jones was also dead. He had died just over a year before Jimi Hendrix and Janis Joplin. He was found motionless at the bottom of his swimming pool. The coroner ruled that Brian Jones had died as a result of drowning by immersion in fresh water associated with severe liver dysfunction caused by fatty degeneration and ingestion of alcohol and drugs. Brian Jones was twenty-seven. A month earlier he had announced he was leaving The Rolling Stones, but the reality was that Brian Jones had been asked to leave the band.

Exactly two years to the day after Brian Jones was pulled out of the bottom of his swimming pool, Jim Morrison was found dead in Paris. He was twenty-seven. Jim Morrison, who had been heavily addicted to drugs and alcohol, was found dead in the apartment on Rue Beautreillis, on the Right Bank, he had rented with his girlfriend Pamela Courson. No autopsy was performed as the medical examiner found no evidence of foul play and therefore, in accordance with French law, no autopsy was required. Later, Pamela Courson told friends that Jim Morrison had died of a heroin overdose as he had thought, after a day of heavy drinking, that he was snorting cocaine. She said that earlier in the evening Jim Morrison had vomited up blood and then decided to have a bath. She said he had appeared to have recovered, so she went to sleep. When she woke up, hours later, Jim Morrison was dead. Pamela Courson herself died of a heroin overdose three years later. At the time of her death, she was twenty-seven.

In Jim Morrison's will, made two-and-a-half years before he died, Jim Morrison had left his entire estate to Pamela Courson.

After Pamela Courson's death, Jim Morrison's parents and Pamela Courson's parents fought over who had the legal rights to the estate. Jim Morrison's parents contested the will. But Jim Morrison's will was clear. Everything he owned was to go to Pamela. And because of that, Pamela's parents inherited the estate. Jim Morrison had really managed to erase his parents and his brother and sister out of his life, Lola thought.

After two weeks of mostly sold-out concerts at the London Palladium, during which she received wild applause and standing ovations, Mama Cass was elated. After the very last performance, she went to Mick Jagger's thirty-second birthday party. She stayed there talking to various guests until well into the next day, before going home to the apartment she was renting in Curzon Street, Mayfair. The apartment belonged to the singer/songwriter Harry Nilsson. Harry Nilsson had asked Keith Moon, who usually lived there, to move out for a few weeks. From the apartment, Mama Cass called Michelle Phillips to say how happy she was.

After talking to Michelle Phillips, Mama Cass went to another party in her honour, then came back and went to bed. The next afternoon, Mama Cass's naked, cold, dead body was discovered by one of her staff. Mama Cass was thirty-two. The doctor who examined Mama Cass initially thought she may have choked on a ham sandwich he had seen by the bed. He had overlooked that fact that the sandwich appeared to be untouched. The findings of the coroner's inquest were that Cass Elliot died of a fatty myocardial degeneration due to obesity. She had died from heart failure.

The rumour about her choking on a ham sandwich never died down. People still believed it. It was such an ugly rumour. Such an ugly picture. A fat person choking on a ham sandwich. It fed into peoples' prejudices. And carried a subtext that read a fat, greedy person eating a ham sandwich she shouldn't have been eating died of her own gluttony. Mama Cass would have been mortified.

Keith Moon, The Who's drummer, whose animated, spirited, almost manic drumming style was highly admired and whose erratic, eccentric, destructive behaviour was well-documented, had moved back into the Curzon Street, Mayfair apartment. Four years later, he was found dead in the same apartment.

Poor Otis Redding was dead, too. He died less than six months after his appearance at the Monterey International Pop Festival. Otis Redding's twin-engine Beechcraft plane crashed into Lake Monona, in Wisconsin, killing Otis and four members of the Bar-Kays, his backing group. Otis Redding was twenty-six.

All that life force, all that energy and intelligence and talent and level-headedness was gone. His body was found the next day when they searched the lake. No one was able to determine the cause of the crash. Otis Redding was buried on his ranch, in Round Oak, Georgia. One month later, 'Sittin' on the Dock of the Bay', which Otis had recorded four days before he died, came out and went straight to the top of the charts. It would have been Otis's first number one.

Lillian Roxon was also dead. Lillian, who didn't smoke or take drugs and hardly ever drank alcohol, had died of an asthma attack. She was forty-one. Lillian, who had looked after so many people, died alone, with no one to look after her. Lillian, who had been a compulsive phone caller, had called no one. Lola hoped this meant that she had died swiftly.

Lillian had just published *The Rock Encyclopedia*, the world's first rock encyclopaedia, and was one of the stars of the New York music and art scene. Friends said she had looked very tired on her last trip to Australia, ten months before she died. Lola hadn't seen Lillian on that trip. Lola felt Lillian hadn't forgiven her for going back to Australia and marrying Mr Former Rock Star. Lola thought that Lillian saw her as yet another person who had made an uninformed choice and disappeared into good-wife, good-mother land. Lillian was right. Good-wife, good-mother land had very firm boundaries and ill-marked exits.

Lillian Roxon had also fallen out with Linda McCartney. After Linda married Paul McCartney and moved to London, she had seemed to drop all her closest friends in New York. Lillian had been very hurt. Lola was told that Linda had been bereft when she had heard the news of Lillian's death, as Linda had hoped to restore the friendship. Lola herself had cried when she heard that Lillian had died. She too had planned on seeing Lillian again and apologising for not taking her advice. Advice Lola had thought about for years after she had ignored it.

Linda McCartney, who lived on for twenty-five years after Lillian's death, died of breast cancer at the age of fifty-six. She died in Tucson, Arizona, on the ranch she and Paul owned. Lola was told that Linda McCartney was still riding her beloved horses one or two days before she died. Lola hoped that if there was an afterlife, Linda and Lillian would be keeping each other company, phoning each other every day and going out together at night.

Sonny Bono was also dead. He had skied into a tree at the Heavenly Ski Resort near Lake Tahoe, in California. His widow, Mary Bono, asked Cher to deliver the eulogy at Sonny's funeral. Cher's eulogy had been very touching and very moving. Cher spoke, through tears, of how some people thought that Sonny wasn't very bright. But she said he was smart enough to take an introverted sixteen-year-old girl and a scrappy little Italian guy with a bad voice and turn them into the most beloved and successful couple of their generation.

'Sonny was a short man,' Cher said. 'But he was heads and tails taller than anyone else. He had a vision of the future and just how he was going to build it.' The epitaph on Sonny Bono's headstone said, *And the Beat Goes On.*

The beat didn't go on too well for John Phillips of The Mamas and the Papas. His drug use kept increasing. He himself said that at one stage he was shooting cocaine and heroin every fifteen minutes, for two years. In 1973, Mick Jagger tried to help John Phillips record another album, in London, but the project came to an abrupt end because of John Phillips' heavy drug use. John Phillips' years of drug and alcohol addiction had wrecked his liver. In 1992, he had a liver transplant. A few months after the transplant, he was photographed in a bar in Palm Springs, drinking alcohol. 'I was just trying to break in the new liver,' he explained. John Phillips died nine years later. He was sixty-five.

The list of the dead was endless. Lola had been trying not to think about the dead. She had been trying not to think about Janis Joplin, Jimi Hendrix, Jim Morrison or Brian Jones or Mama Cass. She had been trying not to think about Renia or Edek's dead. Or anyone else's dead.

Lola had grown up with the dead. She was trying to remove herself from them. She was trying to discard the dead. She felt glued to them. And she wanted to unglue herself. She wanted to ditch her past and her parents' past. But it wasn't easy. You couldn't ditch the past the way you could ditch last year's coat or the shoes that weren't quite the right fit. You couldn't dump the past in the way you could dump a lover or a disloyal friend. The past seemed to be as much a part of you as the fact that you were short or tall. Lola was discovering you couldn't will either your height or your past away. Her past was always going to be full of murdered people and barracks and fear and disease and the barbaric aspects of very ordinary human beings.

Lola thought that part of her relief at the fact that Mick Jagger and Cher had not only survived but had thrived, stemmed from her own episodic ambivalence about surviving and her attraction to the dead. This ambivalence, which had surfaced in her forties, had, two decades later, mostly abated.

All of the guests had been seated for dinner. Lola was sitting eight people away from Mick Jagger. She had to stand up to see where Mr Someone Else was seated. He was sitting opposite Phyllis-Elissa Earlwood. According to the menu, the waiters were bringing plates of seared peekytoe crab salad with a spicy peach chutney. This would be followed by a pan-roasted Long Island duck breast with cumin and cardamom-seasoned black beans.

The guest on Lola's left introduced himself. His name was Irwin Keller. He was a veterinary nutritionist and behavioural specialist.

'Does that mean you look after the dietary and emotional health of animals?'

'Yes,' he said. 'That about sums it up.'

'I didn't think animals needed nutritional counselling,' said Lola. 'Don't they naturally eat what's good for them, or do they suffer from vitamin deficiencies like we do?'

'Some of them do,' he said.

'Oh,' said Lola. 'I was joking. I thought I was being funny.'

'It's not funny,' Irwin Keller said. 'Take fish, for example,' he said, looking at his peekytoe crab salad. 'In the food fish industry, fish generally require a high-protein diet.'

'You mean they eat other fish?' said Lola.

'They are fed fish meal,' said Irwin. 'But there is a problem. Most fish don't synthesise ascorbic acid, Vitamin C, so you have to give them supplements. A Vitamin A deficiency in fish, which is not as common, can lead to poor growth and retinal atrophy.'

'That sounds terrible,' said Lola, trying to picture a fish with atrophied eyes. 'It wouldn't look great either in the fish market or the fish store.'

Lola tried to eat her peekytoe crab without thinking about what it had been fed. 'Do animals have food disorders?' she said to Irwin Keller.

'They can have,' he said. 'A horse that has a thiamine deficiency could suffer from anorexia.'

Lola started wondering whether an induced thiamine deficiency might be an aid to dieters. She wanted to ask Irwin Keller, but Irwin Keller had moved on and he was now talking about sheep. By the time Irwin Keller had finished, Lola knew that thirty per cent of sheep were homosexual and that fourteen per cent of dogs had separation anxiety. She also now knew that dogs had fears and phobias and that social maturity in free-ranging chickens occurred at about one year of age, although most chickens were slaughtered before they reached that age. That meant that most of the western world was eating socially-immature chickens.

The peekytoe crab salad had been replaced by the pan-roasted Long Island duck. To Lola's relief, the woman on her right tapped her on the arm. 'Frances Withers,' she said. 'Has anyone ever told you you look like Cher?'

'Occasionally someone has suggested it,' Lola said.

'She's still very beautiful,' Frances Withers said.

'I think so, too,' said Lola.

Phyllis-Elissa and Elwood Earlwood's apartment didn't look like the sort of place where Cher was regularly discussed. Lola was pleased to be talking about Cher.

'Her hair is not curly like yours,' Frances Withers said, scrutinising Lola's hair.

'I think Cher is fabulous,' said Irwin Keller, who must have been listening. Lola was surprised that Irwin Keller had even noticed what Cher was like. He seemed to spend all his time absorbed in ascorbic acid and chickens and pigs and goats and fish.

Lola felt an almost maternal pride in Cher, even though she and Cher were the same age. Lola was thrilled that Cher had been so successful, and had grown up into an independent, powerful and accomplished human being. Cher hadn't become bloated with celebrity. In interviews, you could see her humility, her grace and her intelligence. She also had a great sense of humour. 'The trouble with some women,' Cher was quoted as saying, 'is they get all excited about nothing and they marry him.'

Lola was pleased that Cher had done so well. Thrilled that Cher had been so resilient. It hadn't been an altogether bump-free ride. Cher's daughter with Sonny Bono, Chastity Bono, had come out as being gay when she was a teenager. Cher had handled Chastity's news with the same sort of fear and confusion any mother might feel, but she had adapted and become a staunch supporter of lesbian and gay rights.

At high school, Chastity Bono had begun to feel more and more certain that she was meant to be a male, not a female. Just before she turned forty, she decided to make the physical transition from being a woman to being a man.

Lola was pleased that Cher hadn't pretended that it was easy to have a daughter who had become a man. Cher had looked almost shell-shocked when she was trying to come to terms with having her daughter become her son.

In interviews, Chaz Bono reminded Lola of a young Cher. Chaz got such joy out of very small things. He seemed unspoiled. And not at all bitter about the struggle to address the imbalance between his body and his psyche. He was the sort of child any mother would be proud of. Lola was sure that Cher, whom Lola had noted with joy was still wearing false eyelashes, was proud of Chaz.

Lola ate much more of the dessert than she had intended to. The flourless chocolate cake, with its molten chocolate interior, was one of Lola's favourite desserts. She looked at her plate. She hadn't left a crumb of cake or a drop of chocolate. She wondered if Mick Jagger had eaten his flourless chocolate cake, but she couldn't tell. Someone was leaning forward and blocking Lola's view of Mick Jagger's plate.

Lola still hadn't worked out what this fundraising dinner was for. She didn't feel that she could ask anyone without coming across as not only stupid, but crass. Lola tried to catch Mr Someone Else's eye. But he was talking to two or three people and didn't notice. Lola wanted to go home. She wanted to go home and make some notes about a dialogue Pimp was having with Schlomo. Three days in a row, Schlomo had lost the suspect he was trailing because of his frequent bathroom stops. This was an important case for the Ultra-Private Detective Agency. It was fraud on a large scale. Pimp couldn't tell the corporation that had hired them that her head private detective kept losing the subject because of a frequent need to pee.

Lola looked up. Mick Jagger was looking at her. She looked away and then she looked back at him. He was still looking at her. He had a slightly quizzical expression on his face.

Lola smiled at him. He smiled at her. She wondered whether she should go over and say hello to him. She felt awkward about it. What would she say? 'Hi, I'm the fat Australian journalist who interviewed you when I was nineteen and you were twenty-three.' Or 'Hi, I'm Lola Bensky, I argued with you about the meaning of the word "propagate", and you were right. It was a long time ago. I also talked about the flood of cabbage into the Lodz Ghetto, in Poland, which was followed by mass diarrhoea.'

Lola didn't think so. What else could she say? 'Hello, I met you years ago. I talked about how in Auschwitz they cultivated diseases like cholera, typhus and pneumonia to inject into prisoners as experiments and they grew the bacteria and other microbes in cultures made from live human flesh because it was much less valued than anything that came from a cow or a pig. And you made me a cup of tea.'

Lola could see that Mick Jagger was still looking at her. She smiled at him. He smiled at her and nodded.